Binjamin Zwi

Hannah

Family saga

Novel

Bibliografische Information der Deutschen Nationalbibliothek: Die Deutsche Nationalbibliothek verzeichnet diese Publikation in der Deutschen Nationalbibliografie; detaillierte bibliografische Daten sind im Internet über dnb.dnb.de abrufbar.

Proofreading: Andreas Weissenberger

Othercontributors: Andreas Weissenberger

Verlag: BoD • Books on Demand GmbH, In de Tarpen 42, 22848 Norderstedt

Druck: Libri Plureos GmbH, Friedensallee 273, 22763 Hamburg

ISBN: 978-3-7597-7942-7

Table of Contents

This book I dedicate to our beloved Hannah

(* 1934, † 2017)

INTRODUCTION

My name is Hannah. I am Jewish. I mention it right at the beginning because it has shaped my life. And this book is about me and my life - a completely happy life, even if it did not seem that way at first. But then success became evident, and today we belong to the upper class.

Our happiness became visible to everyone when my husband, Hans, and I bought one of the most beautiful villas in Freiburg. At that time, it was named Villa Else, after Else Weil, who once lived there with her husband. Now I am sitting here at my desk in Villa Mangold, which now bears our last name, writing this book in my elegant study and letting my life flow freely.

Today, it is a normal feeling to move freely on the street as a Jew. No one pays attention, and Jews are no longer humiliated in public. Only I know who I am and that my freedom is anything but self-evident today.

Of course, anti-Semitism has been around for a long time. It has embedded itself deeply and firmly in large parts of society. Has established itself there as a bacillus. So, no one should think that we have finally overcome this form of barbarism. Some people had and still have their prejudices, but few put these prejudices into practice. But that has become rare today. In such cases, there will soon be a social outcry.

But when I was a young girl, people were not just persecuted because of their background; no, they murdered them for it. It was not even that long ago. I remember that very well. I was about 12. It will forever be in my bones, no matter how peaceful the circumstances become.

I was a beautiful girl, ready for my first love. But nothing came of it. A nightmare came true when the war started. My people were hunted down, kidnapped, and mostly murdered, even though we were not a warring party at all. So many men, boys and girls, but also mothers and fathers, were brutally murdered—until the last days of the war when the war had long been lost.

My family and I were lucky. Together with a few others, we escaped a death line, hid, and survived this terrible time.

We had been kidnapped from our home and treated like dirt by the Nazis. Some were murdered because they refused to leave their homes. We were sent to so-called resettlement camps and then herded into railway carriages like dirty, smelly cattle. There were so many people in one car that you couldn't sit down or go about your business. They just let it go and tried to survive. With a bit of luck, the survivors were sent to an internment camp. They didn't know that death also lurked in the internment camps.

We were lucky. Our train was attacked by fighter planes and derailed, and we escaped. We sought shelter in an abandoned mansion, and a small group of us ventured back to Berlin. There was a shelter there. Many of us survived there, thanks to our hero, Eliam Katzenstein. He was the leader at the shelter and welcomed us.

Karl, a young Wehrmacht soldier, even killed a comrade to save Eliam Katzenstein and Adam, my brother. Karl and Eliam had been best friends before the war and had sworn to each other eternal friendship by their blood. Karl proved his loyalty by killing our enemy, even if it was only one soldier.

At that time, when Eliam heard the shot from Karl's gun, he first thought that Karl had shot himself, and he and Adam remained in this belief for years, for they fled as fast as their legs carried them. It was only in the last days of the war that Eliam found out that Karl was still alive, and now Eliam has saved Karl's life.

Karl was deserted because he saw no point in a worthless war and had never wanted it. He was captured and was to be attached to one of the lanterns in the Wilhelmstraße near the Reichskanzlei. But he stumbled and almost starved to death in front of Eliam's vehicle, but managed to escape in the bomb hole. Because the soldiers who were supposed to hang him were almost all young, they fled. They left Karl behind with unfinished things.

Yes, Eliam was our hero. But he did not want to hear that. After the war, he went to Holland to find his girlfriend, Rachel.

Even in an era of horror, time does not stand still. Despite all the threats, life must go on. Whoever wants to survive the whole thing and eventually be among the survivors must never give up. There are always allies and righteous ones. They will not be left alone, but they will find allies, even righteous ones. I found my beloved husband, Hans Mangold, in the struggle for survival. I married him later.

There were also good people, like the peasant couple Adaja and Gustav, who helped us a lot. We had to have something to eat. Gustav and two other farmers from the outskirts of Berlin gave us what they could be lacking. The two have grown very close to our hearts. It was only later that I learned that Gustav had also saved Adaja from the Nazis. She was Jewish, and he was an evangelical Christian. An allied priest married the two and provided Adaja with false papers. Since then, her name has been Marta, but in her heart, she remains Adaja.

Without Adaja and Gustav, we would often have starved, and I would never have met Hans. The two found him almost dead in the forest and kept him healthy. We took him to the shelter. It was love at first sight. The two also took Eli with them. His family was murdered by the Nazis. Eliam had saved him and given him a home in the refuge. Eli was snorted in Adaja, and once we got food there, he decided to stay with the two. Eli became her son. That was the best thing for him, and they also helped him not to be bitter in the face of his difficult fate. Eli became a fabulous man. He still lives with his family on his parents' farm and is a cattle breeder. The rural region around Berlin offered itself at the time and still offers itself very well today.

After we had survived the war and Eliam Katzenstein (God bless him) had agreed with the Russian commander, Marshal Konstantinovich, we were finally free again! Because of Eliam's remarkable negotiating skills, we got from Marshal Konstantinovich an old camp, which had served youth recreation before the war. There, we relaxed and built our community. Today, there are only the remains of the wall. The GDR did not want to remember our history. The Jewish flag with our David star has long been out there.

What a feeling it was to suddenly walk underground through the bombed streets of Berlin after so long! Well, it was a precarious freedom, and we only owe it to the Russian liberators. If it had gone after the Germans... We Jews were no longer murdered, but they hated us nevertheless, even more than before, because we knew now what they would have done to us if they had not been handled at the last moment.

We saw it in their eyes when they saw our shattered figures, and they did not allow themselves to take relevant comments such as, for example, "Na! Have you been forgotten? The furnaces are still burning in Auschwitz!" Not everyone wanted to know about it later, but at that point, everyone was well-informed. They couldn't say they had a fist behind their back because they wouldn't have been able to resist. No, that is not all true, and they do not think differently today; they do not trust each other anymore.

Or that old, bitter Nazi widow from our neighborhood who poured a bucket of ice-cold water out of her window on us. I will never forget that. I still felt the cold shock today when I dropped the water. She was the one who always insulted me as a Jew. Just because I was wearing a black dress that no longer looked nice.

Jews wore most of their clothing in black. Black suit, white shirt, and vest. Depending on the faith, the head covering is either a kippah or a Schtreimel. Women wore or still wore black dresses with long sleeves and a black knitted jacket. The head cover is either a wig (Scheitl) or a scarf, depending on the faith. (We Jews also refer to an older coat or dress that no longer looks as good as a Jewish skirt.)

We wanted to move back to Levetzow Street, where we had lived before the war, but there was nothing like it once was. The synagogue was almost destroyed. It was also not restored or demolished by the DDR authorities in the 1950s. But for so long, she stood there and was—inaccessible and profaned for us—a constant silent reminder of our destiny!

As a child, I always went there with my family. We prayed, met our friends, and discussed our religion with Rabbi Lewkowitz. It hurt me to see my synagogue looking so destroyed before our eyes.

(In 1960, a wall with a memorial plaque was erected. After the fall of the Berlin Wall, I was at my synagogue and was shocked. From a religious place, it has become a playground and a bowling field. In 1988, a steel flame wall, a ramp, and a wagon were erected on only half of the plot, with figurations abstractly depicting 'human packages' knotted in iron. Thank you!)

Otherwise, the East and the GDR were never a subject in my life. I never wanted to live there; I hated this regime and the views of Ulbricht. Only my dear mother Sarah was still happy in Levetzow Street, but the house was technically no longer to be saved, we thought at the time.

My father bought us an apartment in the district of Mitte, and we all went soon to the west of Berlin. He only picked up the last things from our old apartment and what was left in the cellar. As I learned shortly before his death, he seemed to have extracted far more from the basement than we could have known. The documents and photos he had saved at the time were good for a bestseller. But with me, my father knew the secret was in good hands when it ended with him.

Who knows, maybe in our family there will be another writer who takes up the subject. I promised my father I would not do it. Of course, I kept it to this day! Not just because I promised it to him—I don't believe it, or I do not want to believe it. Only my own story can tell it.

Young Luck
(1945–1951)

HANNAH EPSTEIN (CENTER) WITH MOTHER SARAH (LEFT) AND BROTHER ARI (RIGHT) BEFORE THE PERSECUTION, BERLIN CA. 1940

NEW LIFE AND THE MOVE

Since no one in Hans's family was alive, my dear father Yaron wanted Hans to stay with us even after his liberation. Not only had we become a family in the underground: My father already knew that we loved each other, and I also soon had my Bat-Mizwar; I became religious, and I was allowed to have a friend.

Then, we moved to our new apartment in the Mitte district in 1946. Hans came with us, as well as my older brothers Ari and Adam. Adam with his fiancée Rosa and their son Leon. Together, we got a 4-room apartment without a toilet, and there was neither electricity nor running water, but after all, we lived.

Father started as a housekeeper in the residential block, because he had shown his versatile talents in the war many times enough. The residential block was taken by the Russians at the time. But when the sectors were divided among the four occupying powers, we came to the British sector – fortunately! This residential block was one of the few residential blocks on this street that remained almost intact. Father enjoyed a good reputation among the occupiers thanks to his craftsmanship. Before the war, he had run a carpenter's workshop in Levetzow Street with a shop business. Eliam had told the new gentlemen enough about the deceptively real-looking twisted door in the old railway tunnel, without which we could not have survived so long.

My father did not want Hans to live in my room, but I knew how to wrap him around the finger. (My granddaughter Leah is the same today as I was back then. I think with a smile as I write this sentence down.)

In any case, Hans lived with me, and Adam and Rosa also shared a room. Ari wanted to live with Zuria, the wonderful shepherd. Of course, mom and dad also had a shared room. Then there was the kitchen and a living room, but there was nothing inside. What are chairs or a couch if you could also sit on boxes? (Yes, today you can laugh at it!)

My father took away our fate and admonished us to humility. He always said: "What are material values when you have yourself and live!" He was right! Yeah, he was often right, even though I didn't always understand him at the time.

We volunteered for reconstruction. We children were allowed to do easier work because school was not yet. Let no one say that we Jews are lazy! Quite often, we were kept pretending that we were to blame for all this. Hitler had seen this before, or at least he had claimed it. And they still liked to believe it.

My mother cried a lot, but she was a strong woman. She would have liked to work as a teacher again, but the country was on the ground, and no one thought about education in the first few months. But I was glad that we Jews were then allowed to go back to school from September 1946. Our occupants had ensured that our imperialist and militarist views were transformed into a democratic attitude in the school. It was no different in West Berlin than it was in the East.

It was good for us Jews. We could only win. The occupier saw us no differently than the other Germans. But the Aryan children refused to sit next to a Jew. Something like this was speaking around quickly in the class, especially since we were from Berlin. At least I was more fortunate than Ari. He had to sit alone in the back. I was allowed to sit next to Hans.

After school we had to go to reconstruction every day, knocking mortar from the bricks. The occupants wanted to reuse the bricks, and so many new living blocks for the population – it said. Often, however, the damaged buildings had to be renovated first. That's where the invaders moved in. We came to the end; And from this point of view, we were suddenly a single German people!

We met with our fellow sufferers from underground in temporarily furnished synagogues. During the long time together under the earth, many friendships had arisen. Some of them hold to this day. I often went to such meetings at the time. They were the only friends I had.

There was always a lot to tell. We were all getting better from day to day, no matter how bad it was. Hans also occasionally came with me, but he had never been happy down there and did not want to be reminded of that time. He said, "The only good thing about my salvation was that I met you." That touched me deeply at the time.

My mother and father always liked to accompany me to meetings, because they had many friends there. She had a very good relationship with the Bundschuh family. After the war, Jakob Bundschuh managed to regain his banking house in the American sector. Adam was allowed to work in his bank because he and Eliam had saved the family Bundschuh.

(In the American occupation zone, the restitution procedure was regulated in the Military Act No. 59 of 10 October 1947, which was also introduced two years later for the British occupation area and Berlin, but not for the French occupation Zone. The law provided for the restitution of all identifiable deprived property, primarily commercial property and real estate, and assigned the individual cases to local reparation authorities, before which the two parties should agree on a settlement, if possible.)

Bundschuh reopened his bank as one of the first in Berlin but allowed only the Jewish population as a clientele. So, my family got a bank account. It was exciting at the time! Today it already has a child, furnished by grandma and grandpa.

Due to the war and the lack of Rabbis and synagogues, I was not able to celebrate my Bat-Mizwar until I was 15. However, I have been practicing for this event since I was 13. My mother told me faithfully what I had to do and what the others would do, but in reality, it was different. Rabbi Chajm, who himself had been in the shelter, performed my Bat-Mizwar in the synagogue on Joachimsthal Street, and I was happy that it was him.

It was one of the most beautiful parties I've ever had. I can still see my mother crying in front of me today when I sat on the chair and was pushed up. Apart from the many gifts, I got things that I have until now in my jewelry box. Mr. Bundschuh gave me a gold coin, which had been poured out in old Jerusalem. How he saved this gold coin through the war was a mystery to me, but he never revealed it.

Mother and father melted their wedding rings and made a gold-smith make a ring out of it. Inside, there was a message saying, <Mom and dad, always connected with you> Until I had always thought that father had given his gold ring to this brown bastard of a Wehrmacht soldier, who didn't want to leave him with us when we were driven out of our apartments in Levetzow Street. But he told me that the ring that this soldier got was worthless. Today, it is fashion jewelry or tin.

The greatest gift was that all our friends were there. Even Eliam came from Holland. He brought us a bunch of Gouda. Today it is noth-ing, but then it was like gold. The friends who didn't have much gave me homemade. I didn't want anything. I just wanted everyone to be there and be happy. I was never materially attached, on the contrary: I preferred giving rather than assuming!

Adam even brought wine. Supposedly, he was able to rescue a few bottles from the basement of the old cargo railway station in Moabit. I was not allowed to drink alcohol yet, but I accepted a bottle as a gift. This bottle still standing in the display case next to my desk today.

(Also, by the way, a drawing with all the persons who were near me in the shelter. A friend, a painter who had been there once had the idea of creating this painting. I won't inherit all these things that I'm thinking about to my son Samuel. He can't appreciate that. Aaron is the Mangold who has the same blood as me. He is benevolent, sensi-tive, and flattered by religious customs. I have so many things he'll get when I go on my last journey. But right now, I feel fit and don't think about my last trip.)

After my Bat-Mizwar I had to go to school for another year. I left with a good testimony, but what was it for me at the time? I wanted to study as a hairdresser, but no hair salon accepted me because I was a Jew, and there were no Jewish hairdressers in Berlin at the time.

I was sad, but I didn't give up. I went to the housekeeping school – a new model to bring girls closer to the household. The Nazis had set up the first such school on Lake Wannsee. The occupants liked it and allowed this schooling. I learned a lot there, but it didn't make me happy. Hans always said that it's good if a woman can cook and clean. Men were real puppets at the time!

Hans had just learned that there were Note boards. You could put your data there. If someone from the family came and read the note, they could find you in this way. So, Hans also did this in his old street, waiting daily for a sign from someone from his family. So long time!

To our knowledge, his whole family was dead. But one day, a young man spoke with a Swiss accent. His name was Martin Hornmann, a lawyer from Zurich.

It was a knocking at our front door, and I still get gooseskin when I think of that moment.

I went to the door and opened it.

He said. "Good morning, lady!"

I said. "Good morning. Do you want to?"

"My name is Martin Hornmann. I am a lawyer, and I come from Switzerland. I got notice that Hans Mangold is supposed to live here."

"Yes, that's right. But what do you want from Hans? He is afraid of strangers."

"Oh, he doesn't have to. I am here to say something pleasant to him."

"Please come in. I will get Hans."

He politely said, "Thank you, dear lady!" and entered. I offered him a chair in the kitchen.

Then I went to Hans to pick him up: "Hans, there is a man who says his name is Hornmann, and he comes from Switzerland!"

"What does he want?"

"He says, he has got notice that you live here, and he has something good to tell you."

"Well, I'm coming."

Hans went with me to Mr. Hornmann, who was sitting in our kitchen.

"Mr. Mangold, I have been looking for you for a long time!"

"Good morning, what can I do for you?"

"Do you know a Samuel Mangold?"

"Yes! This was my father. He and the rest of my family were murdered in a massacre in 1944. But why do you ask?"

"Your father survived the massacre! He was able to flee to Switzerland."

"I can't believe it. Father lay dead next to me!"

"He was shot, seriously injured, and survived. My uncle rescued him and smuggled him to Zurich. I'll give this to you!"

Hornmann gave Hans a passport; it was his own. His father had taken all the papers for security reasons at the time.

Hans started to cry. He couldn't calm down.

He asked with a crying voice. "Is my father still alive?"

"Yes, but he doesn't want to set foot on German soil! That's why he's sending me. I read in your old street that you live here."

"Hannah, my father lives!"

"Yes, incredible, almost seven years have passed!"

"Is there anyone else in my family alive?"

"Unfortunately, not!" said Mr. Hornmann sadly.

"My mother, my brothers, all dead?"

"Yes, but her death is not unpunished! I'm going to sue the Nazi regime in Nuremberg. Hundreds of us Jews have already done this!"

Hornmann suddenly felt anger. He was considered a warrior advocate. Well, in Switzerland, a Jew would like to become a lawyer, but especially in Nuremberg. Were the Jews a victorious power?

Hans didn't want to go on such a sluggish terrain. He preferred to stay with obvious family matters: "When can I see my father?"

"When you want! I can take you right away!"

That was too much! Hans had not even perceived that his father was still alive. Now he should even visit him! Hans had found a new life by my side here a long time ago. He slipped onto the kitchen chair and sat there sinking into himself for a moment.

He thought about it, he was ripped apart. But he could hardly wait to see his father again. So, he took a moment and explained to me in a serious voice: "Hannah, I'm going to my father, but I'll catch you up!"

I didn't want to make a lift. I understood Hans. In our time, nothing was lasting. So, I reinforced his determination: "Go first to him, and someday we will see each other again."

At the time, I didn't think we'd ever see each other again. Hans was one of his own, and that's where he was going. It was a tough breakup, but it had to be. Hans had to bury his ghosts and arrange his life.

The day he and Mr. Hornmann left was the worst day for me since the end of the war. I had cried, and my family was trying to comfort me. Adam wanted to go to a romantic movie with me, but I couldn't.

I had to give up Hans for almost three long years. He did not forget me. I received letters from him – a great consolation – in the end, he kept his word.

I still have the letters. They're tied up in a bunch and lie in my vitrine next to my desk. I just took one out and quoted it here:

"Dearest Hannah, how much I miss you here in Basel! My heart hurts from longing for you. We haven't seen each other in so long! My father is fine. I only hear him at night. He calls for mom. Suddenly he is quiet. Tomorrow, we have an appointment with Martin Horn-mann. It is about my father's company and my inheritance. I promise you. When I finally get back to you. I'll ask you if you want to be my wife. Be excited, dear Hannah! You and father are my only stops; I would give my life for you. I hope you answer my love. With a beautiful girl like you, it's hard not to think about it. Dear Hannah, I have to go to an appointment, but in my mind, you're always with me. I love you with all my heart. Your Hans"

I'm still melting today when I read what he wrote to me at the time.

On my 17th birthday in September 1949, it rang at our front door. (We've had electricity for almost a year.) I ran to the door and was scared as I opened it. A well-dressed young man in a black suit, a white shirt, and a striped vest stood before me and said to me. "Hello, dear, here I am!"

I jumped into his arms and knocked him off. Yeah, I didn't kiss him like a long time ago. "Hans, here you are! What do you look like?"

"I promised you in every letter that I would come back. My father would love to meet you. Can you come to Basel with me?"

"I would go anywhere with you, but we have to talk to father and mother first."

Hans frowned. I knew he had respect for my father. But then he asked me: "Are your parents there too?"

"Yes, today is my birthday! We have cake and coffee!"

"I knew that you do have your birthday today, my love. Happy birthday. Honey, this is for you!"

He gave me an elegant-looking box and a small drawer. Of course, I immediately opened the little drawer and yelled when I saw what was in that little fine box. It was a gold ring with a brilliant. However, I did not think too much about it. It was a ring for my birthday, I thought.

I pulled Hans by the hand towards the kitchen: "Come, Hans, my parents will rejoice!" And so, it was.

Hans seemed nervous. Then he began to speak with a slightly stumbling voice: "Before I have no more to speak, I will make it brief." Hans kneeled before me and said: "Hannah Epstein, do you want to be my wife?"

I shouted without waiting, "Yes, yes, I will!"

Everyone wished us good luck. Then Hans went to my father and picked up his blessing for the wedding. Dad loved giving it to us.

I said to my family. "I have something else to tell you. I'm going to Switzerland with Hans for a while. Hans' father wants to meet me. I hope you don't mind!"

At first, my parents still had doubts. I was not yet a major and wanted to go abroad. But I was able to change her mind. Then there was cake and "coffee vomit." It was coffee laced with chicory and tasted like sleeping feet.

My father asked me. "When are you leaving, and why do you have to go to Switzerland?"

Hans replied. "Good morning, Yaron. We have to go to Switzerland because my father lives there and I work in his company. You know Hannah will do much better there. Above all, I can't leave my father alone. He has no one. You have your family, and they have you.

Father frowned. You could see that he was hurting, but he let me go. With Hans, I was well-raised after all, we loved each other and were engaged. So, it was the last afternoon with my beloved family for a long time. (I would stay in Switzerland longer than I thought.)

On my last night in Berlin, I slept very restless, was very excited, and had stomach pain. In the morning, Hans and I slept out. We had a long train ride ahead of us, over 14 hours from Berlin to Munich, where we would take the train to Basel.

We had to be at the station at ten to six in the evening. Hans wanted to make another appointment with Mr. Bundschuh. His father wanted to cooperate with his bank. I would have liked to go with him, but he said in a firm voice. "Dear, stay with your family and enjoy the day. I am just having boring conversations in a dusty old office."

I didn't say much about it at this time. After all, I was still a young girl. I enjoyed the last day with my father and mother. Later came Ari, Adam, and Rosa with my nephew Leon.

At four o'clock, Hans came back from his appointment and had to drink something first. I gave him some more cake and offered him coffee. That afternoon, I also opened the box that Hans gave me for my birthday. It was a beautiful dress: black, long-sleeved, and elegant (not a Jewish skirt). I would wear this dress on our trip and shine next to Hans.

Father and mother took us to the train station in Friedrichstrasse. We could walk; it was not far. From there went the long-distance train FD 150. We had to say goodbye on the platform edge. "Was it forever?" I wondered in secret.

Dad looked at me and shook his head. He wanted to hold me back, didn't he? No, he asked Hans: "How long will the train to Munich take?"

Hans drew out a timetable and looked. "From Berlin to Munich. We will take almost fifteen hours. We will surely have a longer border stay in Probstzella again."

Father looked at us with uncertainty and continued: "Will Jews cross these borders without any problems?" I saw the fear in my father's eyes.

"Don't worry, Yaron. I have a passport and a visa for Hannah. They were issued for her by the Swiss Government. My father has many good contacts there."

Mother looked at me and cried. Then she said quietly, "My child, take care of yourself. And you, Hans, take care of my daughter. May Adonai accompany you on your way."

"Mother, don't worry so much. Hans will take care of me."

"I will take care of your daughter, and we will call you by telegram."

My mother was more realistic. She knew this was not a fun trip. It was a life choice.

Father just hugged me. I saw the tears in his eyes. We got in and looked for our seats. Hans packed the suitcases in the luggage net, and I opened the window to wave to father and mother.

I called out to them again, and the train started moving. "Take care, I love you!" Mom and dad waved after me, and I watched them until I did not see them anymore.

"Oh, Hans. I am excited, what is in Basel? Are they better to the Jews there?"

He had hinted at it often enough in his letters, but I could not believe it. Maybe he just wanted to calm me down or deceive the censors.

"Basel is a wonderful city, and yes, they have nothing against us Jews there. Let yourself be surprised, my love!"

"I will, my dear!"

The first route was from Berlin to Munich. It was a pleasant route. The evening sun was shining, and I turned my face to the sun. I could feel the warmth, breathed on the pane, and drew figures with my finger on my breath. The most beautiful stories emerged before my eyes. (I have always been very imaginative).

Our first stop was Leipzig. The clock said quarter past nine in the evening.

"Look, Hans, how beautiful the train station is. And the huge hall, so much steel."

Hans was thoughtful. Was he worried about the zone boundary? Nevertheless, he gave me an answer. "Yes, dear, it looks huge."

Twenty minutes later, our train started moving again. The next stop was Saalfeld. The station was damaged during the war. Trains could still run. The only strange thing was that no one got in or out.

Hans told me our next stop was Probstzella. It was the border point. We would all have to get out there and walk to the zone border. I was afraid. Hans could see it and held my hand.

The train started moving again. I was shaking all over. When we arrived at quarter past one, you could hear the German Shepherds. The barking reminded me of our deportation back then. Tears welled up in my eyes. Hans noticed and took me in his arms.

"What is wrong with you, my love?" Hans protected me always and everywhere. (I knew that!)

"I am scared, and the howling of the German Shepherds reminds me of Berlin and the deportation." (Since all of this, I have had a disturbed relationship with Moabit. Years later, we visited the Moabit freight station memorial and stood at the former platform 69. We both shed tears. Although Hans rarely cried. To this day, I cannot come to terms with it. No, I just cannot.)

Hans took his white handkerchief and wiped away my tears. "Do not be afraid. We have all the permits, and I am a Swiss citizen."

The train stopped!

We had to get out with our luggage. On the platform were young Russian soldiers, not heavily armed, but with a dog. I was afraid of this. We had to pass by to get to the checkpoint. The young soldier in Soviet army uniform just stared at us. Fortunately, Hans knew where we were going. He had gone this way twice before.

When we arrived at the checkpoint, we had to stand in a queue and wait. Luckily, things happened quickly at this point. A little further ahead, I saw a young couple being dragged away. The girl was crying, and I tried to stay calm.

I managed to do this until it was our turn. In front of us stood three Soviet Army soldiers and two German police officers. The two police officers checked the passports and our luggage.

Luckily, we only had two suitcases with us. Nevertheless, the policeman asked, "Do you have any Eastern money with you?"

Hans said very calmly, "No, only Swiss francs. Not more than 300 francs."

The police officer seemed bored, he looked at the passports, saw the necessary stamps from the outward journey, and also that of course I did not have one. Hans explained this to him using the documents he had from the Swiss government. The police officer took a closer look at them, and I inevitably thought of that young couple from before. When the policeman called a Russian officer, my heart sank.

Thank God the Russian officer spoke German, although somewhat broken, but good enough. He looked at the document and read it, looked at it again, looked at me, and asked me my name. I told him: "My name is Hannah Epstein." Immediately, I fell silent again.

He took my passport from the policeman, looked at my paper again, and then he said: "Okay, go!" The policeman let us through. I was relieved and happy that Hans had this document from the Swiss government!

(Years later, I learned from my father-in-law Samuel that it was a letter from the then Federal President Ernst Nobs. He was also head of the finance department and a good friend of Samuel. However, how much money he gave him for this favor remained secret. I still remember meeting him years later at a banquet.)

"Now, dear, we have to walk a few meters. Then comes the American border checkpoint, and once we get through there, we have made it."

I rolled my eyes and felt tired. But I had to persevere; I was tried and tested in that. After 200 meters and a curve, you saw the American border checkpoint. Again, we had to stand in line and wait. This time it happened quickly. It was our turn after just fifteen minutes. Three soldiers stood in front of us again, this time Americans. German police officers carried out the checks.

The policeman took a look at our luggage, looked at our passports and of course the document. (I was shocked, but the policeman smiled at me.) Then he wanted to know if we had Ostmark with us. We quickly said no, and he let us move on. I liked him. He looked nice and smiled.

Although, I had to assume that his father had been one of our murderers.

Luckily the bus was already there. He would take us through the Loquitz valley to Ludwigsstadt. The driver took our luggage. We were able to get on, and the transfer was already included in the train ticket. (What a luxury!)

When the last passengers had boarded, we could get started. Our path led through the Loquitz Valley - a very beautiful place since the wall was opened. A few years before Hans' death, we allowed ourselves to have fun and walked this arduous path again.

Due to the steep mountain climb, the omnibus arrived 20 minutes late at the station, but we still had time. Our train did not leave until three past two. We were hungry, we were cold, and we were tired too.

"Dear, I am going to see if I can get something to eat. There must be a kiosk or something like that in the railway building."

It was in vain; Hans came back after five minutes. He looked furiously, and I froze.

"There is nothing there!" And Hans said with a crunch. "Come on, let us go inside the train and rest."

On the train, we searched our compartment. When Hans saw a fat woman bite into a meat sausage in the third class, his mood did not improve. We ran through the train and arrived in our compartment. Hans put the suitcase in the baggage net and threw himself into his seat. I sat in front of him and looked at him.

I did this until he smiled and kissed me: "I love you, Hannah Adriana Epstein. I loved you then, I love you now, and I will love you till the end of my days."

I melted and was frightened when the train started moving. "Finally, we're leaving!" I relieved.

"That's right."

Hans took my hand and kissed her. He kissed my hand often and with pleasure. I looked out into the darkness and saw the lights of the houses passing through us.

(I found an old Timetable on the Internet. So, we stopped at three o'clock in Lichtenfels, at about half-four we were in Bamberg, at just before four in Erlangen, at a quarter to four in Fürth, ten minutes later in Nuremberg. Twenty minutes later it went on to Treuchtlingen. At ten past seven, we were in Augsburg, and after ten minutes we went on to the destination station. Man, there were many railway stations!)

We arrived in Munich at ten o'clock. There was nothing left of the former magnificent building and the large railway hall. A few months previously, halls and buildings had been blowed up. The railway continued operations at a temporary station.

At that time, the signs of the devastation inflicted by our liberators could still be seen everywhere in the city. The population was shrinking in reconstruction. If you see the result today, they have done a good work.

Our train left only in the afternoon. We could walk to the hotel in peace. A cab took us and our luggage to the Hotel Four Seasons, where we wanted to rest for a few hours. (It was called the House of Dollar Guests. Except for the occupants, only civilians who paid in hard currency were allowed to stay there. Hans paid in Swiss francs, and they are still 'hard' today.)

When we arrived at the hotel. We could not get out of our amazement. The building was not finished yet and had been severely destroyed in the war. Still, its splendor was undeniable. Only a part of the work could be done in certain areas, But the finished area was beautiful.

We checked in at the emergency reception. A lady wrote down our dates, a page brought us to the room. Of course, the furniture was new. The room was completely renovated and elegantly decorated. Unbelievable that in the war, this part of the Hotel was completely burned down. The page put our suitcases in the room, and Hans gave him a tip. I was very exhausted and had to sit down.

Hans, on the other hand, was restless and tense. First, he took off his jacket and hung it on the coat rack, then he went to the window and looked out. Suddenly Hans ran back to the cloakroom and took his Jacket.

"Dear, I'm going down to reception for a moment."

I couldn't answer as quickly as he was gone. What was he planning to do? A surprise? He always enjoyed making them for me very often. I wanted to freshen up and thought about whether I should put on a fresh dress too. Hans' father certainly attached great importance to this sort of thing. Anyone who could obtain such important documents had to be very distinguished.

I went into the bathroom and freshened up. Hans came back and sat down in the armchair that was part of an elegant seating area.

When I came out of the bathroom I was wearing a black long-sleeved dress. First, he looked at me, then he smiled and said. "Dear, I have a surprise for you."

I stood there and waited, but he had nothing in his hand.

"Dear, I thought we would stay overnight here in the hotel and not drive to Basel until tomorrow. We could take a look at the city, so much has already been rebuilt."

"Yes, but is that possible?" I clapped my hands together and was happy.

"Of course, that is possible! The hotel extended without any problems. After all, I pay with Swiss francs, and I've already checked the new train connection. We have to exchange the tickets at the train station."

31

"How beautiful!" I exclaimed and was looking forward to exploring Munich.

Hans also went into the bathroom and freshened up. Later we wanted to go to the train station and then go for something to eat. We were starving, but we were still able to control ourselves. We were civilized Jews, after all. (Wink in eye)

When Hans came out of the bathroom, we were ready to go. We left our key at the reception and walked to the front of the hotel. Cabs were waiting there, and we decided to use one of them. A younger man offered to drive us. Hans agreed the journey could begin from Maximilianstrasse via Maximiliansplatz and Karlsplatz. The cab only had to make detours at the piles of rubble. But in the end, we happily reached the station square. We asked the coachman if he wanted to wait and show us Munich later. He agreed; Hans paid in advance.

We went to the makeshift station building and looked where we could buy tickets. It wasn't that easy, but a nice woman from Munich helped us. Rubble was also cleared away from the station square, and the lady in her fifties helped, as she said, to rebuild her city. (These rubble women later went down in history)

She walked with us around a corner to a makeshift sales room. There was a lot of activity. Hans went in alone I looked around. But I was careful not to be recognized as Jewish.

(The Protestant theologian Johann Jacob Schudt (1644–1722) from Frankfurt am Main devoted a chapter to our appearance in his Jewish Oddities (1714). In it, he wrote: "That one can immediately recognize a Jew among so many thousand people." G-d has endowed the Jews with unique "characters or characteristics" "that one soon sees them as Jews at first sight." Schudt particularly emphasizes the face, "that the Jew immediately stands out ... at the nose ... lips ... eyes also of color and the entire physical posture." Schudt sees the body as a medium of character and way of life (like his contemporaries), but the external appearance is determined by the social role (and not by the theological one, as his contemporaries saw). According to Schudt, Jews disrupt the divine order because of their appearance. What nonsense!).

I was standing at one of the few remaining lanterns, watching a group of older men drag a large iron girder down from a pile of rubble.

I heard. "Darling, are you dreaming?" Hans stood in front of me and looked at me with a smile.

"No, why should I? I just watched the men at work!"

"I was able to exchange the tickets. Our train leaves tomorrow morning at ten o'clock and goes via Freiburg to Basel."

"Okay, then we still have a lot of time. Let's go to the cab. Our coachman has been waiting for a long time."

Hans took me by the hand, and we walked together along the station square. When we got to the cab, the coachman took us on a little tour through the city.

It was not pretty because most of the sights he showed us were damaged or destroyed. I quickly lost the desire to see the rubble of the city.

I was hungry, and I'm sure Hans was too. I asked Hans to stop somewhere to get something to eat. That was harder than expected because there wasn't much, but the coachman knew something commoner. He drove us to the Hofbräuhaus. Like almost all other buildings, it was seriously damaged in the war. However, the Schwemme, the large beer hall, was largely undamaged and could continue to be used. There wasn't much going on at that time of day, and my dear Hans invited our coachman to dinner. (Hans was always so generous.)

We entered the large hall, and I was amazed: what a beautiful ceiling! The paintings were a feast for the eyes - motifs from different areas of life, such as agriculture or fishing, and Bavarian flags. I loved this blanket and kept looking at it, even as we sat. Worth mentioning are the wrought iron candlesticks that hung from the ceiling.

There wasn't much to eat. I was happy when there was soup. And yes, there was soup. To be more precise, it was potato and cabbage soup, and it tasted delicious. Hans and the coachman drank beer, and I got lemonade. We enjoyed our time at the Hofbräuhaus.

Hans paid, and the coachman drove us back to the hotel. We passed all the piles of rubble and people trying to move these monsters away. An older woman looked contemptuously in my face as if to say: "Get your ass down there and lend a hand!" Did I have to feel guilty? Certainly not, because weren't those who were now on the ground the ones who wanted it that way? Only they had just lost.

When we arrived, Hans paid the coachman, and we said goodbye. We picked up our key and went to our room. We made ourselves comfortable there. Hans went for a bath, and I read a book that I found on one of the shelves in the room. We went to sleep early. Hans wanted to get up early.

The following morning, Hans got up first and then me. Hans was coming out of the bathroom, so I was able to go straight in. I got ready, put on my black dress, and went to Hans.

When he saw me, he looked at me and asked, "Why are you wearing this dress?"

I said, "Because I want to make a good impression on your father."

"Do you think my father values something like that?"

"Someone as powerful as your father would certainly value it!"

"Powerful? My father is not powerful. He is a broken man who will be happy when he finally can meet you."

I said, "I'm looking forward to seeing him!", and went to pack my suitcase.

"Shall we go?"

"Yes, Hans."

A page came to get our suitcases and brought them downstairs. We followed him, and Hans went to settle our bill.

"Dear, there is a cab in front of the hotel. That will take us to the train station."

The page took our suitcases to the cab, and Hans gave him a tip. When we were seated, the coachman drove off past Maximiliansplatz to Bahnhofsplatz. We got out there, and the coachman gave us our luggage.

I wanted to know, "Which platform does our train come from?" Hans looked at his piece of paper.

"Platform 11, we have to walk a little there. We still have time, love."

We took our suitcases and started walking. You could see how quickly the people of Munich wanted their train station back because the new pillar hall was already being built everywhere. There was so much to see that I almost didn't notice that we had already arrived at platform 11. The train was already there, and we could get on, but a conductor first wanted to know which compartment we had reserved. Hans showed him the tickets and the reservation. The conductor took us to our compartment and wished us a safe journey. We were able to get in and take a seat.

I said it almost too frantically to Hans. "I sit at the window!"

"Dear, we are sitting opposite each other. So, we both sit at the window."

I smiled at Hans, and he smiled back. People got on the train. After a while, we could hear two blasts of the conductor's whistle. The train started moving.

The first stop was Augsburg. Following train stations: Ulm, Tuttlingen, Neustadt am Titisee, Freiburg at Breisgau.

I sat at the window the entire journey and couldn't get away from there. I almost didn't notice the customs officers they were traveling with us from Freiburg.

I would have been scared in a situation like that. As I was eight years old, dad and I were thrown off a bus. This was still in my bones. On the bus, on a train, practically everywhere it said: "FORBIDDEN FOR JEWS!" If one of us Jews became caught, he disappeared and was never seen again.

I had nothing to fear from Hans. He became a courageous and strong man in Switzerland. Most importantly, he had a Swiss passport, and I, as his fiancée, was able to enter with my visa. I only was accepted in Switzerland. Hans' father Samuel had to pay a lot.

When the customs officer came to us and wanted to see the papers, Hans gave him our IDs and a letter. The customs officer looked at the documents and said nothing. I was afraid. Upside-down world: Hans was once afraid of strangers and didn't want to meet them if possible. He then preferred to send me ahead. But he had changed in Switzerland.

The customs officer gave the letter back to Hans and went on without a word. Shouldn't he at least be grumpy that he couldn't harm us? His hands were tied in our case. But of course, I didn't understand these connections at the time and wouldn't have wanted to understand them. I was just happy.

A new life began for me. Hans had become an influential man who could not be harmed by a German customs officer. For him, it was all a matter of course for a long time. When he noticed my worried expression, he immediately reassured me: "Don't be afraid, my love, they won't hurt you!"

The following stations were: Müllheim, Weil am Rhein, and finally Basel, Badischer Bahnhof. How amazed I was! What a splendor, what a company! The magnificent platform hall that stretched from platform to platform seemed so powerful to me. My mouth just hung open. Only when the train stopped did I close it.

We got off. The people waiting on the platform were all dressed elegantly, except for me in the black Jewish coat! How we were always easy to recognize, even here! I have worn my new and, above all, more elegant dress.

Hans took my hand, and together, we ran towards a middle-aged man who was waiting for us on the platform. We stopped in front of him.

Hans introduced me: "Father, this is my Hannah Epstein! Her family rescued me and took me in after we were both separated."

Hans' father beamed at me: "Hannah, welcome to Basel. Come and let me hug you!"

I said in a halting voice, "Mr. Mangold!" But that disappeared when I realized that he was a very kind person. After squeezing me, he said, "Come on, children, let's go home!"

"Father, I'll get the suitcases."

"Let Sebastian do it!" Mr. Mangold turned to a young man in an elegant suit who was accompanying him and asked him: "Sebastian, would you do that?"

Sebastian simply replied. "With pleasure, Mr. Mangold!"

I could hardly believe my eyes: The Mangold family had a servant!

Then Mr. Mangold turned back to Hans and me: "We are going to the car."

I asked, surprised. "What, you have a car?"

"Yes, even two! You will see all that, my darling."

I did not even realize what kind of wealthy family I had fallen into. I was still completely overwhelmed by Basel as a city. With all the people here, I almost forgot that I was Jewish and should keep a low profile. At some point, someone would figure me out and send me off.

So, as we walked through the large domed hall of the station, my mouth was wide open again. Hans said it was a building from the imperial era. In 1852, the Grand Duchy of Baden and Switzerland signed an international treaty for the construction of the Baden train station on Swiss land.

Well, this was yesterday's news. The splendor had long since continued. At the front of the station forecourt, the cars lined up, each more beautiful than the last. But there were also numerous horse-drawn cabs there. Taxis, as you could see from the large number of visitors.

"As soon as Sebastian comes, we can go." Called Hans' father over the noise.

"Where do you live?" I wanted to know.

"In the villa district, directly on the Rhine."

Great! I just thought. It was an understatement, as I soon realized. What kind of fairy-tale land had I come to? And what was Hans doing here?

When Sebastian came with the suitcases and stowed them away. We were ready to go. He drove us leisurely through the area, and at some point, the houses became more and more beautiful and valuable.

Hans took my hand and said. "One Jew after another lives here, but Swiss people also live here, and everyone gets along!"

I said to him quietly. "I cannot say much right now. I almost cannot breathe!" Suddenly, we stopped in front of this elegant villa.

Hans' father said: "Well, here we are! Welcome home, Hannah!"

(We sold the villa after the death of Hans' father. His widow Renate wanted to return to Zurich, where she originally came from, and simply leaving the magnificent house empty was out of the question for us. The consul of Italy asked us at a garden party to see if he could buy the villa. We agreed because I had always loved Italy.)

I got out and walked through the park first. I was happy, feeling joy for the first time since our unexpected arrival in paradise.

"Come on, Hannah, I will show you the house!"

"Yes, I am coming, Hans!"

When Hans showed me the villa, I was so amazed that I couldn't walk straight any longer. What a beautiful building! The rooms where Hans and I lived from now on were amazing!

"Do you like it?"

"Yes, Hans, I am so fascinated by all of this. I have never seen such luxury before!"

"You get used to it very quickly. When I think about how I felt!"

"Weren't you shocked by all the luxury?"

"Yes, but it is not our doing. My father and I have so much money since everyone in our family died."

"Yes, you've changed a lot!"

Was that a hint of distrust? Today, I cannot remember exactly what I felt at that moment. But I do not want to dismiss the assumption. I had a suspicion back then that things weren't going right here. I knew Hans came from a respected family but not a rich one.

Perhaps Hans sensed my doubts, however subtle they were, because he immediately tried to dispel them.

"Do you find? But inside, I am still your Hans!"

"Yes! Who I love more than anything!"

"If you have time to think about it, think about when we want to get married."

Oh no, that was too much of a good thing! I first had to get used to the new surroundings and wanted to gain security.

So, I first weighed it down: "I will do it, but let us wait a little longer. Now we are engaged!"

"Of course, my dear, we have all the time in the world."

"Where do I sleep?"

"You can sleep alone or in the same room with me!"

"Of course, I will sleep with you now that we are engaged!"

"Come on, I will show you where we sleep!"

He took my hand and walked with me to the second floor. There we stood in front of a room door.

Hans said, "Open it!"

I did not trust myself. I asked. "Should I?"

Hans rolled his eyes and said again: "Yes, do it!"

I grabbed the door handle, pushed it down, and pushed the door open.

"Oh Hans, I think I am dreaming!" In front of me was a room decorated entirely in white.

"Come'! Let us go in and take a look!"

Hans took my hand and walked with me into the very large room. It was decorated with light damask wallpaper and white carpeting. There was stucco on the ceiling and a chandelier hanging in the middle of the ceiling. Only the dark suitcase and my black dress stood out from the surroundings.

"You think you are in heaven, but I do not want to go there yet!"

Hans said with a laugh: "No, my sweet Hannah, you can stay down here with me!"

Sebastian rang the dinner bell downstairs.

"Come on, let us go eat! I hope you like our cook's food."

"Certainly! I am not spoiled."

We went to the ground floor. The meal was served in the large drawing room.

"Ah, there you are. So, Hannah, how do you like it here?"

"It is simply wonderful, Mr. Mangold!"

"I am glad, child."

"What is there to eat, father?"

"Roast beef with pasta and salad!"

My eyes got bigger and bigger when I heard that. When was the last time I had a roast? I do not know! Such a meal was normally for Switzerland, but certainly not for us bombed-out Jews.

"Do you like two slices?" Because I was so amazed, I did not even hear Hans. He asked me. "Hannah, are you dreaming?"

[03 VILLA MANGOLD BASEL]

(VILLA MANGOLD IN BASEL (TODAY ITALIAN CONSULATE)

(I can still hear his voice. He has been dead for 20 years now and died of a pulmonary embolism. That day, I wanted to die myself. I missed him so much. But at night, I saw him in my dreams; he promised to wait for me on the bridge. I did not know I had to wait so long.)

When we had finished eating, Hans asked me if we wanted to go into town together. I was a little scared, but he told me it was unfounded. In Basel, no one had anything against us Jews. So, I agreed and went to change my clothes. After about fifteen minutes, I met Hans downstairs in the large entrance hall.

"How beautiful you are!" He welcomed me enthusiastically. I went to meet him. Hans was now also dressed entirely in black.

"You look good too, Hans! So elegant and beautiful."

"Shall we go?"

"Yes, I am ready!"

"Then come!" Hans took my hand and discovered the big city that I had never heard of before.

We walked along the esplanade of the Rhine to the very front, where the Café Spitz was and this big bridge. Hans told me what kind of bridge it was, and I was just amazed at what he knew.

"This is the middle bridge over the Rhine! Look, there is a tram coming."

"Yes!" Hans took my hand and pulled me behind him.

"We have to jump up!"

I shouted to him. "Yes, then let us run!" Hans paid for the tickets and sat down with me.

"We are going to the town hall. Today is Market Day!"

"How beautiful! I love markets!"

"Even! I know, and I want to give you fresh flowers!"

"I am glad!" I had not been afraid to go out for a while. Unfortunately, the tram was only a short drive, so we had to get off.

"Come, here we are. Well, what do you say?"

"So great a market and so many stalls!"

"When you are in this market, it is obligatory to eat a sausage called Basler Klöpfer."

"But I am not hungry!"

"Such a Basler Klöpfer always fits in the stomach!"

"Do you?"

"Yes, come!"

Again, he grabbed my hand and ran to the next barbecue stand. Unfortunately, I hardly understood what they were talking about. But Hans knew this dialect perfectly. He had learned it in the last three years. It even sounded almost like German – just speaking with chewing gum in the mouth, as we knew it in Berlin from the American occupation soldiers.

But what Hans said worked out. He was given two Basler Klöpfer with bread and mustard. When I first bit into a real Basler Klöpfer. It was an indescribable moment. Hans was right, a Basler Klöpfer always fits in the stomach. Of course, the bread was also fantastic. Mustard belongs to the Klöpfer.

"Well, how do you like it?"

I could not say anymore. "Tasteful!"

(I am running water in my mouth right now. Would you not like to eat a hot, delicious Klöpfer from the charcoal grill right now? After that, you are doing so well, my dear readers. In our Basel years, we always had the Sausages from the Bell butchery. They are still among the best slaughterhouses in Switzerland today.)

Hans asked impatiently. "Are you ready?"

I said with my mouth full. "Yes!" I have never been able to eat fast.

"Come, let us buy fruit, vegetables, and the flowers, of course."

We were crawling over the market when I suddenly asked Hans what this was for a Klöpfer. He said it was pork, but he had never done much of our faith and had rarely gone to the synagogue, so apparently, he did not take the dietary rules seriously. Well, Adonai had hurt him very badly.

I, however, felt bad now, but we had also eaten pork during the war and had only been able to survive. Only I can never tell my father that I ate the pig. He does rather starve than eat pork. father and mother did not even eat pork during the war. They ate potatoes and other food. Just what was acceptable before Adonai.

I must have looked around sadly, for Hans tried to comfort me, and excite me: "Love, let this be our secret! Sometimes, you have to do something where others do not like it!"

"Yes, Hans, that is the best way to do it!" Nevertheless, I did not feel good.

But Hans made every effort to get me to think differently.

"Well, we have bought everything. Should we go to the little café in front of it?"

"Yes, I do like to drink coffee now. I hope the coffee is real!"

"Of course, it is real! We are in Switzerland!" Hans laughed so loudly that other passers looked at us.

"Shh, do not be so loud! The guests are already watching us."

Hans said and waved with his hands. "It does not matter, dear."

In front of the café, we sat at a small table with a direct view of the market. Hans ordered two Café Crème, whatever it was. Cake I refused, but it looked very seductive! When the coffee came, I looked at it: it had such a light brown foam on top.

I asked. "What is this supposed to be?"

"Café Crème! On top is the coffee cream. It arises when the coffee leaks out of this modern machine, like a dense foam."

I tried and loved Café Crème. After the first cup of coffee, Hans asked how it tasted. I just said as I said before, "Tasteful!" Hans was happy because I had smiled. (As I write this, I realize again how much I loved Hans. He could have changed so much or changed later.)

It was already dark, and Hans wanted to leave. After all, the cook also needed the vegetables. We went and decided to walk to the villa. It had been such a beautiful day, and the evening air was splendid.

We walked past all the shops. Hans got another piece of bread from the baker. Did not we want to go home quickly? But then he came out without having to wait long. There was everything in abundance here.

He took my hand and pulled me towards the big bridge. As we were in the middle of this bridge, I dared to look down into the shimmering green water. I had high anxiety, but Hans held my hand, and nothing could happen to me.

As I was slightly embarrassed, he pulled me out of the tray and kissed me. Then we went on.

"Come! It is down the stairs in front of you. We will walk again along the Rhine."

"Yes, let us go down there. We could have a cup of coffee at this Spitz Cafe. And thank you for this beautiful day!"

"Yes, my dear, and so it will always be!"

"This Café Spitz is a little beauty." I noticed as we passed by it.

Hans whispered and then said to me. "Yes, dear, you will also get the famous Basel Läckerli there. You have to try them!"

"I do like to!"

So, we walked the last piece home comfortably along the Rhine promenade. I recognized fishermen sitting on the bank and holding their fishing rods in the shimmering green water. One of them waved, and Hans waved back and said to me. "This is Rudi, the man of our cook."

He looked friendly, I thought, and waved at him. Hans started laughing because I looked so shy, but I started laughing too.

"Why are you laughing?"

I said to him. "Just because you are the love of my life. I only love you, and that is all my life."

Hans stood still and kissed me again.

"When are we going to get married?"

There she was again, this question that many young ladies dream of. But I was afraid of it unfounded. For a moment I thought about it, and then I said, "Surely, Hans, give me a little more time!"

When we arrived home, we were already expected by Mr. Mangold.

"Well, you two, did you have fun?"

"Yes, very much, father!"

"I have allowed myself to invite a few friends to celebrate the day. That is why we changed the dinner. There's an Appenzeller Fondue. Hannah, you will love it!"

"I am looking forward, Mr. Mangold!"

"Oh, darling, please say Samuel. Mr. Mangold makes me so old!"

I had to laugh and say, "Yes, Samuel!"

Hans laughed and said. "Well, let us go!" (How I miss his laughter! He could always infect everyone with his laughter.)

I apologized to the two of them because I wanted to refresh myself for the food. Hans said I did not have to apologize, I could go wherever I wanted, and I did not need to ask.

It is a change to change so much from yesterday to today. In my family in Berlin, all this would not have been possible, even if the conditions in Germany had continued to improve.

I went to refresh myself. When I got out of the bathroom, a beautiful dress lay on the bed. It was light blue, had white rods, and was made of silk.

I said surprised. "Oh, what is this!"

I ran to the bed, took the dress in my hands, and smelled it. It smelled so wonderfully new. I heard a laugh behind me. It was Hans who sat on the chair in the corner.

"I see, you like the dress!"

"It is wonderful and so elegant!"

"I thought you wanted to paint your beauty with this dress."

"You are a slanderer! Thank you, Hans!"

"Well, my love! Put it on. I will wait outside!"

"Good!"

I wore it, but it was not that easy. After almost ten minutes, Hans knocked on the room door.

"Is everything okay with you?"

"Yes, come in! You have to close the zipper."

Hans came in and almost became blind! "You look like a princess, so beautiful!"

He came closer and pulled my zipper.

"Come, look in the mirror!"

I turned around. I saw myself in this dress for the first time and was totally in love with my mirror image.

"Wait, I have something for you!"

Hans put a chain of pearls around my neck.

When I saw her, I had to swallow! I have never worn anything so valuable before.

"It is from my mother, and father said you should wear it."

"Thank you, Hans!"

"Ready, sweetheart?"

"Ready!"

"Come! Let us go down, the guests will be waiting."

"I'm afraid!"

"You don't have to be afraid. The heart of a warrior beats in you!"

We went hand in hand to the stairs, and I saw all the guests.

There must have been 30 guests, and everyone was waiting for me! Hans made the start, and step by step we got closer to them. The guests clapped, and I enjoyed it. We stood downstairs, Samuel came to us, and I will never forget his words.

"May I introduce you to my daughter Hannah Adriana Epstein! She and Hans will soon get married and continue our family history. Welcome all Hannah!"

They all lifted their drinks and said. "Welcome, Hannah!" I should be touched! But I felt oppressed. Hans must have noticed that my hand was cold and damp. He gave me a glass of champagne and took one for himself, and then we stumbled upon each other. So, my nervousness immediately disappeared, and I drank my first champagne – from that point, I loved this sparkling deliciousness.

After everyone had struck me, we all went together into the big salon. There were already some butlers, and each of us was brought to his place. Hans and I sat in the middle. Samuel Mangold and the widow of lawyer Hornmann senior sat opposite us, both widowed. I immediately suspected something was going on between them. But why not? Both were alone and not too old for a new love.

But when we all sat down, it suddenly began to smell awful. What was that? I thought, but before I could ask Hans, I saw them: seven men in strange clothes came into the room, each with a pot of stone in his hand.

What they brought us there was disgusting at the time, but that was before I tried it. Today, I love this dish, and when I go on vacation in our villa in Basel, I almost always eat such a delicious Fondue. It is best with the Appenzeller cheese. It is pretty spicy, and when it is melted, deliciously creamy.

Music sounded. Four dairymen (shepherds) in the same costume played an instrument, which in Switzerland is called an original 'Schwizer Örgeli'. In German, they call it harmonica. These seven gentlemen walked past us to the music as if at a ceremony, then stopped at one position. Where a small warmer was burning at the table, they put down the caquelons and began to yodel. I had to laugh.

The others looked at me in surprise, but then they laughed. I later learned that the clothing the dairymen were wearing was a traditional costume from the Appenzell region.

(The dairymen have yellow breeches made of leather, and the farmers have long brown trousers made of cloth or half-linen without a fly, but with a square bib is closed with buttons at the waistband - hence 'loading trousers'. The trousers include a Chüeli broscht = Kühlein chest): black leather suspenders have rich brass fittings with rosettes, cows, and shepherds.

The shirt has a double-breasted design, is decorated with white embroidery, and has short puffed sleeves. Instead of a tie, a red button with a gold-plated silver brooch is worn. The scarlet vest worn open – Broschttuäch or Liibli – has a small stand-up collar, embroidered lapels, and two rows of silver buttons.

The 'Sennenfetzen', a large handkerchief printed with pictures and sayings, is folded into a triangle and worn around the waist with the yellow trousers. Includes a wide-brimmed, flower-decorated felt hat when driving cattle.

The knitted stockings are tied below the knee with black leather straps. The shoes are heavy-low shoes with silver buckles.)

I understood that it was possible to live well in Switzerland, even if I had only been here for a day. But well, I had found heaven on earth in the Mangold villa.

Regarding the food itself, I can say once again that it smells terrible - not just the melted cheese, but also the schnapps (liquor) in it, which makes the mixture thick - but it tastes irresistibly like more. But please do not put too much liquor in the fondue. Otherwise, it won't taste good!

Hans gave me a small glass. Back then, I was so naive and thought it was water. He raised his glass like everyone else and said proudly: "To my fiancée, Hannah!"

I saw everyone downing the glass in one gulp and tried to do the same. Then I noticed that this water was kirsch water and belonged to every fondue. I was drunk later! I was allowed to do that because I was yet a fine lady at the time. I was at home here.

Of course, the other morning I woke up completely hungover. I had never drunk alcohol in my life. I was sick and hated that kirsch but after my first coffee. The world looked better again.

On this day, I wanted to go into the city alone; Hans was in Zurich with his father. I decided to get dressed and go. Maybe there was a sausage stand somewhere. I was impressed by the Basel Klöpfer. I loved them even if they were pork.

"Sebastian, I am going into town."

"Shall I accompany you?"

"No, I can have fun alone. But thanks for asking."

"At least take Peter with you. Peter can carry your shopping!"

"No offense, Sebastian, but I won't be shopping that much. I want to explore a little Basel in peace!" I took my jacket and left.

Finally, alone! I thought to myself as I stepped out of our villa. Sebastian is always so clingy, but of course, he means well. I was completely new here and in a world that was foreign to me.

I decided to take this tram. I first had to walk along the Rhine. I saw the fishermen again, and they gave me a friendly wave. I could see it was the husband of our cook again, so I waved back.

What a beautiful day! The birds were singing, and people were sitting in the garden restaurant of the Hotel Merian and were happy. (The

Hotel Merian burned down in 1969 – a disaster!) I ran up the stairs and went up to the tram. The friendly conductor gave me the ticket, and I paid for it. How funny that was! I did not know how to handle money, but I just did it the way women have always done it, and then I learned along the way.

I took the tram to a place that I had not seen or heard of - Barfüsserplatz. What a strange name! Were you only allowed to enter it barefoot?

The conductor told me that if I got off there, I could experience something. So, I got out and saw a small market in the square. I was happy because I liked going to markets. I slowly strolled through the narrow streets of the stalls. There was so much to see! The smells of spices, flowers, and especially the smell of the barbecue stand. I bought flowers and was even given a rose by the seller, a young man.

He said: "A rose for a rose! May it bloom as long as your beauty lasts!" What a charmer!

"If you do that to every woman, you will soon run out of roses."

He bowed to me and kissed my hand. I blushed. I quickly moved on to a stand with spices.

"Do you like spices? They are all from the Orient!" I waved him off, but he did not give up. "I have the best cinnamon from Ceylon, the best cloves spice from India, and the healthiest herbs from our Alps! Come buy something, I will give you a good price."

I decided to buy something from him. "Okay, I will take these herbs. What can I do with it? "

"For in the salad, or you can mix it with liquor!"

"I'll think about it - well, I want to take two bunches."

He gave me two bunches, I gave him the money. I did not want to buy more, but who knows? I kept walking, there were still so many beautiful stalls. I had to stop again at one stand. There was lace and tulle. I was totally in love with this lace apron, but it was expensive.

The dealer suggested. "I will give you a discount if you take them."

I asked him. "How much do you want?"

He wanted five francs. I looked in my wallet and saw I only had four francs left.

"Unfortunately, I only have four francs left. The other herb dealer was so expensive."

He smiled at me in a friendly manner. "I will take the four francs."

I gave it to him, and he gave me this wonderful apron. I thanked him and left. But now I wanted to move on. I ran up the narrow alley. There was a beautiful church upstairs that I wanted to see up close.

It was the famous cathedral in Basel.

I walked around the cathedral to the wall. From up there you had a beautiful view of the other side of the Rhine! You could even see our villa on the other side of the river and the fishermen, who were still fishing.

I continued walking and saw this sign that said 'Rhine ferry'. I have to see this! I thought to myself as I ran down the stairs. There it was, the ferry with the beautiful name Leu. (The Leu is one of four ferries still in use today. These ferries were named after the coats of arms of the three honorary societies of Kleinbasel. The main characters in the traditional procession of the Gryff bird.)

I shyly asked the young man on the ferry if he could take me to the other side. He said he would be happy to do so. He called me Miss, how nice! He helped me get in, then we set off. He cleverly let his ferry drift to the other side all by itself. I wanted to pay him there, but he didn't want any money from me.

Instead, he said in his Swiss dialect: "What am I supposed to do with your money? It is enough for me to see your beauty!"

I felt my face turn red, thanked me quickly, and ran up the granite stairs. I only stood up on the shore promenade but had to look again at the ferryman. This one saw me look around and waved at me. I smiled at him, but he turned and lay down again.

At home, Hans and his father had already returned from Zurich. I quickly ran into the villa to see my beloved. Sebastian said he was still in a conversation with his father. I thanked myself, went into our bedroom, and got out. I refreshed myself in the bathroom. I thought about what to wear and chose the simple blue dress.

I heard the two downstairs. Hans and his father were done. Hurry down and greet him, but not without shoes! I ran to my shoe wardrobe, put on my shoes, and ran to the stairs. There we met, and I still know how my heart was pounding.

I shouted, "Hans, you are finally back." I walked down the stairs straight into his arms.

"Hannah, my love!" I kissed him.

His father had to laugh. He said, "It was just four hours, and you act as if it was four years!"

"Father, this is because we love one another infinitely."

"Yes, yes, son!"

"Hannah, I need to talk to you."

"Is something going on, Hans?"

"No, my love but I just have to tell you something."

"All right, Hans, it is time. I was alone in town today, and I drove a ferry!"

"Yes, that is great, but I want to tell you something. Father wants me to go to Zurich and conduct our new company there."

I said without long thinking. "That sounds good! When are we leaving?"

"Are you ready to come with me?" He asked me, and I said, "Of course! I love you, and we belong together, Hans."

He kissed me and was happy that I wanted to come with him.

"My dears, let us eat!"

After dinner, we had enough time to talk. We sat down in the small lounge. Hans drank whiskey, and I drank tea.

"Hans, what kind of company is this?"

"My love, I do not know if you will understand this. I am trying to explain it to you. Very many Jews have very much money or other valuables. Martin Hornmann knows many of them, and our company will take care of this money and these valuables. We deposit these things for a fee. Or we invest the money in profitable projects. Or we buy houses and rent them."

"You are right, I did not understand anything!"

"No matter, my love, I will show you it there personally. If you like, you may also work a little."

"I do not know yet. I would rather learn something. I do like to be a hairdresser!"

"It's out of the question!"

I was angry, but I was good at hiding it. Jewish women suffered and endured everything in silence, but I did not want to give up at the time.

"Hannah, understand! My wife cannot be a haircutter. We are rich, and you do not have to do anything but represent, give parties or receptions, and be my wife."

"I understand, Hans! I am supposed to be the mistress at your side!"

"Forgive me if you misunderstand me. But that is our life."

I did not understand it at the time. Today I know that I had a good life.

"I am going to bed, sleep well!"

I got up and left. Hans did not say much except "Night!" Oh God, our first dispute!

The other morning was yesterday's news. Hans was lying next to me, and I looked at him. He smiled and said. "Do you still love me?"

"Of course, very much!"

I kissed him and snuggled up to him. I did not know how to have sex back then, but that came with time. I did not know whether Hans wanted sex at this time. I was still young and did not want to know anything about it.

"Let us get up. We still have a few things to do."

"Good!"

Hans immediately got up and went into the bathroom. Oddly enough, he left the door ajar. So, I could see him undressing. So, he looked so great naked! I noticed my face blushing. I quickly pulled the blanket over my head.

I heard Hans ask as he came out of the bathroom. "Are you freezing?"

"No, Hans, everything is fine. I thought I was going to sneeze, but there was nothing."

"I am going downstairs, I have to talk to father."

"It is okay, I still have to go to the bathroom. A lady needs longer!"

"Don't worry, take your time, my love."

He came to me, kissed me, and then left. I went into the bathroom and got ready. Today I wanted to make myself pretty for Hans. I wanted to hear the famous "Ahh!"

When I was ready, I went downstairs. Hans and his father were already sitting at the table and eating breakfast.

"Good morning everyone!"

"Good morning, Hannah, how pretty you are, my Daughter!", said Samuel.

Hans was speechless. He could hardly concentrate on his sandwich. There it was: "Ahh!" Hans said it, and I was happy. I sat down opposite Hans. Sebastian served coffee, and I helped myself to a roll and some cheese. Hans and his father were talking about business. I was sitting next to them. When I finished breakfast, I got up.

Hans stopped me: "Where do you want to go now?"

"You talk and take no notice of me. I can do something else!"

"No, I would like to speak to you about another matter. Let us go out to the park."

"Yes, I do love to. Some fresh air is good!"

I went to the cloakroom to get a cardigan. Hans was already wearing his suit jacket. As we were walking outside in the park, I said to Hans:

"The weather today is wonderful."

"Yes, Hannah, it is already warm in the morning."

"You wanted to talk to me?"

"Yes, Hannah. I wanted to ask you if we wanted to go to Berlin for a few days."

"What? Yes, I do love to see my mother finally and everyone else."

"Yeah, that is why I thought you missed them."

"That is great! But when you are with me, longing is not that great."

"Dad got tickets, we will go tomorrow if you like?"

"Yes, Hans!" I hugged Hans and kissed him. "I still have so much to do! Can we still go shopping?"

"Yes, sweetheart, whatever you like!"

"Then come, I do like to buy some gifts for home." I ran to get myself a jacket.

When I came back to Hans. He was already standing by his car, waiting for me.

"Please forgive me, it took a little longer!"

"Now you are here, my love!" and helped me to get in.

I wanted to know. "Where are we going?"

"To Riehen, this is only a few minutes away by car. There is a nice market and small shops."

"I am looking forward, Hans."

Sebastian drove the car, and after 15 minutes, we were already in Riehen. This is a small border town to Germany. Sebastian parked the car and got out to help us both get out.

"Hannah, look, there is the market!"

"How nice, Hans, let us go!"

Hans took me by the hand and aimed towards the market. He stopped at one of the stalls where soap was sold.

"Do you think your mother and Rosa are delighted with soap?"

"Sure! Soap is precious and rare in Germany."

"Then let us take four pieces of lavender soap and four parts of rose soap!", said Hans to the market woman.

"Well, the gentleman! Can there be anything else?"

"Yes, two pieces of kernel soap, then we have everything."

"I'd like to!" The market woman took them all in. "Twelve francs, please!"

Hans paid, and we went on until a stand came with goods made of lace. I stood there and admired all the beautiful tablecloths and bedding.

"Would you take something with you?"

"Yes, please!"

"Let us go!"

Somewhat shy, I said to the seller. "I do like tablecloths."

"I do love to. Find something for yourself!"

I looked at a few pieces and then chose three tablecloths.

"These, please!"

"I'd love to! Can there be anything else?"

"Yes! Two more Aprons. Do you have colored?"

"I have to go look."

He came back with colored clothes, beautiful pieces. I picked up two nice Aprons.

The seller packed everything.

"That is twenty-four francs, madam."

Hans paid for the goods, and we went on to buy a few more things for Adam, Ari, and especially for father.

After more than an hour, we had everything together. Hans was already exhausted. He just wanted to go for a coffee.

"Would you come with me, or would you like to go look at the market?"

"No, Hans, I will come with you. I do like coffee and cake, my love."

Hans smiled contentedly at me. "Come on, let us go, there is a nice café up there!"

The café itself was in an old villa. With the nice weather, we were able to sit on the terrace, which we did. Hans ordered coffee and cake. When the waiter came, I was amazed. There was Black Forest cake! My eyes widened.

"Oh, how beautiful, Black Forest cake! How I would love to take a piece for mom."

"I do not know if she will be able to eat the cake when we get there."

I said sadly. "I know!"

"But you could ask for the recipe!"

When the waiter passed us again, I gathered up the courage and asked him if I could get the recipe for this delicious Black Forest cake.

He politely said that he would have to ask in the kitchen. He did this, and when he came back, he had a piece of paper in his hand.

"Look, madam, the pastry chef gave me this for you."

I said delightedly. "This is fantastic! Thank you!"

Hans gave him a little tip for his effort. I was so happy and decided that. I would bake this great cake in Berlin.

"Should I pay, or would you like something else, love?"

"No, we can go. I am excited about tomorrow!"

Hans waved to the waiter. He came, and Hans paid. I thanked him again, and we left.

Sebastian was already waiting in front of the café. When he saw us, he got out to help me get in.

"Thank you, Sebastian!"

"With pleasure, Miss Epstein."

Sebastian got in, and then we were off.

"Sebastian, please stop at the nearest shop where you can buy pocket knives."

"You are welcome. Someone is coming, I will stop!"

"Thank you, Sebastian !"

I jumped out and ran to the store. Hans called after me to wait. However, I only heard this in passing because I had seen a great hunting knife in the shop window. It is what it should be, and Adam is happy about it. The salesman greeted me politely and asked me what I would like. I greeted him politely and showed him the knife I wanted. He looked at me with wide eyes and then said: "Miss, are you not too young for a knife like that?"

"No! I'm 21 years old, not too young, sir!"

At that moment Hans came into the shop and said: "Dear, you cannot hear! I called you because you cannot just buy a knife!"

I asked curiously. "Why not?"

The shop owner said: "It's not common for young women to buy knives in Switzerland."

I said awkwardly. "I understand!"

"But I can buy it for you!"

"Then please do that and buy another tobacco pipe for father. He loves to smoke in the evenings."

I pointed to the knife I had chosen. Then I thought of Ari. He could use one too.

"Can I have two of these, please?"

"Of course!" It was, after all, a good deal for him.

"That makes 52 francs, and here is a gift for you." He held two small stones in his hand, which he grabbed with them. Hans paid, I took the goods, and we went.

He said politely and whispered. "Goodbye!"

"Goodbye!"

I was already outside when I got in. When Hans sat down, we could move on.

Hans asked me. "Do we have everything now?" and taking my hand into his.

"Yes, my beloved, thank you for having bought all this!"

"My money is also your money. Darling, you don't have to thank me. What your family has done for me, I can never thank you enough!"

"I love you, Hans!"

"I love you, too, Hannah Epstein!"

Sebastian bowed into the Rhine promenade, where our villa is. Samuel stood upstairs on the stairs when we got out. He waved at us; he was always very kind.

At the top of the staircase, Samuel asked us if we had nice shopped. He could see all the bags that Sebastian was dragging into the villa.

"Yes, father. Hannah wants to take presents to Berlin."

"Yes, I can understand! We can never thank you enough for what you have done for my Hans!"

"Samuel, we didn't do this alone. Many have helped!"

 Samuel said to me. "Thank you, Hannah!"

"When is dinner ready, father?"

"I think it would serve soon. You have to go to bed soon."

"Yes, we have to get up at five in the morning."

"I will not accompany you. That is why I will say goodbye to you later. Let's go eat now." The cook was already ringing the bell.

We went to dinner. There was a Pasta bake today. It was so delicious, and there was almost nothing left. The cook had Tessinian roots. The Tessinian cuisine has Italian origins. Pasta bake and gratin are very popular.

After we had finished, we sat in the small salon for a little while. There were always cigars and whiskey there. People talked about the day or whether any rumors could be passed on. That evening, however, we only talked about our forthcoming trip to Berlin.

Samuel wanted to know how long we were going to stay in Berlin. Hans said we would stay for a week. On the other hand, I would have preferred not to leave Berlin in advance.

When it was time to sleep, we said goodbye to Samuel and went to bed. That night I slept very restless because I was excited. I'll finally see my family again! They do not know that we are coming, so the joy will be much greater!

At some point, I had to fall asleep, because when I woke up, Hans was already sitting on the bedside and wanted to get up.

"Good morning, my dear. Did you sleep well?"

"Good morning, yes, but it took me a long time to fall asleep!"

He bowed to me and kissed me.

Since that night we were no longer strangers.

(You know what I mean. At the time, it was not customary to have sex before marriage, not even between fiancés. We had our first sex that night, and I think we made our baby there.)

"Will we get up? It's almost five o'clock!"

"Yes, my beloved! Do you want to go to the bathroom first, or should I?"

He joked. "I am done, but we can go together!" I shouted, "No, you madman!" He laughed and went into our bathroom. However, he left the door wide open. (My G-d, he had a beautiful body! How I loved him then! You can paint it yourself.)

Ten minutes later, he came out of the bathroom refreshed, in a good mood, and whispering, sat next to me on the bedside, and kissed me.

"I am going downstairs and arranging breakfast! Or should I help you in the bathroom?"

I screamed, and he laughed, and then he went. I got up to see if he came back. When he was gone, I quickly ran into the bathroom. Today, I think, how could I have been so stupid then?

When I was ready, I dressed elegantly. Then I went to Hans to have breakfast with him. He was already sitting at the table in the salon and drinking coffee.

"Hannah, there you are!"

"Yes, Hans, sometimes it takes a little longer."

"Do not worry! Do we want to bring some more coffee for your family?"

"Yes, please! I am sure the coffee there is not as good as here."

"Do you like coffee?"

"Yes, please!" Hans gave me coffee, I took some fresh bread and ate some butter with cheese.

After 20 minutes, Hans said, "When you are ready, we can go. I packed the coffee and some chocolate!"

"Thank you!"

Hans and I cleaned the table, and then Sebastian came.

"Good morning!"

Hans greeted him, and I said, "Good morning, Sebastian. How are you today?"

"Thank you, well, Miss Epstein. I have already brought the suitcases to the car."

"Thank you, Sebastian. We will be right back! All I have to do is get my coat."

"No hurry, we still have some time."

Hans was already in front of me when I picked up my coat. He was still in the room on the chair. I took it and put it on as I walked. They were already waiting downstairs. Sebastian held the car door open for me. Once I got in, we were finally able to set off.

Shortly, we arrived at the station. Sebastian let us out, and then he picked up the suitcases. He took them to the platform with a trolley. I still had an open mouth and made big eyes when I saw this large entrance hall at the Badischen Bahnhof. We walked to our platform, past the German customs.

It was not like today, then. Today, there are very few customs officers at the border crossing, and there were many more at the time.

Our train was already there when we arrived at the platform. People ran back and forth, the conductor waved, and we were in the middle.

This time, we took the high-speed train to Frankfurt am Main. From there, it would then continue with the transit train FD 1/2. The route led from Frankfurt am Main to Bebra (border crossing), then from Wartha (Werra) via Erfurt and Sangerhausen to Berlin Friedrichstraße. The journey took only 7.5 hours from Frankfurt am Main to Berlin-Friedrichstraße. The journey time from Basel to Frankfurt am Main was a good 6-hour route. We drove a good 690 kilometers and had to pay 552 Reichsmark. That was, after all, 281 Swiss francs.

Sebastian said, "Train carriage three, compartment two!"

I looked and saw that carriage three counted for the first class.

I said to Hans. "Hans! There must be something wrong, we are in first class according to the train number!"

"That's right, father booked the trip for us, and he always books first class!"

I was shocked when I saw the setup on the train. So classy and so modern for this time! Today, the first class is no longer so noble.

"I'm finally sitting down, and I feel bad too!" I groaned.

Hans laughed. He was pleased that everything had gone smoothly so far. "Are you looking forward to Berlin?"

"Yes! I finally see my family again. I miss them and I am excited to see how Berlin has developed." Like so many other German cities, Berlin had to be rebuilt, and that did not happen as quickly back then as with today's technical possibilities.

At the start of the journey, it was very restless on the train. People walked past, and now and then, the door was opened, and people asked if there was anything available, but Hans just growled: "No!"

Little by little, it became quieter. Everyone was sitting where they were supposed to. Customs officers also passed through in between. One of them looked briefly into our compartment and nodded in a friendly manner. I read "The Red Zora" - A young adult book. I know! When I was younger, we couldn't read books like that. Hans, on the other hand, was leafing through the newspaper.

The first stop was Freiburg. The train stopped, and a few passengers and customs got off. New travelers boarded and walked around again. Finally, it was quiet again. I continued reading; Hans studied his documents and took notes. Now, and then he would say quietly, "Good!" and I would look up because I thought he meant me.

The next stop was Karlsruhe. Travelers got off and on again. I was getting bored. Luckily, the coffee cart finally came past our compartment. The train employee looked at us in a friendly manner, and I waved to him.

He asked politely. "Hello, would you like something?"

I answered: "Yes! I want a coffee with milk and sugar. Would you like something too, Hans?"

He was engrossed in his work but looked up when I asked him.

"Yes, dear. A coffee and two pretzels. The coffee with sugar."

The train employee gave us coffee and pretzels. I paid him, and he left.

"Finally, coffee, I am already tired. I could have had a pretzel too, too bad."

"Dear, I took two extras because I know you will want some afterward."

Hans gave me a pretzel, and I was happy.

We arrived in Mannheim, and the train stopped. Soldiers were standing on the runway, Americans, some Afro-Americans. They wore their olive-green uniforms and smiled. They were glad they did not have to do a favor. It got loud when they got on the train, but it did not bother me. They traveled in second class but ran past our compartment. So young and friendly! Someone whistled because of me when he saw me! I felt like I was getting red. Of course, Hans had not heard of anything. The train operator whistled in his whistle, and the train set in motion. I looked at the train information and saw that the next stop was Frankfurt.

What am I doing in just 45 minutes, reading my book? I thought. Hans kept looking into his records, noting something in silence. I liked to watch him at work, and when he looked at his papers, he had to laugh because he caught me.

The time passed, and we finally arrived at the train station of Frankfurt am Main. I could already see the imposing building with the arched buildings when we crossed the Main. I knew from the travel information that it was a terminal station.

"Hans, we have to get out of here."

"Yes, my dear, I have heard the message."

Hans packed his documents in the suitcase and locked it. He pulled the suitcase out of the luggage net, and I took my bag.

The train stopped, and we could get off. On the platform, you could still see the remaining damage from the war. In the hall buildings, almost everywhere, there was a lack of glass.

I wanted to know from Hans. "Which platform does our train depart from?"

He looked at his note and said, "Platform 12 in ten minutes."

"There are only three tracks away."

Hans put the suitcase and bag on a trolley, and I took my bag. When we arrived at platform 12, we saw that the train was already standing. As the passengers boarded, Hans decided to board as well. The train was a little simpler and had no first class.

"Wagon 3, places 12 and 13, there we have to go."

We walked on the platform to Wagon 3 and got in there. A railway employee helped us bring the suitcases and bags onto the train. Hans gave him a tip, and he was happy. We found our seats; it was a four-place. Hans was already turning his eyes because he wanted to sit alone. On the other hand, I was looking forward to possible acquaintances.

"Well, we have the windows."

I immediately sat on my seat, looking forward to the train ride. Hans kept the suitcases in the trunk and sat down next to me.

Hans asked, "Do you like baked bread?"

"Yes, what is there to drink?"

"Water!"

"Only water?"

"No, there is also table water."

I had to laugh; it was the same bottle that Hans had given me.

"Then I will take a table water and bread."

"It is coming!"

We ate our bread and drank the table water.

"No one comes next to us. The train will leave right away."

Passengers ran past us. They ran like we did before, and they had travel documents in their hand. We also had our documents in the suitcase, in which Hans was very accurate. You could already hear the train operator's whistle. The train set in motion: the next stop was Border Station Bebra, the last western station.

I looked out the window. Hans was glad that our side seats remained free. How beautiful Hessen was! I loved the landscape. Although it was rough, you could see reconstruction progressing everywhere.

"Dear, did you know, we are going on from Bebra with a steam locomotive?"

"No, that's certainly interesting."

"We have to be there soon."

We still had five minutes after the time, and the announcement came that we would arrive in a few minutes.

Nobody got out in Bebra. Three police officers and three US soldiers got on board. The familiar fear spread within me again. But I had nothing to fear. We had all the papers, including the necessary stamps.

Passport control was not bad. One of the police officers had a Hessian dialect and was very nice. He asked where we were going, and Hans said we were going to West Berlin. They took a closer look at our passports, and one of the officials also saw my Swiss visa. We received our counting card for visa-free transit travel. They already left us alone and tortured a few poor GDR citizens. I was happy and had to take a deep breath. Hans smiled at me and continued working.

"Did you notice that we continue without changing engines?"

"Yes. I thought that they did it in Bebra, but no. Maybe not until Wartha."

As one of the police officers walked past, I seized the opportunity and asked him: "Excuse me, do you know why we don't go with a steam locomotive?"

"You will have to wait a little longer. The locomotive change will only take place in Wartha."

"Thank you very much!"

The officer nodded in a friendly manner and continued walking.

Hans was surprised that I had more courage than he expected.

He said, "Wartha is coming soon!" and looked out the window bored. "Look how barren it is here, gray and dreary! I could never live in an area like that."

"Me neither. We're not country people either. Look, there's the train station ahead."

When the train stopped at the platform, we were greeted over the loudspeaker: "Wartha, it's Wartha! Dear travelers, we welcome you to the German Democratic Republic! All travelers who were not going to Berlin would be asked to get off immediately, as this train does not stop until Berlin! I repeat: ..."

Apart from a few GDR citizens, the police officers and US soldiers got out. I opened the window and looked out cautiously. Soviet soldiers stood at the railway building and were armed. When one looked over to me, I quickly pulled my head back into the train.

You could hear work being done on the train outside. Our electric locomotives have been replaced by a steam locomotive. You could feel a jerk. From now on the steam locomotive was our traction engine. We could see our electric locomotive on the siding.

The conductor whistled twice, and the train slowly started moving. The steam locomotive whistled and became faster and faster.

"From now on, there is no stop to Berlin. We should sleep a little, the journey is still four hours."

"You can sleep, I am looking out the window. The landscape is interesting. You can see ruined houses."

"Well, no one wants to live in such a desert."

"I think that the residents were driven out by the GDR regime."

"As I said, they didn't want to live in the desert."

Hans laid his jacket over his upper body and slept a little. On the other hand, I had nothing better to do than to think about the empty farmhouses or smaller residential buildings. There is a different fate behind every vacancy. I inevitably had to think about our escape from Poland to Germany. We lived in uninhabited buildings. I liked the little cottage on the edge of the forest the most. We should've stayed there! Instead, we went on and came to a village where the Nazis had carried out a massacre. We saw a bunch of bodies burning in the market square. When we searched the buildings for food and convenience, we found that the inhabitants had been of Polish descent. The church that was burning was Catholic, and I had compassion for everyone who was there burning on the market square.

The train stations I could see as we drove past were: Eisenach, Gotha, Erfurt, and Sangerhausen. At some point, I fell asleep for a while and woke up only when we were near Berlin. Wannsee was such a nice station, and it was a pity that the train did not stop there. I remembered that Hans told me at the shelter that he was from Wannsee. When the train passed, Hans also woke up and stretched himself. He had gotten a stiff neck from lying down.

"Dear, we have to get out of here."

"Yes, we're here."

ENGAGEMENT IN BERLIN

After more than 13 hours we arrived in Berlin at Friedrichstraße train station. Finally, I thought. When the train stopped, we got out, Hans had the suitcases, and I had the bags. Fortunately, there were luggage carriers on the platform. Some young boys wanted to earn some money. Hans was happy when one of the men asked him if he should help.

We gladly accepted his offer. He immediately took three suitcases at once out to the courtyard, where Cabs and taxis were waiting. We decided to take a taxi. That was faster; It was already getting dark.

The taxi drove us to the hotel at the zoo. It was already a good address then, and I still like to go there today. (It was built as a residential house at the end of 1800 and was inhabited by architect Walter Gropius Senior with his family. In 1911, it was converted into a hotel by the Charlottenburg merchant Adolf Koschel.)

How much Berlin had changed! New residential blocks and shops was created everywhere. I was already looking forward to my first tour of the new Berlin. Of course, I wanted to make this first walk with my mother. She didn't know we were in Berlin. Immediately after breakfast, we wanted to go to the family and surprise them. Everybody was out of the house, because it was a normal day of the week. Father, Ari, and Adam had to work, but Rosa and mother took care of the household.

When we got out of the taxi I saw the hotel facade I already liked the bay windows and the bosswork cladding on the ground floor back then. We were greeted by the car master. He called a page to get our luggage out of the taxi. The car master let us into the hotel. Only the entrance area with lobby and reception was an eyepiece. We were welcomed very kindly. Hans completed the registration. Then a page brought us into our suite. Hans gave him a tip in Swiss francs.

"At last, we have arrived!" I said to Hans.

He said nothing, went to bed, and threw himself down to the length. Stretching and lamenting, he said. "Man, I am tired! Let's go to bed, sweetheart!"

"Yes, sweetheart! I'm tired, too, and tomorrow, we want to leave early."

So, we went to bed, but not without bathing in this beautiful bathroom, which was furnished in Art Nouveau. It was the first time we had a bath together. How beautiful it was! We also got closer there.

When we were lying side by side in the bed, Hans kissed me and said, "Good night, my dear. I love you so much!"

"Good night, my dear! I love you so much too."

Then we fell asleep. I had wild dreams of our bathing together and how it ended in a dream.

The next morning, I woke up very early. Hans was still asleep. I went to the bathroom to refresh myself. Just as I was done, Hans knocked on the door.

"Love, can I come in?"

"Yes, Hans!"

"Thank you. I need to pinch!"

Oh, my God, I thought and ran out.

Hans, on the other hand, laughed, already sitting on the toilet. I closed the door and got dressed. It knocked on the door, it must have been the room service. He brought our breakfast.

I went and opened the room door. The young butler said kindly: "Good morning, Mrs. Mangold. I'll bring your breakfast."

"Good morning, that looks delicious!"

"I wish you a wonderful day here in Berlin. Enjoy your breakfast!"

I gave him a tip, then he left.

"Hans, breakfast is here!"

He called from the bathroom. "Coming!"

"I'm starting!"

He was already coming out of the bathroom.

"Ah, that looks delicious!"

"Do you like orange juice and coffee?"

"Yes, with pleasure, dear!"

I poured both for him, then we ate our leisurely breakfast.

"The butler called me Mrs. Mangold earlier. How that sounded!"

"Definitely because I registered us as Mr. and Mrs. Mangold."

"Does not matter. I can get used to it."

"Do I need a jacket?"

"It's already 19 degrees outside! You can go in your shirt."

"Doesn't that look a bit sloppy?"

"No, Hans, walk around a little more casually! We are in Berlin and not in Switzerland."

"I have to go with a jacket, darling. I forgot I still have appointments!"

I said sadly. "It's okay, you and your appointments!"

Suddenly, he grabbed me and kissed me.

I shouted at him. "You boor!" Then I smiled and kissed him back.

"Come on, let us go!"

I grabbed Hans' hand, and we started going. We took the elevator to the lobby and handed in our key. Outside the hotel, we got a taxi and drove to the Spree.

The weather was so warm, and a walk would do us good. We decided to walk towards the Brandenburg Gate. I was thrilled by the new cityscape. Where we went, there were still tanks driving around during the war and soldiers walking around!

I thought of Adam on the Spree. He, Doctor Levin, and Moses Benmon had to cross the Spree back then. All they could do were swim, otherwise they would have been discovered and killed. Only a few kilometers from there, was the tunnel complex, where we had to wait until we were all rescued.

Unfortunately, there was now this horrible GDR that had existed since 1949. I would have liked to see this place again.

"Shall we go to your family?"

But I was so lost in thought that I didn't hear Hans. It wasn't until he pulled on my coat that I was back to the present.

"Sorry, what are you saying?"

"I asked you if we wanted to visit your family now."

"Yes, gladly!"

"What were you thinking about?"

"Back then! About the war and how we suffered."

"You do not have to cry. This bad time is over, and hopefully, it won't come again!"

Hans took his handkerchief and wiped the tears from my face.

"Let's walk along the Spree here. We can then go up to the street at the front."

It was nice to walk along the Spree with Hans. He held my hand, and I looked at him in love. At the front of the big bridge, we took the narrow path up and walked along Friedrichstrasse to the apartment block on the corner of Mittelstrasse.

We looked at the doorbell signs and looked for the name Epstein.

"Ah, there he is, Epstein!"

I was just about to ring the bell when the door opened. A younger lady came out of the house. She greeted us, and we went inside.

"I'm so excited to see how they react to us!"

"What should they do? Of course, they're happy!"

We walked up the stairs to the second floor. My heart was pounding a little faster, and I rang the bell. The doorbell rang, and we could hear footsteps.

"Quick, turn around, we're joking!"

We turned around so only our backs were visible as mom opened the door. The door opened. "Yes, please!"

It was my mother who was startled when we turned around. Fright turned to screaming and screaming.

"My Hannah!"

"Mother!" I shouted and ran into her arms. She squeezed and kissed me. Then, it was Hans' turn. He was also hugged and kissed. "Mom, how I missed you all!"

"We missed you too. Come in!"

Mother directed us to the kitchen, where we sat down. I was amazed at the new furniture.

"I've only been gone a few months, and you already have new furniture."

"Yes, my child, things are going well for us. Everyone has a good job, and Rosa helps me around the household. Zuria sleeps a lot, and her age is noticeable. Rosa is out with her right now."

I wanted to know. "When are the others coming home?"

"Only in the evening! Ari will be at home for lunch."

I said. "Nice, we have time!"

"Would you like coffee?"

"Yes, gladly!"

Mother made coffee. She also made squiggles.

"Oh, mother, you made the squiggles!"

"Yes, of course, but no one did it better than you, Hannah!"

Hans said, "That's right, darling, they were always delicious!"

When the coffee was ready, you could hear the front door in the corridor. Suddenly, I heard a whimper. Zuria had smelled me. She stormed into the kitchen and jumped at me.

"Zuria, my love, how are you?" Zuria nudged her nose against my leg as if to say, "I'm so happy!"

Rosa was curious. She wanted to know who was in the kitchen. She knew those voices.

"Hannah! I can't believe it. You are finally back!" She shrieked. "And Hans, you're here too!" She squeezed Hans and didn't want to let him go.

"Hello Rosa, my dear Rosa!" I hugged Rosa when she let go of Hans and kissed her cheek. "What? Are you pregnant again?"

"Yes, Hannah! Second month."

"Adam gave it his all!" (If I had known that I was also pregnant, I wouldn't have said such nonsense!)

"Sit down, Rosa. How are you?"

"Thank you, I'm fine. Tell me: How did you do in Basel?"

"Oh, Basel is a wonderful city! I fell in love with Basel so much!"

Hans interrupted us with: "Darling! Sorry, but I still have two appointments. I can pick you up later."

"Good, my darling, have fun with your appointments!"

"Thanks, I will be back in three hours!"

"It's okay, Hans, see you later!"

Rosa also said before she continued gossiping with me. "See you later, Hans!"

Mother had just finished the coffee when Hans left.

"Please sit in the living room. Rosa, tea or coffee?"

"A cup of coffee is good."

We then went into the living room. It was newly furnished.

"You've bought a lot of furniture!"

"Yes! We didn't have much!"

"Ari should be home soon. He'll be amazed when you sit here!"

"Yes, I'm looking forward to seeing my brothers!"

"Who would like a piece of apple pie – or would you rather have a squiggle?"

"I like apple pie! Mom, I have something to tell you. I will stay in Switzerland with Hans. Hans will manage his father's company in Zurich."

"I thought so, Hannah. Good! If it makes you happy."

"Makes it! I can learn a lot there. Switzerland isn't that far away by plane, and you can come and visit us."

The apartment door opened in the corridor. Ari came home and was amazed when he saw me.

"Sister! You've become so pretty!"

"Thank you, dear brother! You've grown too, or is it because of your shoes?"

"No! I've grown five centimeters taller!"

"Come here, big brother, let me hug you!"

"How was it in Basel?"

"Great! I've seen so much, and Hans' father is so nice!"

"Fine, and when are you going back?"

"In a week or two! Hans still has a lot to do here in Berlin."

"I will go to the kitchen then. I have to eat and get going again soon."

"Where do you work?"

"With an architect! I am doing my training there alongside my studies!"

"As a Jew?"

"Yes, my boss is also Jewish. He likes what I do."

Mother said proudly, "Yes, our Ari will be famous!"

Ari went to the kitchen to eat. From there, he shouted: "Did you hear that there are riots? The Soviet zone of occupation is acting up. They want this GDR to become official!"

My mother asked worriedly. "Do you think so?"

"Yes, when the time comes. We have to be careful where we are. I don't want to live in the GDR, and you certainly don't either!"

Mother shouted, "For God's sake, no! I can't understand this view of the GDR. How can a few people secede from their people?"

"Well, my children shouldn't grow up in this GDR either."

"Fortunately, we work all in the Western sector. So, we don't have to worry about our jobs."

"That's right, Ari!"

"This was long overdue! The Russians have had influence over the so-called GDR for a long time!"

"Oh, mother! Who needs something like a GDR!"

(Nobody could even imagine how it wouldn't be long before the regime built the wall!)

Mother had already gone into the kitchen and was warming Ari's food.

"What is there?"

"Sausages and potato salad!"

"Yummy, mom, you're the best!"

When Ari finished his meal, he quickly came into the living room to say goodbye to me.

"Sister, do it well! Will we still see each other?"

"I think Ari. We will stay a few more days."

"Okay, see you soon then. Missed you, little sister!"

"I like you too, big brother!" Ari hugged me and disappeared out the door.

"Ari has grown up so much. Does he already have a girlfriend?"

"I don't know, but he'll find a woman by his side soon. Times haven't gotten much better for us Jews here in Germany."

"Are people still being persecuted here?"

"No, not that. But some groups make us Jews feel it differently. For example, when shopping or on the tram. Sometimes, I don't like leaving the house."

"I am sorry, mother. I wanted to ask if we wanted to go out with Zuria for a bit. Maybe Rosa and Leon will come with us!"

"I'm happy to come with you, and if Zuria is with us, we won't get into any problems."

"Good! Then let's go. The weather is so nice."

Rosa put Leon in the stroller, I put Zuria on a leash, and then we started. We met Ms. Kaiser in front of the house; she lived on the fourth floor with her husband, Klaus.

"Good day, Ms. Epstein. Are you out and about?"

"Good afternoon, Ms. Kaiser. Yes, my daughter Hannah is visiting us with her fiancé Hans. They live in Switzerland!"

"This is nice! Then I'm sure you're having a lot of fun."

84

"Yes, we have got that. We have to go then."

"Goodbye, ladies!"

"Goodbye, Ms. Kaiser!"

"Let's go to the Spree. There is a playground where Leon can swing."

We walked to the Spree and took the small path to the waterfront. There was the small playground where Rosa often went with Leon. But today, I was there, and he just wanted to be rocked by me. However, after a while, Leon became whiny and started crying. Rosa had to put him in the car, where he fell asleep.

"Maybe we should go back home."

"Yes, your father is coming soon. He'll be amazed when he sees you."

So, we started our way home. But we didn't take the same route back. Instead, we walked through a parallel street to the house.

"Those emperors again!" said Rosa when we got to the house.

"So! Are they back? Was it nice?"

"Yes, Ms. Kaiser, it was, but Leo wanted to go home. Now he is sleeping."

"Yes, the children, but we weren't any better before!"

"You're right, but we have to go up now."

Mother unlocked the front door, and we disappeared into the house. Ms. Kaiser stayed behind.

"Luckily, we got rid of her, she's annoying!"

"I think she's nice! Maybe she has no one but her husband."

"You again, you only see the good in everyone!"

I said, slightly out of breath. "Rosa, please open the door. Leo is getting heavier!"

Rosa gave Leon something to drink and laid him in his bed. We were sitting in the living room and heard a door open. It had to be father.

"Quickly, hide behind the door!" Mother called quietly. I jumped up and stood behind the living room door.

"Shalom, my dears, I met Rabbi Löwenstein earlier and am supposed to send greetings."

"Thanks, Yaron. Do you like coffee?"

"Yes, gladly! Ah, there's already a cup for me! But why is it already used?"

"Because of me, father!" I said it quietly, coming out from behind the door. I didn't want to scare him. Not that he had any problems with his heart.

My father turned around, threw up his hands, and shouted: "Hannah, darling, my dear daughter is here!" Then he ran to me and took me in his arms. He was happy at that moment. I rarely saw him like that.

After the greeting, we all sat down. Father asked me about Hans, and I answered him: "He has appointments, but he will be back soon."

"Are you staying for dinner?"

"If Hans has nothing else planned! We'll stay in Berlin for a few more days."

"Tell me: How are you doing in Switzerland?"

"Father, Switzerland is such a beautiful country. I got to know so many things when Hans showed me Basel. Above all, everyone there is friendly. Nobody treats us Jews like the Germans did."

"Maybe we should go to Switzerland too! Things haven't gotten much better here."

"Yes, mother already told me!"

"Are you and Hans going to stay in Berlin?"

"No, father, we will go to Zurich. Hans will run his father's company there!"

"It's a shame, but I wish you only the best."

I could see in his eyes. How much it hurt him that we didn't stay.

"The distance is no longer that far with the new aircraft."

"It's expensive, but you can come and visit us."

"We will, father. But we will stay a while longer."

"You can talk a little more, Rosa, and I will go cook."

"It is OK, dear!"

"If I can help, please let me know, mother."

"I will, but father would probably like to talk with you."

"Wherever Hans stays!"

"How is he?"

"He's fine. He gets on very well with his father, and you can see how much he enjoys being with him."

"Yes, family is important, my daughter!"

The front door opened outside, and we could hear voices. Was that Adam and Hans? When Adam came into the living room, I jumped up and hugged him.

"Adam, how I missed you! How are you, big brother?"

"Thank you, good, little sister, and you?"

"Very good! Hans is there too."

"Yes! He had an appointment with us at the bank."

"Hans did not tell me this."

Just then, Hans came into the room.

"Hello, Yaron!"

He walked up to him and shook his hand.

"You still have respect for me, my boy!"

"Yes! That's probably true", said Hans in awe.

But Yaron hugged his future son-in-law and greeted him like a son.

"Sit down! Hannah, get something to drink."

"No, father, I wanted to greet Rosa and Leo first. I will bring something with me then."

"It's okay, my son!"

Adam went into the kitchen, and we talked a bit about Switzerland.

When Adam returned, the front door opened again. It was Ari, the last family member missing. But he first went into the kitchen to greet his mother and Rosa. After a short while, Ari came over and greeted us.

"I am supposed to tell you that dinner will be ready in five minutes."

"I will go ahead! Maybe I can be of some help now."

So, I went to mother and Rosa. I asked if I could help, but I wasn't allowed. I should get Leo instead. He was still in his crib, sleeping. I went to Leo, or rather, I wanted to get him. He was sleeping so peacefully in his crib that I let him sleep. Rosa had told me that if he was sleeping peacefully, I should let him sleep. Good, he was. So, back to the kitchen! The whole family was already sitting at the table, waiting for me. To come, finally.

"Leo is sleeping peacefully," sitting down in my chair. There was stew, exactly, the kind that Hans loved so much.

"Well, Hans, you were lucky!"

He asked, "Why?"

"Well, there's your favorite stew!"

"Ah, yes, and it's delicious!"

After we had enjoyed the meal, my father wanted to say a table prayer. Hans was already looking contrite, and father began.

"Blessed be You, G-d, our G-d, King of the universe, who created many creatures and their needs. Thank you for all that you have created to sustain all living things. Blessed be He, the Life of the worlds."

We sat together and talked about the GDR and what would happen next. Hans got tired, and we decided to go back to our hotel. I arranged to meet my mother and Rosa the next day. We wanted to go shopping; I was curious to see whether there were more Jewish shops in Berlin again.

"Goodbye, I'm looking forward to tomorrow. It'll be nice."

"Certainly, mother! I'll come around eleven o'clock. We also have presents. I'll bring that with me."

"See you tomorrow, both of you!"

In front of the house, Hans thought about it and looked around. Then he asked, "Do you want to walk, or should we take a taxi?"

I thought and said, "Let's take a taxi."

"Good! There are some there."

When we got to the taxi, a young guy immediately got out and politely asked where he could take us. We said: "To the Hotel Am Zoo!" He let us get in and drove us to the entrance to the hotel. Hans paid him, and we got out.

We were given our key at reception. Instead of going to the bar, we immediately went upstairs. I suddenly didn't feel so good. I didn't know that these were the first signs of my pregnancy.

Hans wanted me to lie down straight away. He ordered a snack and went to the bathroom. I felt sick. When room service rang, Hans was in the bathroom, so I had to get up. A little dazed, I went to the door and let in the young man from room service.

"Good evening. I will bring the club sandwich and wine."

"Come in!"

He put the tray on the table, and I gave him a tip.

"Thank you, Madame, and have a nice evening."

Then Hans came out of the bathroom. He exclaimed happily: "Ah, room service was already here!"

"Yes, just now."

"Would you like some too?"

"No, just eat! I will take a bath."

"It's okay, love, enjoy your bath!"

"I will!"

I kissed Hans and went to fill the tub with water. Later, I took a long bath, and when I came out, I felt deeply relaxed. Hans was already in bed and asleep. Or rather, he snored like a steamboat. (How upset I always was when he snored! Today, I would give anything to hear him snore again.)

The next morning. We were startled awake. A war ruin was demolished opposite. As I stood at the window, I thought of that time. How many times have we had to hide in ruins? We had sat huddled together on the cold floor, hungry - and afraid.

I became so engrossed in these thoughts that I began to cry. As Hans saw it, he came to me and wanted to know what I had. I could not stand to see the building demolished. Hans closed the window, and I sat down on the bed.

"Would you like me to sit with you?"

"No, it's okay."

"I'm getting ready now. You can order breakfast if you like."

"I'm not hungry!"

"Good, and I'll get something in the bank. When are you going to leave?"

"At half past nine."

"Good! I have to go there too."

"Do you have appointments every day now?"

"No, my darling, tomorrow I'm yours!"

"Shall we go to the botanical garden then? I heard it's open again."

"Gladly! I like gardens like this, and there's a little café there too."

"Great, I'm already looking forward to it!"

Hans kissed me and went to get dressed. When he finished, I picked up the presents for the family. It was half past nine, and we left. We handed in our key at reception, and Hans said goodbye to me with a kiss.

"See you later, my love. When are you coming back?"

"Around the afternoon, what about you?"

"I have three appointments, and I think I'll be back around four o'clock. We could go out to eat later."

"Yes, with pleasure, I'm happy."

Hans left, and I looked for a taxi. As I saw one, I tried to stop it, but it kept going. Was it because I looked Jewish? Not, I thought. The second taxi came, I waved to the driver, but he drove on.

"Damn!" I shouted. "Why aren't they stopping?"

Suddenly, a young man stood next, smiled at me, and said in his sparse Berlin dialect: "It will never work like that! You had to whistle!"

When a taxi came, he put two fingers in his mouth and whistled. Sure enough, the Taxi stopped. The man opened the taxi door for me and said to the driver: "The young lady needs a taxi."

The driver said, "With pleasure." I got in, and the young man closed the door and waved to me.

I could not even thank him, but at least I had a taxi now and told the driver I wanted to go to Friedrichstrasse. The Taxi arrived on Friedrichstrasse and stopped in front of my old home. I paid the driver and got out. I walked along the narrow gravel path to the front door. I was just about to ring the doorbell when the door opened, and Ms. Kaiser stood before me. She was like many people. At first, she was friendly, but afterward, she spoke badly about others.

"Oh, hello, are you here again?"

"Yes, I am! Why?"

"Only this way! That's right, you're visiting the Epsteins.'

"No, I'm not! But I have to go upstairs now."

"See you again!"

Without saying anything, I pushed past the horrible person. My mother was already waiting at the apartment door. As I came up the stairs, panting, I saw her smile. (I smile when I think of her smile when I told her I had seen that terrible cow.)

"Leave her alone, she's jealous. Her husband is screwing with the secretary, and she's spending his money in frustration."

"Mother, that's all Tinnef. Let her take a young man and do the same as him!"

"Honey, that's not up to us to decide. But you are right!"

"Shall we go straight away, or does Rosa need more time?"

"Rosa isn't coming. She and Adam are having an apartment viewing."

"Okay, then let's get going. Do we want to go to the Department Store of the West? It recently reopened."

"It is so expensive there! I cannot afford that."

"I will invite you. First, I need to unload the presents."

"Take them to the kitchen!"

"Yes, mother!"

As she looked at my bags there, she threw her hands over her head and shouted: "So many presents, are you meschugge?"

"No, I was just really looking forward to seeing you all, and Hans wanted to make you happy too."

But we could worry about that later when the whole family would be together in the evening. Now we had plans to go on a shopping spree.

We set off. Mother wanted to go to Lehrter Stadtbahnhof and from there go to Kurfürstendamm. Fine, then we would take the train. I preferred to take a Taxi, but my mother was afraid.

I asked her. "What are you afraid of?"

She said anxiously. "They're not taking any Jews with them."

"I drove it earlier. Do not talk like that."

She was still afraid, but it was unfounded. "Okay, then we'll take a Taxi."

I was happy about that, and when a taxi tried to drive past, I raised my hand and waved to the driver. I dared to whistle. But he braked and let us get in.

He asked us kindly. "Where can I take you?"

"To the KaDeWe, please."

"Gladly, Madam!"

Mother looked fearful. The driver kept looking at my mother through his rear-view mirror. Whether he found us attractive or whether he thought we were Jews? My mother got sweaty hands. She looked Jewish, but I haven't looked Jewish since Basel.

After the end of the war, my mother walked hunched over; the war had scarred her like many others. As a child, I had known her as a proud woman. She had been a teacher and loved life. Hitler took that away from her, as it did from many others.

When we arrived at KaDeWe, the driver stopped at the main entrance. He politely asked for two marks. I gave him the money, and another gentleman let us out. "Welcome to KaDeWe, ladies!" Said the wagon master in a friendly manner.

Mother was still afraid. It was something special to enter such an impressive building. You could already see the luxury at the main entrance. I liked the Impressive trellis with the beautiful figures at the entrance. We couldn't help but be amazed: luxury everywhere - marble, granite, and fabrics everywhere you looked! Young Saleswomen offered us perfume. I promptly decided to buy Hans a new fragrance.

The Saleswoman took us to a small stand. We were allowed to sit down, and she showed us her fragrance notes - top, middle, and base notes separately, and we each chose one. At last, we created a perfume that had a spicy woody Note and smelled slightly of bergamot. (Hans loved it. He always bought this perfume at KaDeWe later on.)

I also made mother happy and bought her a fragrance. I hadn't seen her this happy in a long time. I was it too when she was.

"There appears to be a tea room on the second floor. You can get the best tea from all over the world and the tastiest pastries in Berlin there!"

"Really?" Said my mother and her eyes lit up.

"They say!"

"Shall we go check it out?"

"Gladly! I could use some tea now!"

So, we went and looked for the tea room, but there wasn't one, due to the war and the damage when a bomber crashed into the building.

"It's a shame, but then no."

I went and admired the furniture and said: "Look at the beautiful furniture."

"Yes, they do look nice! But they are so expensive!"

"True! Come on, let us go to our hotel. We can also drink tea or coffee there, and if you like, we can eat cake with it."

Mother smiled at me. We were just about to leave a side exit. A young man stood in front of us. He smiled and opened the door for us. We smiled back, and I said, slightly embarrassed: "Thank you, very kind of you!"

"You're welcome, that's my job!"

I felt even more embarrassed, but he smiled and wished us a nice day. As we stood on the street, I had to laugh at my stupidity. Mother just said: "Child, you are a sheep!"

She would never have used a swear word, as it was common practice those days. What kind of blaring you can't hear! One day, I was sitting in a small café on the square of the old synagogue. A young couple next to me and the woman chatted like a waterfall. Most sentences began with "Dude" or "Ey!" But I digress.

We walked along Tauentzienstrasse and Kurfürstendamm. Mother saw interesting shops and wanted to go to a boutique. I was happy for my mother. Finally, she wanted something on her own and wasn't afraid. So, we went to the boutique. My mother wanted a simple black dress. Today, I would say it looked like a funeral robe. It was fancy back then, and I was allowed to buy it for her. It fit like a glove, and when the saleswoman gave a discount, mother was overjoyed. I paid for the dress. Mother wanted to carry it herself.

"Mother, how about some new shoes?"

"It's going to be too expensive!" She replied and quickly walked past the nearest shoe shop.

But suddenly she turned to the shop window because she saw a pair of shoes and immediately fell in love.

"Hannah, just look at those beautiful shoes!"

I walked over to her and looked at a pair of black sandals. (Well, my mother liked them. And she loved to wear black.)

"Come on, let's go in. We will treat ourselves to that!"

"You are meschugge, little one!"

At the store, she put on the sandals. They fit like a glove. I grabbed the shoes, and before she knew it, I had already paid.

"Come on, we can go."

Mother said nothing. She was embarrassed. I was happy. Mother smiled again, and that was enough reward for me. A mother's smile is priceless!

"Our hotel is up there. Maybe Hans is already there."

"Do you think? He has so many appointments."

"Just the right time to drink coffee. There will be cake!"

Since the weather was nice, we decided to sit on the patio in the courtyard. A waiter quickly came running and ensnared us with quick jokes. We ordered coffee and bee sting. Mother took a glass of mineral water, and I took a glass of champagne. It was unaffordable, but I loved (and still I love) champagne.

"Mother, I want to see if Hans is there yet."

"Good, child! I drink up. Should I wait here?"

"Yes, when the waiter comes, tell him it's for suite number 5."

"I do!"

I went to reception and asked if Hans was back. The gentleman at reception looked for the key, but it was still hanging. I thanked him and went back to my mother.

"Hans isn't here yet. I'll come with you."

"That is nice of you." You could almost see how a weight lifted from my mother's heart that she did not have to go home alone. I went to tell the waiter.

"There are Taxis ahead!"

We ran to the Taxi and got in. The driver drove us to Friedrichstrasse. When we arrived, that old cow, Mrs. Kaiser, was at the door again.

"Look, mother, the old woman is standing there!"

"Never mind, little child! I can look at them, smile, and walk past."

But Ms. Kaiser didn't make it easy to ignore her with a friendly smile. She always made every effort to remind herself of those around her.

So, when we returned, she whistled: "Oh, you're late! Has something happened?"

"No, Ms. Kaiser!" Said mother tormented. "I was strolling in KaDeWe with my daughter."

"Well, isn't it a bit too expensive for you? But that's right, the daughter is from Switzerland!"

"Exactly, Ms. Kaiser!"

We could barely push past her, but I gently pushed her aside.

"Have a nice evening!"

"Thanks, you too!"

Was she so alone back then? She was just curious! Mother quickly unlocked the door, and we quickly went into the apartment. Not that that older woman came along and forced us. To have a conversation! The whole family was home, and everyone was happy we were finally back.

"Shalom, dear ones!"

"Shalom!"

"Do you want to sit down? Rosa cooked."

"Later! Mother should first show her new dress and sandals to us."

"I will do that immediately, my child!"

Mother took the two bags and went to dress up. After a few minutes, she came back. Father almost lost his breath. He was so excited.

"Applause for mom!" I shouted, and the others applauded.

"You look wonderful, my darling."

Adam took his mother in his arms and hugged her. He said to her: "You deserve this," and to me: "Thank you, Hannah!" Mother had tears in her eyes – tears of happiness.

After all the excitement, we ate, and I gave everyone their present. They were all happy like it was Hanukkah. It wasn't until nine o'clock in the evening that I took a Taxi back to the hotel. Hans was there, but the key wasn't in the holder. I went upstairs and rang the doorbell. Hans opened the door. My g-d, he was only wearing a bath towel around his waist!

"There you are, my darling! Was it nice?"

"Shalom, my love. Yes, it was!" I went over to him and kissed him.

He wanted to know from me. "Are you feeling better?"

"You mean my nausea? Yes, it's gone!"

"Would you like some wine? I asked for a bottle."

"No, I'd like mineral water."

"Come now, love!"

"I will come back straight away. I have to go to the toilet."

A few minutes later, I came out of the bathroom again. Hans was in bed!

Oh God, I thought.

"Darling, let's lie in bed for a while. I'm supposed to tell you greetings from father. He asks if we already know a wedding date."

"I don't know yet, but don't we have some time?"

"But! We have all the time in the World."

"I went to KaDeWe with my mother today. It might look classy there."

"Yes, there is only the best and the most beautiful. Have you bought anything?"

"Not there, but in a boutique. A dress for mother and some shoes."

"Nice, she was happy about that!"

"Yes, dear. I have something here for you."

Hans looked surprised when he saw the box in my hand. "What is it?" he wanted to know.

I said mysteriously: "Open!"

Hans took the box and opened it. He saw the bottle with his new scent. "A parfum! Very kind of you." He sprayed something on his upper body and sniffed. It wasn't until the right corner of his mouth went up that I saw that he liked the scent. "Dear, it smells great. It smells so wonderfully of bergamot."

I was glad he liked his scent! "Glad you like it!"

We talked some more, and Hans finished his glass of wine. Then I turned off the light, and Hans snuggled up to me. So, we fell asleep.

"Good morning, sleepyhead!" Hans was already in the bathroom and dressed.

"Morning, I'm so tired, but..."

I felt sick and quickly ran to the toilet. Now it was clear: oh g-d, I was pregnant! When I felt better, I went back to Hans.

"Hans, I think I'm pregnant!" I said to him quietly.

He looked at me, said nothing, but sat down. He was silent, and I became afraid: what was wrong with him, and why wasn't he saying anything? Then he stood up and slowly came towards me. He took my face between his hands and kissed me.

"Darling, finally! We are going to be parents. I love you so much, but now we must get married!"

"You're right, as soon as possible. Unimaginable, pregnant, and unmarried, our whole family would laugh at us!"

"Or hate! Now let us go to the botanical garden and enjoy the day."

"Good! I get ready."

"Shall we say it now?"

"What are we going to say?"

"That we might be pregnant!"

"If you like, but remember, we are not married yet!"

"I don't care much about religion."

I disappeared into the bathroom and came out dressed. "Good! Let's go!"

I wanted to take my jacket, but Hans said, "It is so warm outside. Well, let us leave our jackets there!" In the elevator, I had to decide whether we wanted to take a taxi or take the tram. Since I loved traveling by tram, I chose the tram.

"Do you know the way?"

"Yeah, sort of, but I'll get us directions." I went to the porter to ask him how to get to the Botanical Gardens. He was so generous and told me that there was a new S-Bahn connection from Zoo station.

Hans stood outside and watched the pigeons eating. When I came to him, he smiled at me.

"We have to take the S-Bahn, the porter told me. There doesn't seem to be a tram there."

"Okay, then let's go to the train station."

Hans took my hand, and we walked like two new lovers across the Ku'damm and Hardenbergstrasse to the train station. A train had just arrived at the station, and when the locomotive started to whistle, I was scared as hell and suddenly remembered the horrific journey through Poland towards Auschwitz.

Hans noticed my panic, took my hand, and calmed me down. These steam monsters I hated back then. But now I love traveling by train and a modern locomotive.

"Come on, let's go ask where the train leaves!"

Hans pulled me with him but suddenly stopped after just a few meters. A uniformed man stopped us!

"I would have liked to see your ID cards!", he said somewhat unkindly. Hans wasn't afraid. He showed him his ID and gave him mine.

"Mangold and Epstein. According to your name, you are of Jewish origin, right? What brings you here to the Federal Republic of Germany?"

"I live in Switzerland, and this is my fiancée. We are on vacation, and you are welcome to check!"

I was afraid, but Hans took care of it. The uniformed man had no further arguments and said, still unfriendly: "Move on!"

Hans didn't think about cuddling. He looked into the uniformed man's face and asked: "We're looking for the platform where the train goes to the Botanical Garden. Can you help?"

"Platform 4, direction Steglitz!"

"Thanks!"

The policeman left us standing and went after a man.

"Your hands are very cold, darling!"

"Yes. I was afraid. When the uniformed man said, Federal Republic of Germany. I thought we were in the Third Reich!"

"Let's go to platform 4, now."

When we got there, the train pulled in. It looked old and battered. The railway has definitely already has been exposed to a hail of Allied bombs.

"Come'!"

Hans was already pulling me onto one of the seats on the train. I looked around. But there was no sign saying: "BANNED FOR JEWS." I was relieved and thought about our unborn child. Was it right to give birth to a child in such a terrible world? But when was the right time? You can find something at any time.

"Two stops more, and we will be there."

I said, trying to think of other things. "Good, I'm happy!"

We got out when we arrived at the train station near the Botanical Garden.

"I think we need to go up there."

Hans pulled me along again. He had right as always. The stairs up, and after three blocks came the garden. It was beautiful! Unfortunately, there was not much to see. Most buildings had been destroyed or badly damaged during the war. They rebuilt the greenhouses already.

They had lost most of the targets during the war due to pressure waves from exploding bombs. It destroyed many plants; they froze to death in winter. You could only visit the Victoria House, but there was not much to see there.

At the small café, which was not fully operational, we saw a sign "PICNIC BASKETS RENTAL." We rented a blanket and a picnic basket and sat in the shade. I was so happy; the picnic was unforgettable. Hans laid out the blanket, we sat down, and Hans opened the basket.

There were all kinds of goodies: ham, juice, bread, boiled eggs, and butter. Was it normal? Maybe it was because of a product that was otherwise less available. The price of 15 DM was steep for that, but Hans just said at the time that we would not have to go hungry because of it. He did everything to make me happy. He gave up the champagne, and we drank juice. After eating, I laid my head on his lap. He took a book and read it to me. I loved it when he read to me. He could tell stories beautifully.

He suddenly asked me. "Darling, what do we want to name our children?"

I murmured. "Our children?" I had nodded away, but now I was wide awake again.

"You can choose the boys' names, and I can choose the girls' names."

"If it's a boy, his name should be Samuel Yaron."

"If we get a girl, her name will be Leah."

We sat there for a while and enjoyed the weather. When it got cold, we decided to go home. We gave away the picnic basket and blanket. Then we walked back to the train station to go home. On the platform, Hans checked when the train was coming and was satisfied that it was only a few minutes.

"Would you like to sit?"

"Yes, gladly!"

We went and sat down, and Hans took my hand and kissed it.

"I love you so much, Hannah!"

"I love you too, Hans!"

"Come on, the train is coming!"

We stood up and got on as the train stopped. I counted the stations: many were open again, some were still being completed, or were closed because they were still too damaged by the war. We had to get off again five stops further on. We arrived at the Zoo train station.

"Would we go somewhere to eat, in the old Berlin style?"

"Adam told me about a pub called Patzenhofer Ausschank. You should be able to eat well there."

"Do you know where the pub is?"

"Yes, right in front of Meinekestraße, that's at our hotel."

We were looking for this pub and found it in Meinekestraße 26. We went in, and everybody looked at us. At first, I had a bad feeling, but Hans was not afraid, as always.

I was pleasantly surprised. Uschi, the woman behind the trunk, was awful to me. But she quickly became like an old friend when you talked to her. The so-called Berliner Schnauze, as she so beautifully said, had inherited it from Vaddern. Uschi always said, "Here you can make remidemmi even until the dolls dance!" Patzenhofer always had challenges to overcome, and they had overcome a few disasters.

Whenever we were in Berlin, we went there. You were treated there as a human. Nobody is judged there based on their origins. Adam was often there whenever the cry of his children struck him. The last time I was at Patzenhofer was in 1990.

We had a few more nice holidays, and Hans had some appointments. I never asked about the background or what the appointments were all about. I was allowed to go shopping and spend time with my family. Soon, we will be apart for a long time.

Of course, we wanted to make our engagement official in Berlin and celebrate properly. Hans and I planned a small dinner with the family, but father and mother had other plans. Everyone was consecrated, except us. So, came our last day in Berlin.

Dad called and told us we had to cancel dinner. He and mom would have prepared something for us. Hans got up. He did not want a bribe, and I was sick.

"Dear, the guests are coming in 20 minutes. Let us go downstairs."

"Yes, I will be right back. I am sick again!"

"My poor dear, shall we tell them today?"

"Yes, otherwise, we shall not be allowed to look again in Berlin!"

"I spoke to my father on the phone before. He thinks that August is the best month to get married."

"Do you?"

"Yes! It's warm, and we could build anything in the garden."

"That's right, so let's get married in August!"

Hans grabbed me and kissed me. "What would I do without you, my dear."

"Surely you would have a beautiful woman on your side and not a girl like me."

"I am sure I did not have anyone else by my side. No matter where you were hiding. I would always have found you!"

"You have said that kindly!"

I kissed Hans and withdrew from him. I had to go to the toilet.

After ten minutes, Hans knocked on the bathroom door: "Dear, do you need more time?"

"Come!"

The others would arrive soon. The guests will soon arrive. The elevator then went down; the bar manager was already waiting. The bar manager explained: "Moment, we have to wait. There are problems in the small salon; we had to escape into the small hall."

Okay, we stopped in the little hall. I was curious. I could not see: "What is going on there?"

Another waiter came and gave the bar boss two black towels. He said mysteriously to us. "Please put these on yourself. It is a surprise scheduled!"

Now I was a little scared, but Hans held my hand tightly. Did he know anything? He never told me!

We tied up the towels in front of our eyes. They led us into the small hall. Everything was quiet - as if no one was there. Suddenly, we were supposed to stop. Salvation came, and Leon cried. So, there was someone there!

"Should we take off the towels now, or are we here before our execution?"

Everyone started laughing.

"Take it off!"

"Father!" I said when I recognized his voice.

We took off the bandages and looked at them. The whole mixpoke was there, and a few more. I could not believe who I saw there.

Father had told the hotel behind us not to set up the little salon. But the small hall. There were far more friends than expected. I loved my father for this surprise and thought for a long time about this event.

"Eliam!" I shouted and started to cry. I ran to him and threw my arms around his neck. "What are you doing here?"

He said happily. "Surprise!"

"G-d, how beautiful, and who is that?"

"This is Rachel, my fiancée and soon-to-be wife."

"Shalom, Rachel, you are the woman for whom Eliam went to Holland."

"Shalom, Hannah. Yes, I am."

Suddenly, I saw him: Rabbi Chajm had also come. "My g-d, Rabbi, you are here too!"

"Yes, little child! I am so glad to see you again."

Hans had already delved into a conversation with Eliam. Now, he had shook hands with Rabbi Chajm, and they talked some more. I went over to the two of them because we wanted to toast everyone together, and of course, we also wanted to announce the good news.

"Hans, shall we now? Better now!"

"Yes, let's do it, I'll start." He got a glass of champagne, tapping it with a spoon.

"I would like to announce something. Why don't we think we're in the salon? Is there anything better to celebrate today?" He joked, then continued seriously: "Indeed, Hannah and I are getting married in August. Oh, and before I forget. We are going to be parents."

Everyone started clapping. And which was unusual for me at the time, cheering. My father said with delight. "Children, how happy you make us!"

Everyone came and shook our hands and said something nice. I was glad that no one was angry. Why? Because back then, it wasn't common practice to be pregnant before marriage. Is how it is in Judaism. Because the rabbi, who will officiate our wedding ceremony, would check all of this. The Rabbi checks whether we are ready for marriage. The whole wedding would last eight days, but it is often less. It would be unimaginable if our family and friends had condemned us. Because that also would have been reflected in the rabbi's verdict!

Luckily, we are not ultra-Orthodox Jews. Very much tolerance would not have been possible. But then Hans would never have married me anyway. His family was never very religious. They blamed Adonai for the Jews going through such a terrible time. I never said anything about it; Everyone should think as they want.

We sat across from Eliam and Rachel. How lovely it was to see him again! His hair was a little shorter. And he was a little stronger than last time.

"Eliam, did it take you long to find Rachel in Holland? Things happened to the Jews there no differently than what happened to us here."

"It didn't take long. Rachel had registered, and so I found her through Rachmiel."

"Are you still in touch with him?"

"Yes, a little. Rachmiel lives in the USSR, got married, and has two boys."

"What about with you? When do you want to marry?"

"Maybe next year, but we're starting our own business."

"Really? A carpentry Workshop?"

"Yes, exactly! She should be as beautiful as the one your father had."

"Yes, I think father misses his carpentry shop a lot!"

"When are you going back to Switzerland?"

"Tomorrow, if we had known you were coming, we would have extended it."

"We will see each other again soon, I hope!"

"Sure! Or should our child grow up without his second godparents?"

"Ha, and you will be ours!"

The rabbi interrupted our Conversation: "Children! Shall we now officially bless your kiddushin?"

"With pleasure, Rabbi Chajm!"

"Then come and receive the blessing."

Hans and I got up and went to Rabbi Chajm. He stood at a table covered with a white blanket. Above us was a white chuppah (canopy). There was a wine goblet on the table. I recognized the cup immediately: it was the one that father and mother had when they were engaged.

We stood in front of the table. The rabbi stood opposite us. He took the cup and blessed it. Then came Adam and Eliam. They had to witness our engagement.

The Rabbi handed us the wine goblet, and Hans took a sip. Then he gave me the cup, and I also took a sip. Finally, the Rabbi said our blessing: "Be fruitful and multiply and fill the earth!"

Then he gave Hans the engagement ring. (According to Jewish tradition, only the woman gets a ring. However, Hans had other plans, but we'll get to that later.)

Then Hans recited his saying: "Through this ring, you sworn to me according to the law of Moses and Israel."

We were now engaged. We weren't allowed to live together, but Hans ignored this law.

We celebrated for a long time. We had only been in Berlin for a week. But we enjoyed every moment. Father offered to take us to the train the other morning, but we wanted to take a Taxi. The train station wasn't far, and driving Taxis was my new hobby.

We had to get up very early. Hans immediately went into the bathroom, and I opened the door for room service. Breakfast was practically to go because we didn't finish early, but Hans had peace.

I warned him. "The train isn't waiting!"

"I know, love. I am ready!"

After a bellboy got our bags, we went downstairs. Hans paid our hotel bill, and I had already gone to the Taxi. When Hans finally came, we were able to go.

We were just on time. But when I just thought that we would soon be sitting on this train forever again! When we arrived at the station, a porter brought our luggage to the platform. Since he knew his way around, we followed him. The train was already there, and we took our seats.

"The train has to leave soon. I hope it is on time."

"Dear, it doesn't matter. We have time, and we can't change anything."

Hans was always the diplomat of the two of us, always friendly, but if someone did him an injustice, he could become angry.

The conductor whistled, and the fearsome monster made of steel and steam started moving. Without Hans, I wouldn't have endured it here. And again, we passed ghost train stations: Sangerhausen, Erfurt, Gotha, Eisenach, then Wartha as the eastern border station.

From there, we were electrified again and got an electric locomotive. The border officials who got on in Berlin just looked at our passports and kept walking. They were generous today, said Hans. I didn't care. I was glad they were gone. They got off in Wartha. Three FRG police officers and three US soldiers got on board.

The train started moving again - destination Bebra, the western border station. Before we arrived at the train station, we checked. One of the US soldiers was black and looked good to eat. (Yes, I know: Is she meschugge now? Engaged, pregnant, and thinking about another man! Back then, it was allowed to think in silence. But today, it is normal.)

Anyway, the black man kept looking at me, and once he smiled at me, I blushed. One of the customs officers looked at the passports and documents from Switzerland. The gentlemen nodded happily and gave us back the passports with the document. In Bebra, the uniformed men got out, and several US soldiers got on. They were probably off duty and went to Frankfurt. (We will never know because I did not ask as they walked past us.)

I looked out the window. It looked beautiful to see the trees rushing past us, and you could see from the landscape that you were in West Germany. The train took less than 50 minutes to reach Frankfurt. I was happy when the announcement came! After another seven hours, we were finally in Basel.

But first, we arrived in Frankfurt on platform 13. Hans grabbed the suitcases, and I grabbed the bags. And we got a luggage trolley in front of the train. Hans loaded him and drove him to platform 10. Our train was leaving from there in twenty minutes.

"Dear, I will go to the kiosk and get us something to eat and drink."

"Yes, please bring me some table water."

Hans just nodded and ran towards the kiosk. After a few minutes, he came back smiling.

"Look, darling, what I got! Two sandwiches and bottled water."

"That is nice, but you have something else. Otherwise, you would not smile."

"You know me very well." He took a bar of US chocolate out of his jacket pocket. Now, I had to smile. I had not had chocolate in a while.

Back then, I almost liked the US chocolate better than the one in Switzerland. (I still remember the name: Hershey Tropical Chocolate Bar.) Back then, chocolate still had a high cocoa content, and this one also smelled wonderfully of vanilla. It did not melt so quickly either, it was made especially for the bags of US soldiers.

"What this kiosk does not have."

"He did not. A soldier gave it to me. He said I should give it to my missus."

"Then you must be jealous now!"

"Not in the slightest, but only if you give me a rib."

"Come on, we have to get in. We have to go to wagon 4, compartment 5."

Hans took the suitcases, and I took the two bags. We got into wagon 4. Compartment number 5, was found quickly. Hans put the suitcases in the overhead compartment, and I put the bags on one of the seats. I sat in one of the window seats, and Hans sat opposite me. The train started moving - the next stop was Karlsruhe.

I opened the window and looked out. Passengers and train staff were milling around on the platform. A younger woman stood on the platform and was crying. She had no luggage with her but got on the train.

The train started moving again - the next stop was Freiburg. Passengers walked past our compartment again. People would open the door and ask if it was still free. But Hans would always growl: "No!"

The young lady also passed by, and it was only then that I saw she was pregnant. She looked a little lost, but I could be mistaken.

"I have to go to the toilet."

"Do I have to come with you?"

"No, I definitely won't get lost."

"Good!"

I went and looked where the toilet was. On the way, I saw the young girl again. Because the restroom was busy, and I didn't want to wait.

On the way back, I had to pass the girl again. She cried, and I felt sorry for her.

I asked her. "Excuse me, can I help?"

Sobbing, she answered me: "I can't find a place. I'm in pain, but I had to get away from Karlsruhe."

I didn't have to think for long: "Come on, we still have space in our compartment."

She couldn't say more than a "thank you" right now. We went to our compartment together. Hans looked up and looked surprised.

I said hastily. "Hans, we have to help her!"

"Come in first."

"Sit down and take a breath. Then things will look better."

Hans wanted to know from me. "What happened?"

"The girl needed help, and I helped her."

Hans said nothing. He knew I would help anywhere.

"What is your name? Are you hungry or thirsty?"

"My name is Paula. Something to drink, please."

"Is there anything else we can help you with?" Asked Hans Paula worriedly.

"No, I just have to come to Freiburg. My fiancé Emil lives there, and we want to get married soon. He wanted to pick me up, but he didn't come. Now I want to go to him, but I don't have any money, and the conductor will probably come soon."

Paula clutched her stomach again as if she were in pain. Hans noticed this and became worried; me too, of course.

"Do you have pain? Don't worry about the conductor. I will sort this out."

"My stomach hurts so much. I am sure it is the excitement."

I poured table water into a cup and handed it to Paula. She drank and became calmer. Then I cut my sandwich in half and gave one half to her. At first, she refused, but then she took it and ate a little.

Hans went to find the conductor to buy a ticket for Paula. As a precaution, he accepted the return trip - perhaps already knowing that Paula would have to return home without having anything. When he returned, he had the ticket and was smiling at us.

"So here it is, I took a round trip. You might have to go back."

"Thanks! I still need your names and address. Father will send you the money. I am so grateful to you."

Hans wrote down our address for Paula. She seemed relieved and soon calmed down.

I wanted to know from her. "What month are you in?"

"5th month, stomach is slowly getting bigger."

"We're pregnant too, I hope."

"Why do you hope?"

"I still have to go to the doctor. We do not know for sure yet."

"Then I will keep my fingers crossed for you."

"You should get some rest now. We will be in Freiburg soon."

Paula nodded off a bit, and when we were just before Freiburg, I woke her up.

"You look much better; the rest has done you some good."

"Yes, I feel better already."

The train arrived in Freiburg. Paula thanked us again and then said goodbye. I opened the window and waved after her. The conductor blew his whistle, and the train started moving again.

"Honey, we'll be home soon now."

"Yes, I'm glad. What do you think will happen to Paula?"

"I bought her the return ticket because I know how it ends."

"Well, I hope she finds happiness!" (A few weeks later, she sent us the money and a letter. She thanked us and told us that she had moved in with Emil. I love happy endings!)

We finally drove towards Basel at full speed. I looked out the window, and Hans was working. At some point, we came to Weil am Rhein, one of the last train stations on the Swiss border alongside Haltingen. Basel was within reach. Five minutes, and you could already see the platforms. The announcement came, and Hans got the suitcases from the luggage compartment; I took the bags.

After more than 14 hours, we finally arrived in Basel. I was exhausted from sitting for so long, but I was looking forward to Samuel and Sebastian! I was curious to see how they would react when we told them the news.

We were picked up from the train platform by Sebastian. We were exhausted, but when we saw Sebastian, the tiredness disappeared.

"Good evening!"

"Good evening, Sebastian, how are you?"

"Madam, everything is fine with me. Mr. Mangold has planned a banquet for the evening."

"Today of all days!", said Hans.

"Yes! He was so happy when he found out that madam was pregnant!"

He stowed the luggage, and we got in. I looked at Hans warningly. He had told Samuel everything without asking my consent.

When we arrived at home, Samuel waited impatiently at the top of the stairs. Sebastian parked the car, and we got out. Hans took my hand, and we went to Samuel together. He happily took me in his arms and kissed me on the cheek.

"Congratulations to you both. I am so proud and happy."

"Thank you, father. I can hardly believe it."

"Tonight, we are going to celebrate it big!"

Hans took the opportunity and said to his Samuel. "We still have something to announce."

He asked curiously. "May I know what it is?"

"Of course, father! We are getting married in August here in Switzerland."

"You make me as happy as before!"

I felt sick. "I have to go in. I am sick!" I shouted and ran forward.

"We are coming too."

"What time is the reception?"

"It starts at eight p.m. There will be around 30 guests, nothing important!"

"Good! Then we can rest for another hour. Hannah has to take it easy now. It is her first pregnancy."

"She can retire later." He probably did not realize how miserable I felt.

Hans, on the other hand, felt it. "Are you okay again, love?" He asked me worriedly.

To have him by my side. I replied, "Yes, but I have to see a doctor tomorrow first. Samuel, do you know somebody?"

"Yes! He is only three houses down."

"Okay, I take a bath now, and we will celebrate later!" I smiled at them both and went into our room.

But Samuel had long had further plans. He had everything taken care of and wanted to get started straight away.

"Hans, can I still speak to you?"

"Yes, of course, father!"

"I founded the company in Zurich. You and Hannah are the managers. And you already have 40 clients."

"That is wonderful, father!"

"Now go and take care of your loved one."

"See you later, father."

I was just in the bathroom enjoying my warm bath. I heard Hans come into our bedroom, and he asked where I was. I told him I was in the bathroom enjoying my bath. As soon as I said this, the door opened, and he stood stark naked in front of me. Man, that was a guy! Adonis was a cheap copy of my Hans.

"Honey, it is written in the first book of Moses: Be fruitful and multiply and replenish the earth."

"I know, but what are you trying to tell me?"

"I have to make my wife happy!"

"You made me happy! I am expecting a baby from you, and we will get married soon. Come in and lie down with me. We will relax a little."

Hans sat down in the tub with me. I soaped his back, and he snuggled up against me.

"It is so nice to be with you."

"Yes, my dear!"

I stroked his chest and stomach, playing with the foam.

"Guests are coming in 20 minutes! We still have to get dressed."

"Yes, come out!"

Hans jumped up, grabbed a bath towel and dried himself, then wrapped it around his waist. If I had not already been pregnant, I would have become pregnant that evening. Once he was out of the bathroom, I dried myself. I looked at my stomach and stroked it. I silently hoped: Please be pregnant! I took my light blue evening dress, and Hans wore his black tuxedo.

"So, darling, can we?"

Nervously I said. "Yes!"

We walked hand in hand down the grand staircase. My heart was pounding like crazy. We stopped at the bottom of the stairs, and Hans looked around.

"Ah, all millionaires and nobility. Enjoy the evening, darling!" Hans kissed my hand, and we continued walking.

We stopped at the bottom with his father, who gave a short speech: "Ladies and gentlemen, dear friends. May I ask for your attention for a moment!"

Everyone looked in our direction, and I felt my face blush. Hans noticed that my hand was getting cold. He looked at me and winked.

Samuel gave his speech and applauded us several times, and we got applause.

Hans squeezed my hand and said: "Dear friends, I would like to ask for the hand of my Hannah in marriage once again. Dearest Hannah, we have been together through thick and thin and have known each other for a long time. When I saw you, I immediately fell in love with you. That is why I want to ask you: Do you want to be my wife?"

I noticed tears welling up in my eyes, and then I said quietly: "Yes, I want to. Now & Forever!"

Then Hans took a small box out of his jacket pocket and knelt. He opened it, and two beautiful rings appeared. Hans stood up again. He took one of the rings and put them on my ring finger. I was also allowed officially to put the ring on my loved one.

Many of the guests looked a bit cautious. They were high-ranking Jews and deeply religious at that. The family from my Hans was a liberal believer. They had to go through it. My Hans did not care that we were not allowed to be together. We were a couple, I was pregnant, and should I have stayed in a hotel? No!

Of course, we got applause. Everyone cheered and applauded us. Samuel tapped his glass again and wanted to make another short speech.

"My dears! The banquet awaits us in the salon. There is a Swiss delight. Let us enjoy the food, and above all, let us enjoy this evening."

The two white doors opened and welcomed us. Two chairs have been highlighted at the banquet table, especially for Hans and me. It was clear, that we had to sit there. We sat down and waited.

After the meal, I was examined by the guests. They thought: What does Hans want with someone like that? But everyone was very nice to me and wished us good luck and soon to have offspring. If only they knew that we had already been successful!

"What a lovely couple you are!", said one of the ladies. "May Adonai always be kind to you."

When she was gone, I asked Hans: "Who was that?"

"That was Anna Davidstein, almost all of her family was murdered in Auschwitz. Today she has a huge fortune and we manage it for her."

A good-looking gentleman came. He was wearing a black tuxedo and a top hat.

"My dear Hans, we have to meet one day. I expect a very large sum from America."

"Gladly, Arthur! Should I come over tomorrow at eleven o'clock in the morning?"

"Yes please, and congratulations on such a beautiful young lady. Madam, I admire you!"

I said, slightly halting. "Thank you, sir!"

He also moved on. I asked again who it was.

"This is Artur Rubinstein. He is a pianist who lives in Geneva."

"Who you all know!"

"Come on, let me introduce you to someone else!"

I looked around, but since I did not know anyone. I could not get a picture. We walked up to two women, and Hans introduced me to them. They were the Baronesses of Löwenstein, more precisely Wilhelmine and Flora.

"Bonsoir, Baronesses. May I introduce my fiancée, Hannah Epstein?"

"Bonsoir, Hans, what a joy and how lucky you were to have such an enchanting beauty!"

I had to laugh. I also wanted to say something about it. "Madame la Baronne, it was love at first sight!"

Now Hans had to laugh and added, slightly moved. "Yes, and how! I have never had such a crush on a girl, even though none of us knew if we had lived to see the next day."

"Yes, that was a terrible time, but now we do not want to think about that terrible time. Let us toast the engaged couple!"

Today, you would say that the two baronesses were Celebration beasts! Of course, Martin Hornmann and his mother were also there. Samuel walked around them like an amorous rooster. They were definitely in love! Martin came to us with papers with him. He and Hans went into the next room because he had to discuss a few things with him about Zurich. After a while, they came back.

"Dear, you are all alone!"

"I had a great time. Your father and Renate behave like two newly-weds in love."

"That is right. I have already noticed that as well!"

"Do you think the next engagement is on the horizon?"

"The two go well together. Both are unattached, so why not!"

"Let us get something to drink."

Samuel had let a bar specially built in the garden, and you could sit comfortably by the pool. We got our drinks and sat by the pool. It was a wonderful evening, but I had a stomach ache and thought about what it would be like with a child. Hans saw that I was mentally absent. He stood up and stood behind me. Then he massaged my neck. I relaxed wonderfully.

"Sorry, but it is very late. I am tired."

"Just go to bed. No one will be angry with you."

"Is good! Martin, sleep well and say hello to your mother."

"Sleep well, Hannah!"

I kissed Hans goodnight and left.

The night was short. I slept soundly and did not even hear Hans come into bed.

In the morning, he slept peacefully next to me. I got up and went to the bathroom. I dressed up for the day. I had to go to the doctor. I was a little scared, but not much. After getting dressed, I went to the salon. Sebastian made breakfast there.

"Good morning, Sebastian! "

"Good morning, Miss Hannah. Did you sleep well?"

"Thank you very well."

"I will get you coffee. The butter is still missing as well."

"Do not rush, Sebastian!"

As soon as I said that, I heard whispers from the stairs. They were the voices of Samuel and Renate Hornmann. Aha, she spent the night here! They were a little embarrassed when they entered the salon and saw me. I saved the situation by shouting cheerfully. "Good morning, everyone!"

They both also wished me good morning. When they sat down, Sebastian came and brought the coffee and butter.

"I still have croissants if anyone likes them. Good morning, Ms. Hornmann!"

"Good morning, Sebastian!"

You could see how embarrassed the two of them were.

"To prevent rumors: Yes, we like each other."

Sebastian looked at me and I at him, then I said happily: "Indeed, we already suspected that!"

"Really?"

"Yes! Even Martin said it yesterday. It is nice – my congratulations."

"You have your appointment today? I hope they do not find anything wrong."

"No, what is he supposed to find? Except I might be pregnant."

"Yes, I hope so!"

"You will be the first to know. I have to leave now."

"Good luck!"

I got up and went to get my jacket. Sebastian was standing in the hallway and wanted to drive me. I decided against it. The weather was lovely, and it was not far. I stood at the outside steps of our villa and saw our cook's husband. He waved to me, and I waved back. A few meters to the right was the young ferryman who had enchanted me the last time. But today, I only had my appointment in mind. He greeted friendly, and I greeted him back.

I had already reached the doctor's house. I stepped through the open door. I entered the large room and saw a woman sitting at a desk.

"Good day! Am I right here? I want to see Doctor Abt!"

"Yes, you have come to the right place! I am Doctor Abt. You are probably Ms. Mangold!"

"More Miss Epstein!"

"Fine, as you wish. Please follow me!"

"Yes gladly! Can I put my coat here?"

"Of course! Wait a minute, let me help you!"

"Thanks!"

Doctor Abt helped me with my coat and put it on the large sofa. When we entered the other room, I saw it was a treatment room. I was a little afraid, but it was unfounded.

The big chair in the middle of the room was the reason.

"Please sit down!"

I was about to sit in the examination chair when Doctor Abt said to me, with a smile. "Not there, in the chair here. We need to know what is wrong with you first!"

After I sat down, she sat across from me.

"So, little one, what can I do for you?" She wanted to know, but where should I start? I had no experience at all.

"Quite simply, I think I am pregnant. Maybe I need something too for my nausea."

"Good, I need some urine, and a little blood would not hurt either."

I asked incredulously. "Urine?"

"Yes, I have to examine it, and if I detect the HCG hormone in your urine, then you are pregnant."

Good! So, I went to the toilet and filled a tin cup. How unpleasant – I almost spilled! I went back into the treatment room. The doctor was already standing there with the syringe in her hand and wanted to take my blood.

"Sit down. I still have to have some blood."

I gave her the cup and sat down.

"I will quickly stow the cup away."

"Do not rush. I have time!"

She went to the fridge. Putted the cup in and came over to me.

"I hope you did not leave any food there."

She joked. "No, but lemonade!"

She pushed my sleeve up a little, put a dust band around my upper arm, and poked me. The blood flowed, and a test tube full was enough for her. After she took the rubber band off, she put a plaster on the area that was still bleeding a little.

"Okay, done! You will hear back in a day or two, and I will call! Here is something else for your nausea."

"Good, thanks!"

The doctor took me into the anteroom. She helped me into my coat and said goodbye to me. As I leaving the house, I suddenly thought of the little café. Should I go home straight away or to the little café? I chose the cafe. It was not far. I had already noticed it on my way and liked it straight away. I first looked in front of the door to see if there was a sign: **"JEWS UNWANTED"**. Nothing was visible - a stupid habit of mine to look for.

Inside I was greeted by a young waiter. He led me to a small table on the terrace and brought me the menu. I thought silently about what he would say if I ordered a beer. Back then, it wasn't proper for a lady to drink beer in public.

The waiter walked past me, put the card down, and moved on. I picked it up and studied it until I noticed the Café Crème.

I said. "I will take that and a piece of cake!"

"Excuse me?" A young gentleman was sitting there. He seemed interested in me.

"Pardon, sir. I was talking to myself."

"I thought you were talking to me. What would you recommend?"

"Wait, I have to check first." I turned to him and thought. "I would recommend a Café Crème with milk and sugar and a piece of Herrentorte."

"Not bad, I will take that too. How did you know what I was taking?"

"I overheard your order earlier."

We both grinned at each other. I wouldn't have had Hans back then. I definitely would have chosen him. Of course, I would never cheat on my Hans. I did not do that when he was alive, and I did not do it after his death. I loved and loved him too much for that. We had happy years together. Come to think of it, we never really argued.

The young man was now sitting opposite me; we had already gotten coffee and cake.

"May I ask if you are still unattached?"

"I am engaged and happy too!"

"Well, you can ask, right?"

"May one!"

"Does your cake taste good?"

"Yes, very much!"

"My name is Louis. What is your name?"

"Hannah!"

"Hannah, what a beautiful name."

"Yes, I am Jewish. I do better say it now before you wonder any longer."

He laughed at me and said. "I am French!" We laughed again, and I felt freer than ever.

"Louis, unfortunately, need to go, but I will have my coffee here again next Wednesday."

He grinned at me again. "I will be there around two a.m. in the afternoon?"

"Yes!" (I know you are probably thinking, good g-d! Back then, I was not the same as I am today. Only I would never have cheated on my Hans. Allow me a little daydreaming!)

I shook his hand and went to the waiter to pay. Inwardly, I thought: Get out quickly and go home! I left the café and walked along the Rhine promenade. I saw the fishermen again in front of our house. They waved to me, and I waved back to them. I met Hans in the garden. He smiled at me when he saw me.

"Dear, you are finally here."

"I went to the doctor, and then I went to this little café on the Rhine."

"It is okay! You do not have to explain anything to me."

"I am here now. Where are you going?"

"I wanted to go for a walk. But now I can go in with you too."

"Shall we have a drink?"

"Yeah, how was it with the doctor?"

"She is a woman, but she was nice, and I was not afraid."

"I will have a sherry!"

"Okay, I will have some tea, and then we will sit on the cozy couch in the little living room."

"Of course, darling!"

I got everything ready. Together, we went into the small salon. There we sat down on this cozy chaise longue. I snuggled up to Hans and drank my tea.

"I hope I am pregnant. I want to have a child with you!"

"Me too, dear, it will work out."

"Tomorrow or the day after tomorrow, the doctor will call and tell me the result."

"I wanted to tell you that we will go to Zurich soon. Our house got completed quicker than initially expected."

"Nice! I am looking forward to Zurich."

"Me too. It is just a little strange at the beginning."

I asked, surprised. "Why?"

"We will be alone in the big house because our staff won't arrive until a few days later."

"No matter, let us enjoy being undisturbed for once! Won't your father be lonely without us?"

"No! He is used to that, and I think Renate will soon move in here."

We cuddled together for a long time, but eventually, I got tired and went to bed.

The other morning, I felt better. Just as I was about to go to breakfast, the phone rang. Sebastian picked up and answered. It was Doctor Abt. Oh, how nervous I was when Sebastian handed me the phone!

I said quietly. "Hello?"

"Hello, little one. Congratulations: you are pregnant!"

I asked, a little embarrassed. "Really?"

"Yes, little one, come and see me tomorrow."

"Thanks!" I said quickly and hung up.

I ran into the salon and saw Hans.

"Hans!"

"Do you have anything, love?"

"Yes, I am pregnant. I am supposed to come by the doctor Abt tomorrow."

Hans looked at me. Then he jumped up and hugged me. "Wonderful!", he exclaimed.

"Yes, finally. I love you!"

"You have to take it easy now."

"Not yet. I am just pregnant and not sick!"

"First, sit down and have breakfast."

I sat down next to Hans, and we enjoyed our breakfast together. Just as I wanted to ask where Samuel was, he walked in the door and sat at the breakfast table.

"Good morning everyone. Did you sleep well?"

"Yes, good, father."

"I'm going to Geneva with Renate for a few days today."

"Fine, father. It will be good for you."

"Yes, I think the same. Renate would like to look at her house and stay for a few days."

"When will Renate arrive here?"

"Oh, she is already here. What else are you doing that is nice?"

"We want to celebrate something. Hannah just got the news that she is pregnant."

"Really? Congratulations, my love."

Samuel jumped up from the chair so that it recoiled with a screeching noise, ran to me, and hugged me. Renate also came running out of sheer shock. She thought it was something, but Samuel reassured her.

"Hannah is pregnant. Dear, we will be Grandpa and Grandma." Was that the first announcement that Samuel and Renate wanted to get married?

"Congratulations, Hannah, and of course, Hans, you too."

How happy they both were! I did not know how to behave. I was a little scared. Hans noticed it. He took my hand and held it tightly. He always noticed when I was not feeling well.

"Honey, are you ready?"

"Yes. I do not like it anymore. Shall we go to the garden for a bit?"

"With pleasure, should I bring you some lemon balm tea?"

"Yes, please!"

I had no idea that the birth would be difficult, but I wanted to take it easy and thought to myself: moving to Zurich will be difficult for me!

I was sitting in the lounge chair when Hans came with the tea.

"You are all right?"

"Yes! I am just a bit tired. That is completely normal. Something is growing inside me!"

Hans sat down next to me and kissed me. "I will always protect and love you both."

"I know that, and our child will know this too. What do you wish for?"

"A son!"

"I want a daughter."

I was excited to see what would come out of me. We did not want to know what it would be, but we were excited.

"You can still recover a bit. I have to do a few things. I forget! Renate had approached me about a baby shower. She would like to prepare them, and everyone will come!"

"If she wants, it is okay!"

Oh god, was I excited, my first baby shower! I did not even know what a baby shower was. Renate picked it up on US radio. She had this new-fangled stuff on all day long. (It is only today that I also enjoy listening to the station US-POP!)

Hans was in his office. I was lying in the sun.

Renate came! "Sweety, can I disturb you for a moment?"

"Of course, Renate, but do not speak everything in English!"

"No! I forgot you cannot speak that!" (Well, thank you, and so direct!)

Renate was always so rough, never a real Jew, and did not have to go through what our people had to go through. I never held her against me for that. Renate was just Renate, and you had to love her for that.

"Shall we plan the baby shower together? I invite the guests, and then we design the decorations together."

"Can we do? When do you have a party like that?"

"Either before the birth or after, but you have to celebrate it."

"Yes, of course. You are an ace at that!"

At first, she just looked at me, but then she laughed. To this day, I do not know what she meant by that. By the way, we never had a baby shower. I did not come back to the idea, and neither did Renate.

"I will go back then. Samuel wants to leave soon!"

"Yes, I will stay here for a while and enjoy the sun."

I got bored soon and had to think about Louis as well. It was just twenty minutes to two. Was he in the little café today? I quickly clapped my hands and told myself not to think about him. (Hold on, Hannah!)

Hmm, I could have a coffee or something else. That is what I am doing now! I got up and went back into the house. I got ready, put on some blush, lined my lips, and grabbed my hat.

"Do you still want to go into town?"

"Hans, no! Just walk along the promenade. The weather is so nice, and who knows how many more times I can do this."

"You are right, love, enjoy."

"Thanks!"

I walked. Only when I was outside did I turn around. I felt shabby. You might think I would want to cheat on my Hans! But I did not want to.

The sun shone on my face as I walked along the Rhine. I saw the ferryman and the fishermen holding rods and nets into the Rhine. I also saw the house from Doctor Abt. As I walked past, I saw her standing at one of the windows.

She waved at me, and I waved back. The little café came a little further. I went upstairs, and Louis was sitting at the table. I recognized

Louis from behind. I slowly walked towards him and stopped in front of him. He saw me and smiled at me.

"That happened quicker than I thought."

"I just wanted a coffee. Can I sit next to you?"

"Of course, you are allowed!"

"Oh, are we on a first-name basis yet?"

"Forgive me, but we already know each other somewhat."

I sat down next to him and was excited. If he had asked me now, I would have done it. The waiter came, and even he noticed me. Louis ordered two café crèmes, and we talked a bit.

He asked me, "And, how are you?"

And I replied: "Thank you, I am doing very well. I just found out I am pregnant."

"Congratulations!"

"Coffee is coming!"

"Finally! So, you said you are moving to Zurich in the next few days."

"Yes, but the father of Hans, my fiancé, will stay here in our villa."

"All alone in a big villa!"

"No, we have servants, and his girlfriend will live there too."

"Interesting!"

"What?"

"Nothing! Just like that!" I was a little unsettled, but the French have always been mysterious.

"I have to go home now."

"We will meet again?"

"I do not think so, Louis. Farewell!"

I stood up and let him sit. I know it wasn't pretty, but it was necessary. I could never look Hans in the eyes again. So, I could, and I did the only right thing! I walked along the Rhine, looked into the greenish water, and enjoyed the wonderful sun. I sat on one of the benches for a few minutes and paused.

When I came up the stairs to the villa, Hans was standing there looking at me.

"Dear, you have been gone for a long time!"

"Yes! I watched the fishermen up at the bridge."

"Renate and father have already left. I am supposed to say greetings to you."

"Thanks. How nice! Is Sebastian there too?"

"No! He is going to Geneva with father and Renate. Why?"

"I just thought, then only the cook would be there. Creepy!"

"Ha, you are scared!"

"Of course not, but it is strange. Shall we go to the salon? I am sure the food will be ready soon."

"We can do that, but there is a ghost there!" Hans started laughing, and I had to laugh.

Young family

(1952–1975)

ZURICH: NEW HOME, OUR COMPANY

I had my next examination with Doctor Abt. I was excited, but the fear was unfounded. She didn't find anything unusual, except that I had been pregnant for longer than expected. My nausea was the sign. It had to have been at least seven weeks ago. (I actually got pregnant the first time I had sex with Hans!) I got the address of a colleague in Zurich and went home relieved.

Then the big day came. Our move to Zurich was in full swing. We packed everything we had previously chosen to take with us.

"Dear, the moving company is coming at two this afternoon."

"By then I have packed everything up so far. What time do we leave?"

"Three o'clock at the latest."

I continued packing and Hans went to do a few things in his office. The moving company also arrived at exactly two o'clock sharp. They had an old van that looked like it was going to crash soon. The driver and two workers got out, scowling.

However, it soon became clear that they were very friendly: three strong men who had to carry many heavy pieces of furniture. Hans loaded our car with personal belongings. He wanted to leave promptly at three. The cook would look after us on site when we were no longer there. She had come specifically for this.

So, we said goodbye to our cook and the movers. Then the journey began; But luckily it wasn't far to Zurich. We had to use the country road; a motorway only existed in the mid-1960s.

There was something beautiful about a cross-country journey like that. There was a lot to see and you could take a break at an Inn. But we didn't have time today. We wanted to arrive at our new home before dark. Our itinerary was as follows: Pratteln, Rheinfelden in Switzerland, Zeiningen, Mumpf, Eiken, Frick, Hornussen, Bözen, then via

Brugg to Baden, Neuenhof, Spreitenbach, Dietikon, and at the end came Zurich.

When Hans turned into the driveway of the property, my eyes widened. I couldn't stop being amazed. Only when Hans stopped did I close my mouth. The villa, already an older appearance, stood before us. It was a building with a tower, a small bay window and a pointed roof. The facade was shining in yellow and had a few ornaments as decoration. Our property had a park and a small lake, I could see that much. I was excited to see the rest.

"So, dear, do you like it?"

"Yes very! I don't know what to say."

Hans got out and opened the door for me. I got out and staggered. Before things got worse, Hans held me.

"Our child is happy too!" (Well, that was a guess!)

"He and his siblings will be happy here."

"Siblings?"

"Yes! A whole Soccer-team."

He smiled at me and grinned.

"You're crazy!" I shouted.

He grabbed me and gave me a kiss.

"Come on, I'll show you what the villa looks like inside."

I gave him my hand and we walked together to the entrance.

"Let's see, where was the key?"

"Perhaps under the doormat?"

"Exactly!"

He was lying there too. Hans took our key and unlocked this old door. The door began to creak when Hans opened it. We went in. Now I was even more amazed. The large entrance hall lay before us. Marble and oak everywhere! Wide stairs led up to the left and right. This staircase was crowned by a glass roof, the glass used to consist of thousands of mosaics. I couldn't wait for the sun to shine. She will be reflected wonderfully in it.

Hans didn't want to go up the stairs, but wanted to show me the lower floor first. In addition to a large salon, there were drawing rooms and a library. Then there was a dining room. The kitchen was in the basement and was accessible via a separate staircase.

"It's so modern!" I was amazed and thrilled.

"Yes, my darling, only the best for us."

"We don't have any staff, who should cook today?"

"Well, we'll manage that!"

"You're right! During the war, mother taught me to cook with what little we had."

"I am excited. Father's cook packed something for us."

"What's upstairs?"

"Come on, I'll show you."

We ran all the way up the stairs. I finally learned what the upper floor had to offer: several bedrooms and a large bathroom, nothing more. We would convert one or two rooms into offices. I was about to open the last door when Hans stopped me.

"Don't open it! It's in the attic, it hasn't been cleaned up yet and there are probably rats in there."

I had to laugh. All of this reminded me of the old lady, Mrs. von Blankenstein. Marta von Blankenstein had given us shelter during our escape - as the wife of a general in the Russian campaign, who hid a Jew who had previously been her gardener. He was also her lover and stood by her in the war. I liked Chajm. Finally, I discovered him in the attic and uncovered their secret. We visited her often after the war. At some point the house was empty and the old lady was dead, Katja, the young lady who had lent us her car, told us. So, we found out that Marta had died suddenly and Chajm had left the country out of grief.

"I forgot, Hans, you're afraid of rats."

"I? No! You must be mistaking me for someone else!"

We left the door locked and went into the drawing room. Hans had put the basket with the cook's delicacies there.

"Let's have a picnic! Remember when I had that picnic at the sanctuary? You were so happy, my love!"

"That's right, you could already do magic back then and you immediately enchanted me."

Hans spread a blanket on the floor, then we unpacked the basket.

"Delicious, beef salami!"

"There is also bread, wine and butter."

"There's juice for you. But I can also do without the wine!"

"No! You deserve it, enjoy it! I drink juice. Would you please cut some salami and bread for me?"

"Yes dear!"

We enjoyed these delicacies. Later I put my head on Hans' lap and listened to his words. He read Moby Dick to me. The book wasn't finished yet.

At some point he wanted to get up. "Dear, it's getting cold, let me light the fireplace!"

"Yes, I'm already shivering too. Where do we actually want to sleep?"

"I rented a hotel room."

"Aren't we supposed to sleep here on the floor? There are still blankets back there and it's cozy and warm by the fireplace."

"If you like!"

I nodded and Hans kissed me. Had he planned this from the start? He never told me, but I already knew him quite well.

When I woke up the next morning, Hans was gone. Where was he? I got up, pulled the blanket over my shoulders and looked for him. When I found him, he was in the kitchen making tea. What a sight, he was only wearing his boxing shorts (modern: boxer shorts).

"Honey, you're already awake!"

"I was scared because you were gone."

"Forgive'! I wanted to make us tea for breakfast. The transporter will arrive in an hour."

"Then let's have breakfast!"

Hans took the tea and followed me.

"Shall we have breakfast by the fireplace?"

"We don't have a table! How nice, breakfast in bed!"

Hans took the things and brought them to me on the blanket. I already had the tea and had to hold it until it sat down. I always had to look at him, my eyes couldn't escape his body. My imagination grew, my gaze tilted towards my lap.

Wake up, I thought.

"Do you have something?"

"No, darling, everything is fine."

I bit into my bread and felt sick. I quickly jumped up and ran to the bathroom. I had to vomit there for a long time.

Hans followed suit and put his hand on my shoulder. "Is it okay?", he asked me.

I said, deflated: "Yes! It's morning sickness."

Luckily it settled down quickly. Hans had already gone back to the salon and got dressed there. When I came back too, he looked at me and smiled. I said nothing and got dressed too. Hans came to me. He saw me struggling with my zipper. While he helped me, he kissed my neck.

"I'm looking forward to our child."

"Yes, me too, even if it seems a little uncomfortable right now." I turned around and kissed him.

"Look'! The moving van drives up. Let's go outside!" Hans took my hand and pulled me behind him.

One of the employees was already standing at the door: "Morning, Mr. Mangold! We can clear out the van."

"Good morning! Gladly! My fiancée will tell you where the things go."

The men immediately began emptying the car. I showed where the things should go and Hans looked around his new study. The desk and boxes were already there. He started setting up the desk.

"Honey, could you arrange for the furniture for my study to be brought in next?"

"I'll see what's possible, but I can't promise it."

"Please! Then I can work."

I went and talked to the movers. Miraculously, the remaining furniture was in the study within 20 minutes. Hans was happy and was able to carry on.

The last things and furniture were soon unloaded. Afterwards I had enough time to unpack the many boxes. The staff should come tomorrow. You would be able to help me set it up and put it away. (Hans had just forgotten to tell them that we had already moved into the new house. But maybe he wanted to be alone with me for a few days.)

So, we were able to treat ourselves to a relaxing break. Hans had done the bare essentials.

"Honey, do we want to go shopping?"

"Yes! We have to have something to eat."

"There's a market in town today, we could go there."

"Good! I'll get the basket and then we can go."

"I'll get the car, then come out."

I went to get the basket and Hans drove up.

"Ready to go?"

"Yes!"

Phew, I was nervous! A new city, new people! Were they like the people of Basel, or did they have something against Jews? I haven't looked like a Jew for a long time. Except for my black hair, nothing reminded me of it. I would have passed for being from Ticino.

(Ticino people are something special. They are like Italians, only a little more casual. I love Ticino and its people, also the delicious food and good wine. We often vacationed in Ticino. I still go to Ascona regularly today and stay in the Hotel Al Faro.)

We didn't have to go very far, about 15 minutes by car.

"Look, there is the market square ahead. Over there is the Grand Minster and here is the office building", said Hans, pointing in a circle.

"Grand Minster, how beautiful! Everything you know!" I said, slightly annoyed. Oh god, the hormones! (I have a sketch of the Grand Minster by an artist. I love this picture because I have long been a fan of the Minster. You have to climb one of the towers and enjoy the view from high up.)

"I'll park here and then we'll walk."

Hans parked the car and we walked together to Bürkliplatz, where the market always took place. It was big – and there were so many people!

"Do they also have Basel Klöpfer?"

"No! They're called Cervelat here. Should we take one then?"

"Sure!"

We walked through the market and at the other end I could see a pavilion. You could hear music from there. How I would have loved to dance there! The pavilion was built for musical groups and dancing. Hans was distracted and picked up fruit and vegetables, but also a few flowers. We also took bread with us, as well as sausage and meat. Of course, everything from beef!

"Do you like something sweet?"

"Let's see!"

"Look, there's cotton candy."

"What? I've never seen that before."

When I looked in the indicated direction, I got a little lost in the noise of the numerous market visitors. The people in Zurich speak angular Swiss German, city dwellers!

"Can you smell that?"

I asked in surprise. "What?"

"The many different scents! It smells of flowers up front, you can smell the cheese back there and there are grilled sausages here."

"Please order some. I'm terribly hungry."

Hans went to order us two sausages, bread and something to drink. We sat at one of the tables and enjoyed the delicious food.

"We have to go to the company tomorrow; they're expecting us."

"Good! I'm already excited."

"You do not have to be. Do we have everything?"

"I think so, but I'll think again."

After a moment and finishing my sausage I said. "We could take some more cheese."

"Yes, if you like."

We quickly ran to the cheesemonger and bought Appenzeller cheese, Emmental and Gruyère. They were very expensive, but very good. The music started again, now we were close to the pavilion. I closed my eyes and took in the music. It was a pleasant moment, it was so wonderful to let yourself go.

"Love, let's go back to the car. We have everything we need."

I wanted to know curiously. "Yes gladly. Tell me, what kind of little island is this?"

Hans answered me: "That's the Bauschänzli. An island where you can eat well and parties as well."

(THIS SKETCH OF THE GRAND MINSTER AT ZURICH IN HER OFFICE)

As we continued walking, we passed a smaller building. It was strange because it was in the Limmat. "Look, this is the bathhouse for women. You can go there sometime."

"I could, but I have less desire to be alone."

"You will become friends with Ursula. The wife from Martin."

"Let us see."

At our automobile, we loaded our purchases in the trunk and drove home.

I was about to pick up the heavy basket in front of our front door when Hans stopped me. "Are you crazy! I will put it on the stairs; you take the flowers."

"Yes, dear! But you know, I am just pregnant and not sick!"

"Be glad I am so careful."

I smiled at Hans and kissed him. He also smiled at me and was happy that I reacted that way. Pregnant women can be so annoying.

When Hans had driven the car into the garage, we went inside. He took the basket, and I took the flowers.

"Please bring the basket in the kitchen, I will put the things away."

"I do, love!"

In the meantime, I was looking for a vase for the flowers. I found one straight away and took it into the kitchen. Hans was just putting our purchases away.

"Honey, I thought I did this quickly. Get the flowers ready!"

"Yes, sir!" I said it angrily.

Hans looked at me in shock. "Do you have something?"

"Yes indeed! I want to decide myself whether I can do something or not."

Hans put the fruit down and left the kitchen in silence. I was in tears, oh God, the hormones again! Crying, I put the things away, put the flowers in the vase, and went to look for Hans. He stood by the fireplace in the drawing room and stared into the fire.

"Darling, please forgive me. I did not mean to yell at you."

"It is okay, I understand! But please promise that you will tell me if I can help you."

I went to him, took him in my arms, and said quietly: "My body is changing every day. I may say something that I do not mean."

"It is okay." But the tone of voice belied his words. I was worried.

I had been sensitive to Hans. He withdrew.

"Darling, I have to go again. Shall we eat in two hours?"

I asked him. "Yes! Is everything okay?"

"Sure! See you later! I love you."

"I like you too!" Hans kissed me and left.

I wanted to distract myself. There was still a lot to do around the house. First, I want to tidy up the bedroom. The movers had assembled the bed and cupboard. I could not carry the boxes, but I used an old technique: with a blanket under the box, I could drag them wherever I wanted them.

I was able to organize Hans and my closets without much effort. The chest of drawers was also quickly sorted. The socks from Hans and our underwear found their place in it.

The fully furnished dining room and living room were only missing a few glasses from the display cases. I soon admitted that.

I felt bad later. Had I offended Hans? He was not back yet. I decided to make myself some tea.

Just as I went down to the kitchen, Hans unlocked the door.

"Dear, here I am again!" He had a bouquet of red roses in his hand.

I had to cry because of the emotion.

"Honey, I am so sorry!"

"Me too. I was a stupid cow!"

Suddenly, Hans had to laugh out loud. The "stupid cow" amused him.

"I was a stupid ass!"

I laughed too, took his hand, and kissed it. We went into the kitchen together because we wanted to cook.

"What do we want to prepare?" I asked Hans, perplexed.

"I have no idea! I have never had to cook until now."

"Okay, we will make fried potatoes and steak and have salad. I still have to put the flowers in a vase."

"What should I do?"

"You peel the potatoes, I will clean the salad."

"Can't we swap? I have no idea how to peel potatoes!"

"Good! Then you clean the salad and I will do it."

"Are you making hash browns, love?" (It is called Rösti. This is a traditional product from Swiss cuisine.)

"If you want, and if I find the grater."

"I am looking for him!" Hans said quickly and started looking.

"You just want to avoid cleaning the salad!"

Well, Hans looked for the grater in one of the large boxes. I peeled the potatoes and also cleaned the lettuce at the end. Hans finally found the grater and, as punishment. Hans had to grate the potatoes. After a few minutes, he was ready. But I did not want to tell Hans how good he was.

"That took a long time!"

"Sorry, but I have two left hands in the kitchen."

"Men and cooking!"

"Is that bad, love?"

"No! I am proud of you for helping me."

"Should I set the table?"

"Yes! I will get everything ready then."

"Fine, but I will come and help you carry it."

Hans marched away, I continued cooking. Heat the pan, add the Rösti strips, and fry. Then I made the salad dressing, and finally, it was the turn of the meat.

Hans came back: "Dear, I need cutlery."

"It is in the dresser in the drawing room, second drawer from the top."

"Can I take something with me?"

"Yes, the juice and the table water."

"Will be back in a few minutes and help you carry it."

I did not say anything because I had to concentrate on making dinner. My hash browns (Rösti) almost burned. Now, all that was left was to fry the meat, and Hans would come.

"Please take the hash browns (Rösti) and salad with you. I will bring the meat straight away. It just needs steep for a bit."

"What you can all do! We do not need a cook." Hans joked.

When the meat was well cooked, I took it and followed Hans. He was already sitting in the drawing room. The candles were burning, and lovely music was playing on the gramophone.

"I love the music of Gustav Mahler."

"Yes, I know that is why I chose him."

I opened it for Hans and then for myself.

"That was great!" Hans said to me after we were finished.

"Yes, I have outdone myself. Can you help me clear up?"

"Of course, dear!"

We brought the dishes back to the kitchen. But we do not want to wash them until tomorrow. We wanted to sit on the sofa and enjoy the great music.

"Should I put on another record?"

"Yes, please!"

Hans went to the gramophone and held out records to me. I chose Leo Blech! (Yes, I know Blech sounds strange as a name, but wonderful music he wrote .) Hans sat down next to me again, and I snuggled up to him.

He enjoyed his wine, and I drank cherry juice. Well, I would have preferred to drink wine, but our child would not have liked it. At some point, it was very late, and the record was over. I wanted to go to bed, and so did Hans. We slowly got used to seeing each other naked, but we slept in nightwear.

When Hans showered in the morning, I had to go to the toilet so badly that I went in anyway. He grinned at me as I stared at him. What a splendid fellow I had caught!

"I have to urinate. Turn around otherwise I cannot."

"Yeah, it is okay, you little coward!"

I almost could not pee because I had bottom from Hans in front of me.

"Can I turn around again?"

"Better not! I go outside."

"Why? Come and shower with me, it is so nice and warm!"

I found myself thinking about it, but I told him. "I do better go. And hurry up!"

He called after me. "Yes, mom!"

I lay back in my bed and enjoyed the cozy warmth. After a few minute Hans came, only he had a bath towel around his waist.

"Please close your eyes. I want to get dressed!"

Instead of laughing, I threw his pillow at him. He turned around, picked it up, and ran to my bed. He hit me in the face with the pillow, and I could not stop laughing. Only when I begged for mercy did he give up. He kissed me, got up, and went to the closet to get dressed. I watched him. And he enjoyed being admired.

"Love, don't you want to get ready too? Soon we have to leave; the staff is coming in the afternoon."

"I will get ready if you make breakfast."

"Yes, it's good."

Hans went, and I dressed up. I had to dress for the occasion today. It was the first day in our new company. I was looking forward to the employees. When I came into the salon, Hans had already prepared everything. I could sit down and enjoy breakfast.

"Dear, I am excited."

"Why?"

"Well, we are going to the company."

"Yes! But it's not wild, they are all very nice, and your assistant Veronika is already looking forward to seeing you."

"What, I have an assistant?"

"Yes, she'll do everything for you."

Oh, my g-d! I never had my assistant as a hairdresser.

"Let us just clear the dishes! We haven't even washed yesterday."

"No matter, the staff will be here today."

"They run away screaming when it looks like this!"

When I came into the kitchen, I was surprised! The dishes were washed and cleaned.

"Well, you were astonished!"

"When did you do that?"

"Before! You need half an eternity in the bathroom, my love."

Let someone else say that Jewish men are comfortable! I kissed Hans and was glad he had washed the dishes.

"Will we go?"

"Yes!"

Hans picked up the car from the garage and drove forward. I was able to get in, and then it started. Every meter I get closer to the company, my stomach turns more and more. It was so far in the middle of the city. We stood in Stampfenbachstrasse in front of the building, where our company, was located. At the time, I thought she was on the ground floor. I quickly realized that Samuel had bought the whole complex.

"And what do you say, dear?"

"What a nice deal! Is this where we have our offices?"

"Yes! We have the entire area, in the attic only for the offices. Besides, there are a few apartments and shops."

We went in; inside was a reception room. Two young ladies were sitting there, immediately they recognized Hans as their boss.

"Good day, Mr. Mangold! Mr. Hornmann is already waiting in your office."

"Good morning, Mrs. Strecker! May I introduce you to my future wife, Hannah Epstein!"

"Good morning, Miss Epstein I am delighted."

"Good morning, I am so glad to meet you."

"Let us go upstairs. Martin is already waiting."

In the elevator, I had to smile for a moment.

Hans saw it and said, "I love it when you smile."

"I just had to think of our first picnic."

"You mean in the Zuflucht on the boxes?"

"Yes, we were afraid of dying soon, and look where we stand to-day."

"This is only the beginning!"

We got out of the elevator in the attic and went into another hallway. Two other ladies were sitting at two desks. One was Hans' front room lady, and the other was my assistant. When she saw us, she jumped up and came up to us.

"Good morning, Miss Epstein, morning, Mr. Mangold. Mr. Hornmann is in the office he got coffee. Can I bring you coffee, too?"

"Good morning everyone! Yes, please bring two coffees. Honey, this is Rosi, and Veronika is sitting at the desk. She's your receptionist and will support you with everything."

"Good morning everyone! Nice to know you."

Veronika greeted friendly. We went to Martin.

"Morning, you two! Have you settled in in Zurich yet?"

"Morning, Martin, yes, something!"

"Before I forget! I am supposed to give you an invitation from my wife for this evening at eight o'clock. She wants to meet Hannah!"

"That's very nice, we're happy to come. All the rich and well-known people will come back."

"Yes, as always, Hans!"

"Darling, while you're talking, I could get to know Veronika in the meantime."

"If you like, dear, have fun!"

I went out and got my coffee there.

"Veronika, would you please show me to my office?"

"Of course, Miss Epstein!"

She went ahead and showed me to my office.

What it sounded like back then – my office. From a poor church mouse to an entrepreneur's wife!

I liked my office. It was decorated in beige colors, with a large desk in the middle, next to a cabinet for hanging files, and a small conference table with two armchairs. (The desk has been in my private writing room since a renovation. I'm currently writing this book there.)

"What are our tasks, Veronika?"

"Customer care, representation, and preparing events!"

"Oh, that's a lot!"

"We will make it."

"Luckily, you are here!"

I only sat down briefly but then wanted to go to Hans and Martin. They were already coming towards, and Hans asked if we wanted to go. Martin and his company had rented a floor below. He lived with his family directly on Lake Zurich. (A wonderful lake. We had a sailing boat there for a long time. I sold it after Hans died. The memories hurt me too much.)

At home, there was a strange car at the door. Hans didn't know him and drove closer slowly. A man in his mid-50s got out and waved to us. Who was that?

Hans stopped, got out, and went to meet him. They shook hands. The other gentleman smiled, and Hans turned to me and waved. So, I also got out and went to them. I was curious to see who the gentleman was.

"Dear, this is Mr. Brandt." Hans introduced him. "He's our butler! I forgot he was coming today."

"Hello, Mr. Brandt, I'm very pleased."

"Good day, Madam!" He said: "Madam!"

Hans unlocked the front door and let us in. "I'll show you the house and your room." The two of them marched off.

I made myself some tea. After, they had looked at everything, Hans showed the new butler his room.

"We can discuss further details later. The maids will arrive today or tomorrow."

"With pleasure, Mr. Mangold, I'll come to your salon."

"Is good!"

Hans came to me. I had already prepared the tea.

"What do you think is he the right butler for us?"

"I think so! He makes a good impression."

"Yes, I think so, too."

A short time later, Mr. Brandt came, to discuss everything else with Hans. I sat on one of the chairs and listened to them.

"You already know your tasks. I also want you to take care of the maids. You must follow your instructions."

"I'd be happy to do that, Mr. Mangold. I'm going to go and get myself set up and maybe prepare the kitchen."

"Another cook will be coming this week. Until we have to cook for ourselves."

"I can do this. I am very good at cooking."

"Nice! Before I forget, my fiancée and I, are out of the house tonight."

"Understood, Mr. Mangold."

Hans and I drank our tea, and later we had dinner. Mr. Brandt had outdone himself. From then on, we called him by his first name, Georg. Although to everyone else in the household, he was always just Mr. Brandt. (However, our closest friends adopted our habit.)

A little later, we went to the Hornmanns' party. They lived in the posh corner of Zurich, with their boathouse on the lakeshore. We were driving over the big bridge when it started to rain. Hans wanted to put the top up, but I wanted to feel the light rain.

"We'll be with Martin and Ursula in a moment anyway."

"Even! Then it doesn't matter, darling."

Hans turned into the driveway to the Hornmann family property. I had to swallow. They lived in a property that one could only dream of.

"Do you like it?"

"Yes! But ours is much nicer."

"This once belonged to a rich Jew who now lives in Israel."

"He had real taste!"

Hans stopped at the main entrance. One of the servants helped me get out, and another got behind the wheel and parked the car.

I waited until Hans was with me. He took my hand, and then we walked to the house.

The butler opened the door, and we were able to enter. "Good evening, Madame et Monsieur, I will take your coats." We handed him our coats and continued on our way.

"Do you hear the beautiful music?"

"Yes, that sounds like jazz."

"We have to dance today while I still can."

"Let's do it, love, but first, I would like to introduce you to Ursula."

I was curious to see what Ursula was like. Would she become a friend to me, or would she be more of a fine lady?

"Look, they are standing right there." We ran there and were given champagne on the way. Unfortunately, I had to decline, but there was also orange juice.

"Ursula, Martin! What a lovely welcome!"

"Hans! How nice that you are here!"

"Ursula, may I introduce you to my fiancée Hannah?"

"I am honored!"

"Hannah, this is Ursula!"

"I am very pleased, Ursula."

"Hannah, come on! We leave the men alone."

We went into the garden. What splendor and the view of the lake! We sat down on a bench.

"This is all new for you, but it's certainly nice too."

"Yes, very nice. It takes a while to get used to it."

"We can meet up sometime and do something together."

"I would like that, Ursula."

"Let's go have a drink. Of course, we also have something non-alcoholic."

"Why do you think so?" I asked her, surprised. Could Ursula already recognize that I was pregnant?

"I thought you did not drink alcohol."

"Normally yes. But not at the moment because I am pregnant."

Ursula looked at me in surprise and then said happily. "Dear, how beautiful, and it's your first birth! Congratulations to you both!"

"Thank you!"

We went to the bar and drank cocktails, she with alcohol and I without. (Something about her annoyed me at the time, her posturing and all that stuff. It was not until a little later that we became real friends.) A few cocktails later, we went back to our husbands. Hans was visibly happy that I was back.

"Dear, here you are!"

"Yes, we had fun at the bar."

"Shall we go home?"

"Yes! It's already late."

We said goodbye to the Hornmanns and drove home. I felt dizzy a bit on the journey, but it was probably. Because I was up so late. At home immediately put, Hans me in bed and made me a soothing hot water bottle. I quickly felt better, but towards morning, the tragedy began.

I developed a high fever and terrible abdominal pain. What happened to our child? Hans immediately called the ambulance, but it took almost half an hour to arrive. I was in so much pain that I screamed. The doctor who came with the ambulance examined me. He felt my stomach and was worried. I had to go to the hospital.

Hans immediately got dressed and followed. In the hospital I was examined. Doctor Kress wanted to keep me there for a few days and examine me more closely. He was worried it might be pregnancy poisoning. Maybe our child had even died. I was terrified, but deep down. I knew it was still alive.

Hans visited me every day and told me what was new at home. The maids came and a housekeeper; she should support me from now on. He did not trust me to manage the household and raise my children. After all, the noble gentleman had to pay attention to his position and reputation! I hated Hans at that moment, but that immediately went away when he kissed me.

On the fourth day, I was finally allowed to go home; I felt much better. My baby was still alive, and apparently, I had just had severe colic. The doctor advised me to "fart" more = squirm. My face turned bright red, but he was right.

When I got home, the staff was introduced to me. The maidens were nice, but Mrs. Krähling, the housekeeper, was a dragon with hair on her teeth. Her black hair, was styled into a bun. She wore glasses that made her even more unappealing.

Hans had hired her as a supervisor for the servants and probably also as my supervisor. From his perspective, I probably had rebellious views about the role of women in marriage.

But then, over the years, Ms. Krähling grew very dear to me and proved self-sacrificing and sensitive. She was my housekeeper for over 20 years and soon became our child's governess.

THE WEDDING

It was August. Our wedding month was approaching. It was not going so quickly anymore. I had a big belly and was about to give birth. The tailor-made it easy for me: he came to my dressing room.

"Dear! The tailor is here. He wants to take measurements one last time."

"Yes, I come!"

Mr. Steiner and his assistant were already waiting in my study. "Miss Epstein, how are you today?"

"Hello, Mr. Steiner! I am doing pretty well, but the birth is getting closer and closer."

"Yes, you really can't miss it anymore."

"Are you ready to finish my dress?"

"Of course!" He said to me and showed me.

What a beautiful dress, white and pure silk. It cost half a fortune back then, but Hans only wanted the best for me.

"My assistant will help you get dressed."

"Yes, thank you, I can hardly move. God, I am fat!" I cried in horror.

"When is the wedding going to be again?"

"In four days, if I survive!"

Mr. Steiner had to laugh and immediately helped me finish.

"It isn't much anymore. Move two seams, expand a strip at the bottom, then we have it."

"Fortunately! Thanks for your patience."

"Very gladly! Please recommend me."

"Of course, with pleasure."

I changed it again and was happy to be able to take off this uncomfortable dress. Mr. Steiner and his assistant said goodbye and left. Hans came to me and told me that we still had an appointment with the pastry chef. Well, you can always eat. Not if you are pregnant and want to get married.

"Hans, you have to do this together with Ms. Krähling. She knows best what I like. But I will come with you if you want me to."

"No, you rest. We will do it!"

Hans went to try the desserts with Mrs. Krähling, and I lay in bed. One of the maids came and told me a visitor was waiting in the salon. When I asked who it was. She said they wanted to surprise me. I pulled myself together and crawled to the parlor on the ground floor.

What a joy it was when I saw who it was! Standing in front of me was my brother Adam.

"Adam! What are you doing here?"

"Sister! I had appointments to attend for Mr. Bundschuh."

"Ah, certainly with Martin!"

"No, not this time, but tell me: How are you?"

"Well, look at me!"

"You look great, round as a ball, and probably ready to give birth soon."

"You are almost like my doctor! Are you staying for dinner?"

"Yes! But I am looking for a hotel room and will fly back tomorrow."

"Sleep here! I'll have a room prepared for you."

"Gladly!"

Hans was just as surprised as I was when he and Mrs. Krähling returned.

"Adam! What are you doing here?"

"I had appointments here in Zurich."

"How long are you staying?"

"Till tomorrow morning! Hannah offered to let me sleep here."

"Very gladly! Dear, have you told the maids yet?"

"I was just about to do that, but then you came. I am just going to see Ms. Krähling."

"Sit down, Adam, tell me: How are you in Berlin?"

"We are doing well. Rosa had our Hilda last week. The general situation is just getting worse. The conflicts are coming to a head. There are rumors at the highest levels that the GDR wants to build a wall."

(The Wall was not built until ten years later, but the idea for it had already emerged after the Berlin Blockade. Since then, the founding of the GDR state has been discussed again and again, but has always been rejected by the Soviet Union.)

"That sounds very worrying. If you want to emigrate, we are there for you."

"I hope it won't be that bad."

A worrying topic! We wanted to live in peace here. Adam will also have noticed that he could let his worries rest here for at least one evening. He should have a more pleasant time here with us.

"So, the maids will prepare a room for you. There will be dinner soon. By the way. Hans, how was the tasting?"

"I have never eaten so much sweet food! Mrs. Krähling was brave and tried every pudding and cake."

We had so much to tell each other. Adam told us all about Hilda. We had never seen her before, and when he showed us a photo of her, I was excited about our baby. One of the maidens came to get us for dinner. There were roulades, dumplings, and red cabbage.

"What a great meal, little sister! I have not eaten so well in a long time. How lucky you were with Hans!"

"Yes, every minute together is priceless."

"Let us go to the drawing room. Whiskey and cigars are waiting!"

"Oh, you men again! I will have tea."

When he arrived in the salon, Hans lit a cigar. Adam did not want to, but he could not say to a whiskey.

"What is your wedding doing?"

"Look at me! I will be happy when the wedding is finally over. Then the child can come."

"Do you already know what it's going to be?"

"No! We will let ourselves be surprised."

"I was right about Leon. I would point to a boy."

"A Samuel Yaron then! Hans would prefer a boy, and I would prefer a girl."

"The main thing is that it is healthy and human!"

I had to laugh out loud.

It was getting late, and Adam was tired. He said goodbye and went to his room. We soon went to sleep, too.

In bed, we talked about the upcoming wedding. Everyone was invited and accepted. The rooms were all booked, and Hans had already chosen the location for our wedding early on. Both of my dresses were ready, as was Hans' suit. We were able to get married without any worries. I hoped everything would go well.

After a kiss, we fell asleep.

The alarm clock rang. It was eight o'clock in the morning, time to get up. I was in pain and wanted to stay in bed. Hans was already awake. He came into our room to wake me up.

"I am already awake!"

"Too bad, love! Did you sleep well?"

"No! I have pain in my abdomen."

"Should I call a doctor?"

"No! It is bearable. The doctor at the hospital said there would be pain."

"But if it gets worse, say something!"

"Yes, love!"

"I have to go to the office later, you rest!"

"I will, but we have breakfast first, and Adam is here too."

"When does he have to leave?"

"His plane leaves at eleven a.m."

"Good! I will go down then."

"I will come straight away, too."

Hans kissed me and left me.

"Good morning, Adam! Did you sleep well?"

"Good morning, Hans! Yes, very well. Without Hilda screaming, it was pure relaxation."

"Yes, that will soon blossom for me too! "

I asked Hans when I came to them. "What will happen to you?"

"Dear! The flowers at our wedding!"

"Morning, Adam. Did you sleep well?"

"Morning, Hannah! Yes, very good, and you?"

"It worked like that! I have a pain in my stomach."

"Fennel!"

"Fennel, what?" I asked.

"Well, fennel tea helps with the pain. It was like that with Rosa!"

"Dear, I'll tell one of the maids to get fennel tea from the pharmacy."

"Yes, please!"

"I have to go then. Adam, see you. Good flight!"

"Thank you, Hans!"

Hans gave me another kiss and left us.

"Did he say earlier that he would get sick of screaming too?" I asked Adam after Hans had left.

Adam tried to dismiss it. "Yes! You know us men. We always chatter a little too quickly."

"Luckily, yes. Is he afraid of our baby?"

"He had a panic, Hannah!"

I had to smile. Now Adam had to go, too. He took me in his arms and squeezed me.

"Say greetings from us at home."

"I will, little sister!"

"Should Mr. Brandt drive you?"

"No! A taxi will pick me up soon."

As soon as we said this, the doorbell rang: the taxi was there. Adam gave me one last goodbye and left. He and the family would have come for the wedding in a few days. I was looking forward to it.

Finally, one of the maids came and brought me my fennel tea. It worked. My pain subsided. I still decided to lie down for a while. After all, I was about to give birth and was as fat as a goose. Everyone in the house went about their daily activities. Only I was lying on the sofa in the living room and could not do anything.

The doorbell rang. Who was that? Ursula! That is right, she wanted to come over today. I hoisted myself up and welcomed my new friend.

"Shalom, Ursula!"

"Schalömchen, dear Hannah. How are you, my love?"

"Good! I am glad you came. Do you like coffee or tea?"

"Coffee, please!"

"Good, comes!"

I told one of the Maids and led Ursula onto the large terrace. The sun was shining, and some fresh air would do me good. The coffee came, and Ursula asked me what month I was in now. I told her I was close to giving birth but still had some time.

"The wedding has first to take place, then the child can come."

"Well, the wedding is already in three days. Have you done everything?"

"Yes! All that is missing are the guests and good weather!"

"Martin and I have such a nice present for you. I am so excited to see what you will say about that."

"Now I am curious!"

"You could be too, love!"

"Would you like some more cake or coffee?"

"No! I have to go again. Martin will probably be waiting. We want to go out on the lake."

"How nice! I would do that too, but only after the birth."

Ursula had to laugh.

"Take care, I am looking forward to the party."

"Yes, me too. See you soon, Ursula."

Ursula left. I tried to get some rest again. Hans would be home soon, and the food would soon be ready.

The telephone rang. It was the hotel that was supposed to accommodate our guests. The director personally confirmed that all rooms were available. I thanked him politely and hung up. One item more on the list that can be crossed out.

So, I dragged myself to the desk to cross this item off my list. My stomach hurt again, but that was probably just the excitement. I lay down on the sofa in my office; it was only a few meters to get there.

Beforehand, I called one of the maids to ask her to make me some fennel tea. Mrs. Krähling brought me the tea and a box.

I wanted to hear from her. "What's in there?"

"The package has just been delivered. It was a tailor's employee who made your wedding dress."

"Ah, my wedding dress!" I exclaimed with joy.

Ms. Krähling stared at me. She had never seen such a crazy woman like me.

"Should I open it?"

"Yes, please, but only when Hans is not around."

"Is not he! I will hear him."

"Let's go!"

Enthused said Ms. Krähling. "That looks nice!"

"Yes, the tailor did a great job."

"I will pack it up again."

"Please make this and put it on the top of the closet in our bedroom."

"With pleasure, Miss Epstein."

Mrs. Krähling had hidden my box just in time because Hans was already coming home.

"Shalom, dear, I'm back. Are you, all right?"

"Shalom, Hans! Yes, my stomach hurt a bit, but it is okay."

"Nice! Would you like to eat in bed?"

"No! I will come immediately, Mrs. Krähling will call."

"It is okay I will take a shower."

Hans went to take a shower, and I was finally able to get some rest. While I was doing this, Mrs. Krähling rang the dinner bell. Hans was ready and came to pick me up. We went downstairs together to dine. There was a roast with vegetables and potatoes.

"We have a first-class cook. She cooks the best dishes every day."

"True! I hope she stays with us for a long time."

"Shall we go to the little salon later? I can read to you."

"Yes, with pleasure, I enjoy listening to you."

After dinner, we went into our little drawing room. Hans drank his whiskey and smoked his cigar. (He smoked one every day until shortly before his death.) I drank fennel tea because my stomach would not rest.

"What should I read to you?"

"Gulliver's Travels!"

"Good!"

I was lying on the comfortable sofa, Hans sitting opposite me. The evening was so entertaining that it was quickly time to go to bed.

When I woke up the other morning, the bed from Hans was empty. That is right, he had an appointment with a new client very early. I decided to get some more sleep. There was a knock on the room door.

"Come in!" I said, slightly sleepy. It was one of the maidens who was supposed to check on me. Ms. Krähling was worried because it was already eleven o'clock.

"Everything is fine, Marie. I am getting up."

"It is okay, madam. Would you like breakfast or an early lunch?"

"I do not have any appetite right now, maybe later."

After freshening up, I sat down at the desk. Let us see when the first guests expected were. The first ones are already coming today. Samuel and Renate will travel with Sebastian. My family would have to arrive today or tomorrow, the rest of our Mischpoke. I will be happy when the wedding is over and everyone is gone again!

Now, I was a little hungry. I went into the salon, but first, I called Mrs. Krähling over to ask her to have one of the maidens bring my food.

I was looking forward to my family wanting to come. After all, Adam was one of our witnesses. Martin was the other. I would stand at the front with three men.

The food came. There was soup. I did not have any more appetite today. It would still be good for me; I needed strength for the next few days.

"Miss Epstein, a car just pulled up."

"It is okay. I am coming, and you will open the door, please."

I hoisted myself up and ran after the maiden.

"Oh, my family is already coming!"

Luckily, Ms. Krähling was already at the door to greet them. I was excited. My parents were flying for the first time. I looked at the car. They got out. Where were Ari, Rosa, Hilda, and Leon?

Our butler and one of the maidens went to get the suitcases. My parents and Adam came my way. Mother had tears in her eyes. She ran towards me and hugged me. Now I had to cry, too.

I shouted. "You are finally here!"

"Yes, we are finally here! I missed you so much all we did, of course."

Father slowly walked behind mother. When he got us, he hugged me and kissed me on the cheek.

I asked my father. "Where are the others?"

"At the hotel, but Adam wanted to bring us to you earlier."

"Fortunately! I thought they did not want to come."

"But! You would never want to miss this day."

"Come in, and the staff will get your luggage."

They dropped off inside, and we went into the saloon. Mother looked around and exclaimed, "Oh, how wonderful! So beautifully decorated!"

"We tried hard."

"How are you, my child?"

"Oh, dad, I'm doing very well. The child is growing, and everything is going well at the moment. Nice that you are here! Dad, are you okay? I noticed you do so slowly walk ."

"Yes, I'm fine! I am getting older. I can't move so fast anymore."

"Would you like tea or coffee?"

We opted for tea and cookies. Adam immediately said goodbye.

But just as Adam was about to leave, Hans came in.

"Shalom, family!"

"Shalom, Hans. Our Eydem is here!"

"Yaron, you know I don't know Yiddish." ("Eydem" is the Yiddish word for "son-in-law.")

"You will learn that, my son. It is about time!"

"Oh, father, Hans does not have to function like a true Jew."

One of the maidens to us came. "Ma'am, another car has pulled up."

"It is okay, Sandra, we are coming."

"It is my father and Renate. I will go quickly. You can stay here!"

Hans went out and greeted his father and Renate.

"Father, here you are!"

"My boy, how beautiful!"

"Hello, Renate! It is nice that you are here, too."

"I won't miss this!"

"How was your holiday?"

"Very nice! We are simply in love with Geneva, and Artur wants us to send you greetings."

"Thanks!"

Sebastian waved to Hans. He would take care of the luggage. Hans and his family also came to the salon.

"So now we are complete. Father, Renate, these are the parents and brother from Hannah."

"Shalom together!"

"Shalom, how are you?"

"Very good!"

Everyone got along right away. The ice had been broken.

"You must be Yaron. Please excuse me for saying you." Samuel was usually much more formal.

"That's no problem. We are a family from now on, and yes, I am Yaron."

"I wanted to thank you personally for helping my son."

It sounded like polite party chatter, but it came from the heart, and Samuel was determined to say it first when he arrived.

Father felt no different, no matter how cheerful the words sounded in the dignified atmosphere.

He replied: "I was not alone. It was our community, and we were happy to do it."

For heaven's sake! You did not want to start talking about this dark time now? We had left them behind us.

I cheerfully called out to the group: "Please sit down! Who wants a drink?"

One of the maidens made sure everyone got something to drink. Sebastian brought the luggage to his gentlemen's rooms. He was such a patient person. I liked him very much. (Mrs. Krähling was impressed by him. She hovered around him like a cat.)

Mother, Renate, and I wanted to go into the city. I still had to complete my mikvah. (Mother wanted it that way.) The immersion wasn't so bad, but as a bloated pregnant woman, it bothered me. Later, we re-joined our men and enjoyed the celebration until midnight; everyone went to bed tired.

One other morning, Hans ran through the house and shouted: "Hooray! We're getting married today!" I had a stomach ache again, and – oh God! - I was in a bad mood.

"How can you be in such a good mood in the morning!"

"Oh, dear, today you going to be Mrs. Mangold."

"Yes, finally," I said somewhat grumpily.

Hans noticed that I was not feeling well. Did he also notice that I was afraid?

"Hans, I am so scared!"

He wanted to know. "From what?"

"Before the wedding, before the birth, especially!"

I started to cry, holding my hands to my face.

"If you are afraid, let us have a simple, no-frills wedding!"

I looked up at him and said, "Shall we?"

"We should! We dare to meet in the garden of the synagogue under the big mulberry tree."

"Yes, that will be nice!"

"I will call the cantor immediately. The rabbi can also give his blessing there. Chajm will forgive us!"

Hans went to make a phone call, and I was happy.

"Oh God!" I finally sighed. "How should I explain this to our family?"

"What do you want to tell us?" It answered, to my surprise.

"Mother!" It's now or never, I thought.

"Hans and I will not get married, traditionally, but in the synagogue garden. A registrar and Rabbi Chajm will marry us together."

"That is wonderful, my child!"

I did not believe the words that came out of the mouth from my mother. "Did you say wonderful'?"

"Yes! You have to know how to get married."

"What will daddy say?"

"He won't say anything. He'll do anything for his little daughter."

Hans came back. He smiled at me. "The Rabbi of Zurich gave us his blessing. We are allowed to use the garden. He has the cantor prepare it for us."

I smiled and was happy.

"That is exactly how I want to see my little daughter!"

"Dad!" How am I supposed to explain this to him?

"Why do you look so sad? Did something happen?"

"Yes! We do not dare to meet traditionally but in the garden of the Zurich synagogue."

"Nice! Then I will see the venerable building." He smiled contentedly and went to drink coffee.

I had done it; he said nothing except that he was happy.

"Shall we leave in two hours?"

"Yes, my love!"

"I will let everyone know. I will talk to father, too. He is not very religious."

It started after two hours.

"We want?"

"Yes, my love! You, Martin, and Adam go first. I will come with Renate and Ursula. Georg will take my mother and father to the synagogue. He is not feeling so well."

"The rest of us are already on the way. The cantor will lead everyone into the garden. The registrar and Rabbi Chajm are already there."

Hans gave me one last kiss and disappeared with Adam and Martin. I went to change, Renate and Ursula helped me. They drank champagne, I drank water.

After almost half an hour, I finally squeezed myself into the wedding dress. I felt like a sardine in a can. Renate helped me down the stairs, and Ursula drank her champagne. Sebastian wanted to drive me. He stood by the car and clapped his hands when he saw me.

"Hannah, how beautiful you are!"

"Thank you, Sebastian!"

He helped me and the other two get in. Then, the journey to Löwenstrasse began. When Sebastian arrived at the synagogue, only father was standing there. He would lead me under the chuppah – a canopy. Ursula and Renate got out and then helped me get out. When I finally stood on the sidewalk, father came closer.

"How beautiful you are, my child."

"Thanks, dad. Are you feeling better?" I asked him. Since my mom told me he was not feeling well. I was worried.

"Yes, dear. Come and let us go! The others are already waiting."

"Yes, I am ready."

We started walking. I linked arms with my father. We walked halfway through the synagogue to a small gate. There, the wooden door opened. The cantor smiled at me. As we entered the gate, I saw them all. I started shaking, but father held my hand.

Then I saw him. Hans stood under the white chuppah. He looked at me. Father gently pulled me along because I forgot to move. My g-d, I panicked! I closed my eyes for a moment, and then we continued walking.

We had to walk between the guests. At first, I only knew a few, but as we moved forward, the faces became more familiar. The first two rows sat our families and best friends - Eliam and his Rachel, Karl, and his entourage; Rachmiel and his family also came. My God, how happy I was about that!

Only Moses was not in sight. I missed him very much and continued to do so for a long time afterward. (Until one day, I found out about his death. He was buried, in Tel Aviv. Moses was with the Mossad and died during an operation. For that reason, it was never discussed. I commissioned Adam to place a white lily on the grave every month. We had a lot to thank Moses for. His contact with his brother-in-law alone was worth gold to the community back then.)

Only a few more meters until I finally reached my Hans. Adam and Martin were also at the front. Hans looked happy. This type of wedding suited us better. Neither he nor I wanted a pompous celebration.

The registrar and my beloved Rabbi Chajm accompanied me and father under the chuppah. He smiled contentedly; I was happy! Father released me to Hans, and I faced him. My veil was still hanging over my face.

The Rabbi began to recite one of the holy blessings. Before that, he raised a cup filled with wine. He spoke:

Barukh atah ADONAJ

Eloheinu Melekh haOlam,

bore Pri haGefen!

Barukh atah ADONAJ

Eloheinu Melekh haOlam,

shehaKhol bara liKhwodo!

מתחייב לך - נצחי

אלוקינו מלך העולם,

בורא פרי הגפן!

אתה משבח את הנצח

אלוקינו מלך העולם,

שברא הכל לתפארתו!

Praise You - ETERNAL

our G-d King of the world,

Creator of the fruit of the vine!

Praise You FOREVER

our G-d King of the world,

who created everything for his glory!

The rabbi sang and looked at us alternately.

Mi adir al haKhol

mi barukh al haKhol,

mi gadol al haKhol,

hu jewarekh heChathan vehaKhalah!

כולם מעל האדיר

הכל מעל שמשבחים

הכל שמעל זה

והכלה החתן את יברך הוא!

He who is powerful over everything,

who is praised above all,

who is exalted above all,

HE blesses the bridegroom and the bride!

Barukh atah ADONAJ

Eloheinu Melekh haOlam,

asher bara Sason veSimchah,

Chathan veKhalah,

gila rina diza veChedva,

Ahawah veAchavah

veShalom veRe'uth.

Meherah ADONAJ Elohejnu

yisham'a be'Arei Jehudah

uweChuzoth Yerushalaim

Kol Sason veKol Simchah,

Kol Chathan veKol Khalah,

Kol mizhalot chatanim meChupatam,

uNe'arim mimed neginatam.

Barukh atah ADONAJ

mesameach Chathan' in the Khalah!

אתה משבח את הנצח

אלוקינו מלך העולם,

שיצר שמחה ושמחה,

חתן וכלה,

שמחה ,צהלה ,ריקודים ועליזות,

אהבה ויחד

ושלום וידידות.

בקרוב נצחי ג'ט שלנו

מהדהד בערי יהודה

וברחובות ירושלים

קול האושר וקול השמחה,

קול החתן וקול הכלה,

קול החתן והכלה מתחת לצ'ופה,

ושל הצעירים בשירת משתה.

אתה משבח את הנצח

המשמח את החתן עם הכלה!

Praise You FOREVER

our G-d King of the world,

who created joy and happiness,

groom and bride,

Cheering, rejoicing, dancing and joy,

Love and togetherness

and peace and friendship.

Soon ETERNAL our G-d

ring out in the cities of Judah

and in the streets of Yerushalayim

the voice of happiness and the voice of joy, the voice of the bride-groom and the voice of the bride, voice of bride and groom under the chuppah, and of young people singing at the banquet.

Praise You FOREVER

who delights the bridegroom with the bride!"

Hans lifted my veil. Rabbi Chajm handed us the cup. We drank from it, and Hans kissed me. Then he slipped this crazy ring on my finger and said his wedding vows.

I did the same. Rabbi Chajm presented us with the Ketubba (marriage contract). This contract was written by hand and ornately decorated. Hans signed first, I signed then, and finally, the witnesses signed. It was August 15, 1952.

As we did this, Rabbi Chajm celebrated his Sheva Berachot - seven selected blessings. From that point on, Hans and I were a married couple in the Jewish faith.

Martin took a glass, wrapped it in a cloth, and placed it on the floor. Hans and I took turns stepping on the shards. At the end, everyone presents cheered. We deliberately avoided the rice. (The smashing of glass is a reminder of the destruction of the Temple and Jerusalem. And a reminder to the wedding guests about the transitory nature of all earthly things and an excess of joy.)

The wedding ceremony ended with the usual congratulations. Everyone shouted: "Masel Tov!"

Now, it was the turn of the registrar. He did not say much but presented us with a certificate, which we signed, and then wished us good luck. Now, we were also legally married. The ceremony ended with a kiss.

But we were not at the end of the wedding yet, because now we had a big celebration. Samuel had rented the large hall in a luxury hotel. We all went there and enjoyed one of my most beautiful celebrations of the time.

Most of the guests were already present when we entered the hall. We were fascinated by the mountain of gifts. In the hall, we had to sit on two chairs, and we danced. Later, we were allowed to open presents. Most of the gifts contained cash or nice little things. But one present contained a model of a sailboat. It was from Ursula and Martin: they gave us a real sailboat! How happy we were! It had the beautiful name Drago, named after the dog that watched over the people in the refuge. I loved the dog, and he trusted me.

Rosa approached me from behind. "Hannah!"

I turned around and saw her. She had little Hilda in her arms. I saw her for the first time.

"Rosa! There you are. And that is little Hilda! How pretty she is!"

"She takes after Adam!"

"More like you. Just check the nose."

Hans came up to me and wanted to dance.

"Dear, shall we dance the Hora now?"

"Yes! That will be fun!"

He jumped onto a chair and shouted into the crowd: "Guys, we want to dance the Hora now. So, everyone forms a big circle."

Hans jumped out of the chair and grabbed my hand. Things were a little slower for me, but I wanted to dance. Our two families lined up next to them. The music started playing, and we danced.

(During the Hora, all wedding guests dance in a large circle. So that at some point, you will find yourself holding the hand of your sweating cousin, your slower grandma, or someone stranger. Because the family - the Mischpoke - plays a role in Jewish life, you find at all celebrations, especially at weddings, from newborns to ancient grandfathers, every family member, which makes such a special celebration.)

The celebration lasted late into the night. Some of the guests slept in the luxury hotel where we celebrated. We had specially booked the bridal suite. So, we could get to bed quicker. My parents and Samuel and his Renate slept at home with us. Hans was drunk; well, we did not have to have sex anymore. How about a ball like that that I was carrying in front of me?

Two days later, our families left, and peace returned. I desperately needed this rest. I had problems with my pregnancy and had to stay in bed. Georg and Mrs. Krähling did everything to make it as pleasant as possible for me. So, the days passed, and autumn arrived. I was in bed as usual and ready to give birth. Ursula often came to keep me company. But I also had to endure my mood like everyone else. But I could not stand myself. When would the child finally come?

THE BIRTH/THE GROWTH

The first snow had fallen in mid-November. On that day of all days, I went into labor. It is three months after the wedding. Hans was in the office, and I was lying on the sofa in the living room and was overdue. Mrs. Krähling kept me company. She read me a new book; I got it as a gift from Hans.

At that time, the midwife came to the house. When my contractions came at shorter and shorter intervals, Mrs. Krähling let them come. I had pain; I was unbearable.

"Mrs. Krähling, call my husband and ask him to come."

"Yes, Mrs. Mangold!"

She went and called Hans. When she returned, she helped me to stand up and took me to the bedroom. Our child was supposed to be born there. As soon as I was in bed, the contractions started to come more frequently and more and more violently.

Luckily, the midwife came quickly. She wasted no time and immediately ordered hot water and fresh towels. When she came into my room, I saw her face. I knew I did not have to be afraid anymore.

"Grüezi, Mrs. Mangold! How are you doing?"

I could hardly speak because of the pain, but I squeezed out a "Good!"

"Don't push,"

I shouted. "What else?"

"Panting! Like a dog."

She showed me how to pant and how to calm down. That went well until Hans came. He was so nervous that he was on the verge of collapse.

"Mr. Mangold, sit behind your wife and ignore this down here." Hans sat down next to me and panted with me.

I screamed in pain. "Ouch! Damn, that hurts!"

"Let everything out, no matter what, including swear words."

Hans said quickly. "No, dear, no swear words."

"Then make sure it finally comes out!"

"So, your cervix is ready! Now you can push and then pant."

I pushed and panted, and little by little, the baby came out of me. After a final flood, it was out. I still didn't see what it was.

"It's not breathing", said the midwife. But she didn't sound worried.

I was frightened and started to cry, but the midwife took the child by the legs and patted him on the back. Another slap on his bottom, and suddenly he started screaming. Yes, it was a boy!

"Hans, it's a boy!"

"Do you want to cut the umbilical cord?" Hans refused; he was white as a sheet. The midwife cut the umbilical cord and wrapped our boy in a blanket. Hans was shaking all over when the midwife asked him to hold our boy. But Hans became calm; he took our son and rocked him back and forth.

He whispered into our boy's ear. "Samuel Yaron Mangold"

"Yes, that's what it should be called," I added. I was weak and needed to rest.

The midwife had done a great job. She said goodbye to us and wanted to come in the next few days to see how Samuel was doing. Samuel lay in his crib and panted to himself. He looked so beautiful as a baby. (Today, he is grumpy and dissatisfied with himself.)

"Dear, can I get you something?"

"No, sweetheart! I want to sleep."

"I am in the office. Let me know if I can get you anything."

"I'll do it!"

He kissed me, went next door, and called his father: "Father, it's me, our baby is here. It's a boy, and his name will be Samuel Yaron Mangold. ... Yes, the names of his two grandfathers. ... Is good! I will and see you soon."

He hung up the phone and crept into our bedroom. Samuel slept peacefully, and so did I. He sat down quietly on his side of the bed next to me. (He told me later and revealed that it was one of the happiest moments in his life.)

After a while, I woke up and saw Hans lying in his bed. He was also sleeping. Our baby was also a sleepy head and very quiet. I pushed myself over to Hans and kissed him. Hans woke up and smiled at me.

"Darling, can you check on Samuel? I'm still in pain."

"With pleasure, dear!"

Hans went and looked at Samuel, who was sleeping.

"I'll move the crib closer to your bed and get you some tea."

"Thanks! Please reach my family and let them know that Samuel was born?"

"Of course, love."

I slept a lot. The first birth is always one of the hardest and costs me a lot of strength. Hans looked after me, but he also had to do his job. Finally, after four days, I decided to get up. Everything was already hurting, and our boy wanted me.

Samuel was a beautiful presence as a child. (It's hard to believe that he became such a dissatisfied person. Yet he has everything. Three lovely children and a wife who does everything for him.)

Hans offered me that we hire a wet nurse for Samuel. I wanted to think about it. I didn't have much to do, but I was able to fulfill my role as a mother well, and we also had Mrs. Krähling.

It was probably Renate's idea. Great Renata always knew everything better. She was probably still mad at me for not wanting to have a baby shower. This US stuff was not for us Jews. Our next celebration would be Brit Mila, circumcision.

Mrs. Krähling had picked up Samuel for a short walk in the park. She had a lot of fun with our son. I dressed warmly and went to the park too. Ms. Krähling sat on a park bench with Samuel and enjoyed the sun.

"Isn't the sun wonderful? They look happy!"

"Yes, Ms. Mangold, the little darling makes me happy."

I had long since given up my original reservations about Ms. Krähling. I now knew that she had a heart of gold and, last but not least, ran my household with sober elegance.

When I saw that she accepted my son as her own, I spontaneously offered. "Would you like to be his governess?"

"With pleasure, Ms. Mangold."

I could see how happy she was about my offer. And I had great confidence in her.

"Samuel's Brit Mila is supposed to be in four days. I want to celebrate it with close family circles."

But apparently, I had not been asked. Mrs. Krähling explained to me. "Your husband has already arranged everything." Then she bit her tongue and added: "Sorry, maybe I shouldn't have mentioned it."

"It's nothing! I'll look surprised."

"Shall we go for a walk in the park?"

"Gladly, a little exercise will do me good." After we had walked a bit, I added: "I didn't know we had such a beautiful park."

"Yes, one of the most beautiful in Zurich," confirmed Ms. Krähling.

We also walked past this little house. It looked dilapidated and definitely needed extensive renovation, I asked in surprise. "Is this the gardener's cottage?"

"Yes! But it seems uninhabitable."

"I'm getting cold. We should go back. Samuel will probably be hungry soon."

"Understood, Madame. Do you want to take a bath? The warmth will do you good."

"Yes! That's a good idea, and Hans won't be home for another three hours."

We walked around the small lake. Ducks quacked, and birds chirped. Then we returned.

Inside the house, I suddenly screamed: "Jesus Christ! Before the Brit Mila, I have to go to the mikveh. I cannot be unclean at circumcision."

"Should I make an appointment?"

"No! You can't go there. I have to call Ursula. She will come with me."

Ms. Krähling thought about it and then said. "I am not allowed to do!"

"No, it is okay."

Mrs. Krähling took Samuel and put him in his cradle. I went to the phone to call Ursula: "Ursula, it's me, Hannah. Can we go to the mikvah together tomorrow? Yes? That is nice. At what time? Six o'clock in the evening! Good, I am looking forward. Yes, until tomorrow!"

I hung up and went to check on Samuel. He slept peacefully, and I decided to take my bath. Mrs. Krähling will look after Samuel, and I will be able to relax a little. As I lay in the tub, I felt calm for the first time in a long time. But soon, one of the Maidens knocked on the bathroom door. She informed me that Samuel was crying and was probably hungry.

"It is okay, Marie. I will come straight away."

I got out of the tub, dried myself, and got dressed. Then I went into the children's room to Samuel. He lay in his cradle and slept again. One of the Maidens rocked the cradle back and forth.

I whispered to her. "Thank you!"

She smiled and left. I sat next to Samuel and watched him sleep. When he woke up, he immediately started screaming.

"My poor darling! You're probably hungry." I picked him up, sat down, and gave him my breast.

"You're hungry!" Samuel drank and drank, but then he had enough and yawned. I picked him up and made him burp. Once he burped, everything was fine.

"So, my little one, now it's mommy's turn."

I went with Samuel into the salon and heard that Hans had just come home.

"Good evening, dear. Are you okay?" He gave me and Samuel a kiss and looked happy.

"Shalom, Hans! Yes, we're fine. I have to call Ursula again later to confirm our appointment tomorrow."

"You can talk to her in person. She will come to us later. I just agreed with Martin."

"To eat?"

"No, after that! We have something to discuss, and you can talk with Ursula."

"Yes, gladly! Please come straight to dinner."

"Gladly, I will freshen up."

George rang the dinner bell. I took Samuel with me and put him in his crib in the parlor. Hans came too, we could eat.

After dinner, we went into the small salon. The Hornmanns had to come straight away. Just as Hans was pouring himself a whiskey, the doorbell rang. George opened it.

"Good evening, gentlemen, you are already expected."

"Good evening, George."

Georg let the two in. They left there. Hans went to meet them, I stayed in the salon. Hans sent Ursula to me, and he and Martin went to his office.

Ursula asked as she came in. "Hello, darling, how are you?"

"Shalom, Ursula, I'm fine!"

"Nice! The men must have something important to talk about."

"I do not know what you are talking about. Would you like a drink?"

"Whisky, please!" I poured her a glass. I drank tea.

Later, Hans and Martin came to us.

"That took a long time!"

"I know, but it was important."

"Are you telling us, or is it secret?"

"It is a secret!"

Hans looked serious. I'm worried.

"I talked to Ursula about our mikveh tomorrow."

"Good, dear, this will do you good."

Martin didn't speak much either. Ursula suddenly urged to leave.

"See you tomorrow in front of the synagogue."

"We do! See you tomorrow, and sleep well."

"You too!"

When the Hornmanns left, I asked: "Is everything okay?"

"Yes, dear. Do not worry. I have to go again."

Hans disappeared out the door faster than I could ask why. I was angry and went to bed. Late at night, I heard Hans coming home. He tried to be quiet, but I was a light sleeper. Hans got into bed and rolled over onto his other side. I wondered whether he had someone else. Oh, what! It certainly was not bad.

In the morning, I was already sitting at the breakfast table when Hans came.

"Good morning, dear! I have overslept."

"Good morning, honey! Surely because you came home so late."

"I know! Sorry, but I had to check something."

"And what?" I sounded annoyed again.

"Young people have been hanging around the synagogue for days. They are Jewish refugees who are afraid of being deported."

"Why don't you tell me? We have to help them!"

Hans smiled at me and kissed my hand. "That is why I went to check."

"And were they there?"

"Unfortunately, no!"

"What do you want to do now?"

"I will ask the cantor if he can support us."

"We should do it ourselves. Your family has so many financial resources. Why not give something back?"

"You mean: set up a foundation that helps children?"

"Yes, or so!"

After breakfast, Hans got up and kissed me goodbye.

"Today, a lady comes who would like to be our wet nurse."

"You are only telling me that now!"

"I forgot! Do you forgive me?"

"Always!"

Hans didn't know that I did not need a wet nurse. Mrs. Krähling was there for Samuel.

As he was about to leave the house, a maiden came to him. She told him to call Mr. Hornmann as soon as possible. He nodded and left. The girl closed the front door behind him.

"Marie, would you accompany me to the children's room?"

"Yes, Ms. Mangold!"

She ran after me. I was already standing in the room with Samuel in my arms when she finally arrived.

"What did Mr. Hornmann want?"

"I do not know. Mister Hornmann said that your husband should call him as soon as possible. I arranged this. Did I do something wrong?"

"No, Marie, thank you. You can go."

I breastfed Samuel and thought about how I would get to the children. Later, I packed up Samuel and had Georg drive me to the synagogue.

I said to Georg as we got there, "Georg, please wait. I have to do something."

"With pleasure, Ms. Mangold!"

I got out, took Samuel, and went to the synagogue. I wanted to enter the synagogue through the main entrance. But it was midday, and everything at the front was locked. So, I went through the small gate into the garden. There they were, six boys and a girl. They sat under the mulberry tree and ate its last fruits. They remained in that cold place until November.

When the teenagers noticed me, they wanted to run away. They hit the bushes because they could not leave the garden.

I shouted: "Please stay! I do not want to hurt you." But by then, they had already dispersed.

Only the older boy remained seated, apparently the leader. He looked at me. He was dirty and emaciated.

I asked carefully. I also did not want to drive it away. "Do you understand me?"

"Yes, Madam!"

"Are you French?" His accent sounded French.

"No, madame, Jew, and stateless. Before the war, I came from Poland, Krakow!"

"I have been to Poland before when I was a child. On a death train to Auschwitz, but me and my family managed to escape."

"Not us, we came to Bergen-Belsen. The English liberated us there at the end of the war."

I noticed how tears came to his eyes and to me, too. Suddenly, the boy froze. A door opened behind us. It was the Cantor. He recognized me and smiled at me.

"Shalom, Ms. Mangold. Is the boy bothering you?" He did not like to tolerate the children here in the garden. And would have preferred to chase them away under some pretext.

"No! Not in the slightest, but he asked me if he and his friends could take some fruit from the tree."

I did not know whether the cantor had allowed it. He would not refuse me.

The cantor grimaced. "Of course, he and his friends are allowed to do that!"

"I will come to you in a moment, cantor. But first, I have to talk to the boy."

The cantor went back into the synagogue, and I continued the conversation.

"You can call your friends. He won't hurt you."

"Thank you, madame, you are very kind."

I wanted to hear from him. "What's your name?"

"Herschel, madame."

"How many are you?"

"Seven, madame!"

His companions now also cautiously gained confidence. The rest of the boys and the girl returned to the tree and ate the remaining berries. Weren't they rotten long ago? But this was her first meal in days.

(I still feel angry today when I think about this situation. It was the end of November. It was already cold in Switzerland, and these young people lived on the streets and had nothing to eat!)

"I would like to help you if I may."

"How do you want to help us, madame? We don't exist, and apart from this ultra-Orthodox children's home, no one wants us."

"I want to, and I will help you, but you have to allow it."

He spoke quietly with the others, who were still at a distance and came back. "Madame, please help us!"

"Gladly! You continue eating, and I will go to the cantor. Do not go away. I will come right back."

I went to the door and knocked. The cantor opened the door and looked at me disdainfully as I told him my request. He was unwilling to let the little ones eat the berries for an hour. But I was convincing! Even this problem would quickly go up in smoke. For the tree bore but a few fruits. The ripening period was already well over.

"What do you expect from me, Ms. Mangold? I cannot help! We are in trouble."

"No, we won't get it! I know people from the highest society. We are going to help the children now!" I was scared of myself, but I liked myself in this role. "I call my husband and take the kids away from here."

"Until he comes, they can get soup in the kitchen."

"Gladly!" Did the Cantor have a heart after all? But what did I know about his problems?

I went to get the children, and the Cantor served them soup and some bread. In the meantime, I went to call Hans. He was not particularly happy about me going it alone. At that moment, I did not care. He promised to come immediately.

When I entered the kitchen, Herschel was blessing the soup and bread. It reminds me of our time in the refuge when dad did that to our soup. I waited until he had blessed the soup and bread and told them what to do next.

"I spoke to my husband. He will come and help us."

The Cantor listened. He was just happy that the children were finally out of his garden.

(He had already confided to Martin Hornmann the evening before that he would not be able to tolerate them for long if he wanted to avoid trouble with the authorities.)

"Ms. Mangold! How do you want to help the children?"

"Let that be our problem, Cantor! My husband can help you. There is a home for Jewish children in Bern."

But Herschel immediately interjected: "No! We are not going there. Adam escaped from there. They wanted to raise him ultra-Orthodox there."

"What is so bad about being allowed to experience this kind of education?", said the cantor angrily.

"Should not they decide for themselves which faith they want to practice? I was raised left-wing Jewish and will stick with it."

"Shame on you!", shouted the cantor. "Bergen-Belsen did not just take your family."

I was frightened. I could not believe what I was hearing. "How can you say such a thing! Do not you have a heart?" I bitterly accused the cantor.

No word came from him; he got up and went to the door. The bell had rung. It was Hans and Martin. When he opened it, even three men were standing at the door! They were Hans, Martin, and Georg.

"Shalom, cantor! My wife is expecting us."

"Right, come in, please."

The cantor let the three in and showed them the way. The children were sitting in the kitchen and had frightened faces because strangers had arrived again.

"Hans!"

"Dear! What kind of things are you doing, and where is Samuel?"

"Samuel is sleeping next door! These are the children, and they need our help."

"Good! We will get them to safety first."

"Can you all walk?"

"Yes!", said Herschel. He was the one who spoke for everyone.

"It is Herschel! He is their leader, and they only listen to him."

"Shalom, Herschel, you need not be afraid. But you have to come with us. It's too dangerous for you here!"

Herschel looked at the face from Hans and nodded. Then he stood up, and the others followed him. Martin brought the boys and the girl to the car. I stayed with Hans and saw him hand the Cantor a wad of money. He grinned and took the bundle.

Politics and bribery have always been modern. But bribery was not tolerated by me. (Years later, I took revenge on this Cantor. He had to leave the synagogue. The reason: bribery.)

I picked up Samuel and followed Hans to the cars. He continued to sleep peacefully.

"Oh G-d, I forgot Ursula!" I blurted out. I had more important things to do. Only now did it occur to me again.

"She was waiting for you, but your husband sent her away just as he arrived, citing urgent matters," remarked George. But it remained awkward.

Hans sat down with Martin in his car. We did not get to talk to each other.

So, I asked Georg: "Where are we going?"

"Home, ma'am."

"All?"

"Your husband said yes."

I had to smile. These will be turbulent days. That reminds me of the time when we were with Mrs. von Blankenstein. When we drove both cars onto our property, there was a strange car parked in front of our house. Who was that?

Georg parked our car, and we got out. Hans and Martin came to the entrance with the young people.

"That will be Sarah!", said Hans in a tone as if her presence encouraged him.

"Who is Sarah?" I wanted to know.

"She will help us with the children. She has contacts who we can use."

Everyone entered our villa, and Hans immediately set off for the salon. I sent it to Ms. Krähling. She had to take care of the children.

"First, take the children to the free staff rooms. Show them the rooms they can freshen up there."

"I will arrange everything immediately, Ms. Mangold."

"Marie should come straight away and put Samuel to bed."

Mrs. Krähling went with the children towards the kitchen and showed them the rooms. She could not believe these poor children were homeless. She looked at the traumatized faces and had to hold back tears.

"So, dear ones. We have three rooms for you here. Who wants to room with whom?"

Herschel was the eldest and shared: "Madame, there are seven of us, I would say, three of us boys each and one room for Olga."

"As you wish! "

I went into the salon after Marie got Samuel. Finally, I wanted to know who this Sarah was. When I opened the door, they both fell silent.

I asked quietly. "May I?"

"Of course, dear! Sarah, may I introduce you to my wife, Hannah? Hannah, this is Sarah Klein."

"Good evening, Ms. Klein! Very pleased to meet you."

"Good evening, Ms. Mangold! Hans has already told me a lot about you."

Hans pointed to the seating area and said: "Let us sit down!"

"I have quartered the children in the free staff rooms for now."

"Good, dear! Sarah is working with the Americans. She can help us to locate the children's relatives. In case anyone else is looking for them."

"Nice! I hope it works."

"I just need the correct information. So, I can check our registration lists."

"I'll arrange everything tomorrow. The children should rest now."

"That's a good thing! I will come back tomorrow."

Sarah got up and left us.

Martin, Hans, and I spoke, ate something, and then Martin left soon. But it was already too late for my mikveh. I decided to go the next day. We went to sleep, but not without checking on Samuel first. He lay in his crib and slept. I blew him a kiss and went to sleep.

The other morning, I woke up early because Samuel was restless. I got up and brought him into bed with us. Just a few more minutes, I thought. Only Samuel had other plans. He started to cry. He was hungry, or he had wet himself. So, we got up. I changed his diaper and gave him the breast. Today, I had to finish my mikvah. Because the day after tomorrow, the Brit Milah would take place. But first, there was breakfast. I got ready and then went to the salon. The young people were already sitting there and enjoying their breakfast.

"Good morning, children!"

"Good morning, Ms. Mangold!", came back.

"Do you enjoy breakfast?"

Herschel said: "Yes! It's delicious, and I specially blessed it."

"You'll become a rabbi someday."

"I'm too old for that, but I could be a cantor."

The children looked so happy, I felt good.

"Children! There is an empty house in the park that I would like to have converted into a youth home. How do you like that?"

"Very nice, but above all, we want to go back to our families."

"I know, but you have to write down your details. Sarah – the woman from yesterday – will then go look in the lists."

"Good! Then we'll write everything down."

"But first, we have breakfast!"

Adam wants to know. "Where is your husband?" (That was such a sweet boy.)

"Hans? He's already at work and won't be back until the evening.

After breakfast, I prepared for the mikvah. Herschel sat on the steps at the entrance and stared into space. I walked over and sat next to him.

I asked him. "May I?"

He said to me quietly, "Of course, madame!"

"Do you have something?"

"I feel so alone, and I miss my family." He started to cry. I took him in my arms and tried to comfort him.

"Hans felt the same way as you. He lost his entire family in a massacre, and a farming family rescued him. They helped him. Then he came to us at the end."

"And then?", he asked curiously.

"After the war, a lawyer from Switzerland came and told him that his father was still alive. The same will happen to you. Your family is not dead."

He smiled at me. I wiped his tears and hugged him again.

"Shall we check on the little house later?" I wanted to put the children there, but I did not know what condition the former gardener's house was in today.

"Yes, please, madame!"

"But I have to go to the mikveh first."

"Because of your birth?"

"Exactly! And the day after tomorrow, Samuel will receive his Brit Mila."

"I am going to the others. I am sure you will be waiting.

"Good! You are a brave young man."

Herschel left, and I stayed seated for a moment.

"Madame! Telephone, it is Ms. Hornmann."

"Thanks! I will come right away."

I got up and went to the phone. " Ursula! Nice that you are calling. Yes, we can meet at the synagogue in 30 minutes. See you later, Ursula." I hung up the phone and went to get my coat.

Georg drove the car forward. Samuel stayed with Mrs. Krähling. He would only disrupt the ritual.

"Georg, please drive me to the synagogue!"

"With pleasure, Ms. Mangold!"

He drove off; the journey took unusually long.

"Forgive me, Ms. Mangold. But I have to take a detour. Here are women demonstrating for their rights!"

"It's okay, Georg." I rolled down the window and shouted: "Come on, girls, that's your right!"

Georg had to laugh. And I grinned at him. After a short detour, we arrived at the synagogue. Georg helped me out of the car. Then I dismissed him.

"Ursula will take me back."

He drove off, and I went to the synagogue. Ursula was already waiting for me there.

"Hello dear, I thought you were not coming again."

"Shalom, Ursula! There was a demonstration. We had to take a detour."

"Ah, the women's movement!"

"Yes, exactly!"

"Come on, we have to go through the garden. The Rabbi already gave me the key. I will witness your mikveh, dear."

"I am glad you are my mikveh woman."

We walked through the garden, past the mulberry tree, towards the back. There was the bathhouse where we Jews held our mikveh. We entered the first room. There I was able to prepare for my mikveh: undress, cut, and clean my fingernails and toenails. I did not have to take off my make-up because I rarely wore make-up. But I had to take off my jewelry and take a bath.

Then Ursula gave me a cloak. We went into the next room together. There was a nine-square-meter plunge pool with a seven-step staircase. The pool was three meters deep because you had to submerge completely.

I took off my cloak and climbed down the narrow stairs into the pool. The water was wonderfully comfortable and pure. Ursula celebrated the blessing. I submerged three times and was able to get out of the pool. Finally, I was clean, and the Brit Mila could come. Ursula then helped me get dressed. I was still very groggy.

"What will happen to the children now?"

"There is an old, dilapidated gardener's house in our park. We want to convert it and make a home for Jewish children."

"Martin will be there too!"

"Of course! You also?"

Ursula said, "Always!" and holding up her hands.

After we finished, we went to the car, and Ursula took me home.

"Will you come in for a drink?"

"No! Not today. Martin will probably be waiting with the boys and the food."

"Good! Thank you for accompanying me to my mikvah."

"Gladly!"

I got out and walked to the entrance. Herschel sat there.

"Good evening, Herschel. Are you sitting out here again?"

"Good evening, madame! I wanted a moment to think."

"Are you coming in? I am cold."

"Of course, madame!"

"You can say, Hannah. Madame makes me so old."

Herschel grinned, and then he said to me. "You are welcome, Hannah."

We went to the small salon. Hans sat there and drank his evening whiskey.

"Good evening, dear!"

"Good evening, darling! Herschel would like to talk to me."

"Good! Should I leave you alone?"

"No, Mr. Mangold! You can hear it, too."

"Good! Would you like to drink something?"

"Yes! Maybe some tea for me and Herschel. What would you like?"

"Can I try a whiskey?"

I asked him worriedly. "How old are you?"

"Seventeen, Madame! Er, Hannah!"

Hans looked at him sharply, but then he poured him a drink and handed it to Herschel.

"Le'Chaim! To life!", they said and drank the glass.

I went to get some tea. Hans and Herschel got along well.

"There, my son! Where does the shoe pinch?"

"I don't understand!"

"You have something on your mind, and we want to help you."

"Uh! I understand. Yes, I would love to do an apprenticeship and build a life here in Switzerland. Who knows if I ever will find my family again."

"It's not easy, but not impossible. We need to talk to my friend Martin."

"Can he help me?"

"Perhaps!"

Herschel looked down. He seemed sad.

"Hannah and I will try everything, but first, we make sure you can live here legally."

Herschel just nodded. He couldn't say anything. Henschel was sad, sad that everything seemed so hopeless. Why did he have to live a life like that? He couldn't help it. An assassin mob had attempted to wipe out our race and our heritage. Now, he was being punished once again for being a victim.

When I returned to the drawing-room, both were sitting opposite each other. Herschel seemed sad, and Hans tried to strengthen him.

"We will try everything we can. You have never to give up!"

"I do not want to give up. I want to be strong for the others!"

"I got a letter from a friend in Israel today."

I sat down next to Hans. He took the letter and read it aloud: "Shalom, Mr. Mangold, it is my pleasure to assist you in this matter. I see a great opportunity and would like to donate $200,000 to your new foundation. I would also like to serve as a member of the foundation committee. Signed – Abraham Rosenbaum, Tel Aviv."

I said in amazement: "How? Such a large sum?"

"Yes! He lost his two children in Auschwitz and moved to Israel after the war. He would like to help with this donation."

With tears in his eyes, Herschel said quietly. "That's very kind of Mr. Rosenbaum. I will say a prayer for him in the evening."

"Tomorrow, we will put your data on paper and send it to Bern."

"You're welcome, Hannah! I'll let the others know."

"Now go to sleep. We will see what happens tomorrow."

"I will do! Good night together."

"Good night, boy!"

Herschel left, and we talked about Mr. Rosenbaum and Herschel. He was already like a second son to us. Later, we went to sleep, but not without checking on Samuel first.

The new day started rainy, but I didn't care. Like my mother, I also loved the rain. Hans was already up. I went to the bathroom to get ready. After getting dressed, I checked on Samuel. He was still asleep when I picked him up. I sat down in the armchair and gave him what he wanted - my breast. Samuel smacked his lips, and I thought about what we needed to do to get the old house finished as soon as possible.

"I need to talk to an architect!"

"What do we need an architect for, dear?"

I hadn't noticed Hans coming into Samuel's bedroom.

"I thought you were already in the office!"

"I was just about to leave, but for now, I wanted to say goodbye to my two loved ones."

"When will you be back?"

"Towards evening!"

"I'm going to call an architect today about the old house."

But he only listened to me with half an ear, only confirmed cheerfully: "Do it, love."

He didn't even know my plans. Then he kissed me and left.

Samuel was full. I changed his diaper and went with him to the parlor, where breakfast was waiting.

"Good morning, children!"

"Good morning, Ms. Mangold!"

I wanted to know. "Where is Herschel?"

"He went into town with your husband."

"What does he want in the city?"

"He didn't tell us."

"That's fine! I'm sure he'll be back soon."

We finished breakfast, and I suggested the young people take us to the park. The little piece of jewelry was there. I wanted to show them the house, and they loved it.

"Madame, we have written down our details as you asked."

"That's nice, Adam. I will take a look at it later."

So, we went to the park. Adam and Leonard had a ball with them. Martin had brought it with him from one of his sons. The boys played a round with the ball; I sat on the park bench with Olga and had a small talk with her. After a while, the boys got fed up and came to us.

"So, would you like to look at the small gardener's cottages with me now?"

"Yes!" everyone shouted at once.

"Then comes!"

We walked to the little house. I wanted to open the door, but the door to the garden house was stuck. But the boys were strong and pushed the door open. Inside the house, it was dusty and very messy. The boys had fun. They suspected there was treasure behind every bedsheet. It was often garbage, but one or two gems also.

The children were happy. I enjoyed the moment with them. 14-year-old Nikolai was among the boys. His body had scars all over it, but he smiled at me. I liked him, and Nikolai told me how they beat him up - soldiers with batons. They hadn't wanted to spare him the suffering when he begged them to kill him. You have to imagine this: Nikolai was six years old at the time and begged to be allowed to die. And like dirt, the soldiers left him to die.

Luckily, Herschel came, he told me. He helped him, and from then on, they were inseparable. Little by little, more young people joined in. Each of them had a terrible fate. Somehow, they ended up in Switzerland. But they weren't welcome there either.

(How much we would have liked to have adopted each of them back then, but that wasn't possible. Often, the children were found again by their families. Some of them were unfortunately not found. I had contact with each of my protégés for a long time, but friendships fail and all too often are forgotten.)

"Hannah! We found an old box."

"Bring it to me, and let us see what we found."

Two of the boys dragged the box to me.

When I saw the box, I said, "Jesus! It is almost a treasure chest."

The two boys placed them in front of me.

"It is locked!"

Adam gave me an iron bar. That worked.

I asked. "Who wants to open it?"

Leonard shouted, "Me!" and took the iron bar. With one blow, he broke the lock on the box. "It cracked like my bones when the soldiers beat us up." Since then, the boy hasn't been able to move his left arm properly.

(At this point, I have to pause. It pains me too much to write about it.)

We had a great afternoon, but that should never have ended. But now Mrs. Krähling came over with Samuel and reminded me of my duties. However, I didn't want to leave without seeing the contents of the old box. Leonard opened it. It came to light old books, money, and a few trinkets.

"That is what I call a great treasure, children."

Leo wanted to know. "What do we do with these things now?"

"Divide it between you! You have found it, and it is yours."

The teenagers started smiling. You did not want to forget these happy faces anymore.

"I have to go. Samuel is hungry. Are you coming with me? We take the box into the house. We can clear them out there later in peace."

"Yes!", everyone shouted again.

On the way to the house, we met Herschel. He was back.

"Hannah!"

"Shalom, Herschel!"

"I could do an apprenticeship! Now I have to prove that I exist. But how do I do that?"

"That is nice, Herschel! We will do the other thing, too. I will call the lawyer in Bern tomorrow."

"Maybe he will have some advice!"

"Certainly!"

"Were you in the old house?"

"Yes! You missed so much. Where did you introduce yourself?"

Herschel said proudly: "With Martin Hornmann."

"In his office?"

"Yes! I could be a lawyer, and he is a Jew like me."

"True! I am so proud of you!"

Herschel smiled at me and was happy.

"You could go have a drink. I will feed Samuel and come to you. The boys want to plunder the treasure chest.

"Let us do it, Hannah!"

I went into the nursery and breastfed Samuel. When he had enough, I put him to sleep and went into the large drawing room. The boys and Olga were waiting there. They were about to open the box when I entered.

"You have not started yet!"

"No, Hannah, we wanted to wait for you." Leo lifted the lid of the box and opened it. He took out the books. They were handwritten, and they were diaries. The money that was there was already very old and could no longer be used. The jewelry, on the other hand, looked valuable. Olga got the first one and they gave me one too. (It's sitting here in my display case and I can just see it sparkling in the sun.)

"Children! Shall we have a fine dinner in the evening?"

"Yes!", everyone shouted.

"I'll arrange everything with Mrs. Krähling."

Leo looked down and said sadly. "But we're not well dressed!"

"We could look at Hans closet, he has enough clothes and certainly doesn't mind. Olga gets something from me!"

"We'd rather wait until Hans comes and ask him."

"As you wish, children."

Everyone shouted a big "Yes!"

"I will arrange everything with Mrs. Krähling."

Leo looked down and said sadly. "But we are not well dressed!"

"We could look at Hans's closet. He has enough clothes and certainly doesn't mind. Olga gets something from me!"

"We'd rather wait until Hans comes and asks him."

"As you wish, children."

Mrs. Krähling went into the kitchen and had dinner prepared. It was supposed to be an unforgettable evening. The cook prepared one of the best dinners ever.

The boys, Olga, and I were waiting for Hans. When he finally got home, the boys attacked him. They were all talking, and Hans did not understand what they wanted. I went and stood by him.

"We're preparing for an unforgettable evening, but the boys have nothing nice to wear. Can you help them out?"

"Of course, dear! Let them rummage through my closet. It is a party today."

The boys were excited, and Olga looked sad. I went over to her, took her hand, and together, we went to my closet. When I opened it, her eyes started to sparkle!

"I know how you feel now! That is how I once felt, too. You know, Olga. I wasn't always as rich as I am now."

She said happily: "I can't believe it!"

"Choose something nice and keep it."

"A groysn dank!"

"Ah eydish, mayn kind!"

"Yeah, abisl."

The boys demystified this warm moment. It turned into a mess of pants and shirts. Anyway, we all had fun, and Hans laughed like a madman.

"Madame, telephone, a gentleman from Bern is calling."

"Thank you, Marie, I'm coming." That was the lawyer. I called him, but he wasn't available. I picked up the phone in the office and was pleased it was Mr. Stöckli. "Hello, Doctor Stöckli. Yes, I am fine, thanks. Yes, I gave Ms. Klein the children's details, and now we are waiting for her to come to us. - Really? That is nice! I think the kids will like this. Thank you for your call, and see you in the next few days. – Yes, I do, and the transfer goes out. Goodbye!"

I was so happy. I was able to share some good news with the boys and Olga. I immediately ran into our bedroom. Hell was still raging there. By now, the children were all dressed, and Hans was sweating on his brow.

"It was Doctor Stöckli. He had great news."

Herschel wanted to know. "What kind?"

"I'll tell you about it at dinner. Now I have to take care of Samuel, and you and Mrs. Krähling go to set the table. – Hans, can you keep me company while breastfeeding?" I had to talk to him.

"Yes, dear!"

We went to Samuel's room. He was already awake and smiled when he saw us. I picked him up and sat in the armchair. Hans sat down in the armchair that was in the corner. He looked at me, and I smiled.

"What?", he asked me.

"Nothing!" I said and continued to smile. I didn't want to demystify the moment with my news. I might as well tell everyone at the table.

After I fed Samuel, we went into the large salon. I was curious to see how the children had set the table.

As we entered the room, I couldn't help I was amazed. The boys and Olga had set the table festively, and everyone got a napkin.

"You did a good job!" Hans was amazed.

"Yes, you did it beautifully."

"Mrs Krähling helped us a lot!"

The doorbell rang. Who could that be? Marie went to open it. It was Sarah Klein.

"Good evening! Can I speak to Mr. or Ms. Mangold? It is important!"

"Wait, I am asking. Please come in."

Marie told us that Ms. Klein was there.

"Let Ms. Klein come to us."

"Immediately!"

"Good evening, Sarah!"

"Good evening, everyone! I have news for the children."

"Sit down, Sarah, and eat with us."

"Gladly! That looks delicious."

"Marie, please bring another place setting!"

"At once, madam!"

Marie went to get another place setting, and Sarah explained what she had found out.

"I have good news for Adam Widawski!"

Adam was startled, and his eyes widened. I had to return the phone call with Dr. Stöckli. He also told me this on the phone. Now Sarah should get her appearance.

"Your mother survived and is looking for you. But she is not allowed to enter Switzerland. I will arrange for you to go to Germany and meet her there."

Adam's eyes moistened, and tears streamed down his face. "Really?", he asked, crying. He kept wiping away his tears with the back of his hand.

Sarah said joyfully. "Yes, of course, my boy".

I went to him and took him in my arms, hugging him tightly.

Sarah Klein continued. "If you like, we can leave in two days."

"Yes, I would like! What do you say? You are my family now."

Herschel spoke up. "Adam, you should be happy. We are happy when you are. Go meet your mother."

"Okay, then I will come with you."

"I will pick you up in two days, but I am hungry now."

"Yes, us too, and the food is coming."

There was poultry with potatoes and gravy. Of course, vegetables couldn't be missing either. The food was so delicious that I can still smell the smell today.

"How are the other boys and Olga's search coming along?"

"Hans, we search in all available registers and check all lists. Unfortunately, nothing yet!"

I saw the disappointed faces, but giving up was not an option for us.

"Doctor Stöckli also has other contacts. Maybe he will find something else."

"Yes!"

"Thanks for the nice dinner, but I go now."

"You are welcome, and thank you for the good news. Adam is happy!"

We accompanied Sarah to the exit and then said goodbye to her.

"See you again! Ah Hannah, don't we want to be on first-name terms too?"

"With pleasure, Sarah!"

"Goodbye, Hannah!"

We accompanied her out to her car and said goodbye to Sarah Klein.

As the door closed behind us, I sighed with relief: "What good news for Adam!"

Hans agreed: "Yes, dear, I would like more of that."

"Yes, me too!"

We went back to the drawing room and continued eating.

"Children! Tomorrow, we want to celebrate the Brit Mila from Samuel. There will be a small celebration, and you will be there. Important people are coming!" I noticed Hans's irritated reaction. Did he not want to present this to me as a surprise? No matter, I did it faster, and Hans could handle it because he didn't say a word about it later.

"With pleasure, Hannah!"

"I am tired! I am going to sleep. Don't be so loud, boys."

"No, Hannah!"

Hans kept me company, and it was a great night.

The following morning, we woke up in a good mood. Because the Brit Mila of Samuel would celebrate on this day, and it was quiet in the house. What was going on? I went to check on Samuel. Then I wanted to know why it was so. Downstairs, I noticed that no one was there. Only the cook cooked, and two of the maidens worked.

"Marie, where are the children, and where are Mrs. Krähling and Georg?"

"They're in the old house, madam."

"What are they doing there?"

"I can't answer that for you."

"It's okay!" I went to check it out, but just as I was going up the stairs they came in the door.

"Children, here you are!" Mrs. Krähling and Georg also came along.

"Good morning, Hannah! We wanted to show Herschel the old house. Please apologize if we did anything wrong."

"No, boys! It's okay, and they've taken care of you."

Herschel said happily, "Hannah, the house is wonderful!"

"An architect will come and take a look at it tomorrow."

"Hurray!", everyone shouted and ran away.

"Please excuse me, madame, but the children were anxious to leave."

"It's all good, Georg, don't worry."

He nodded happily at me and ran after the boys.

"Mrs Krähling! Please come to the small salon in ten minutes. We need to discuss everything later."

"Of course, madam!"

I went to the door and sat on the stairs. I was there so lost in thought that I didn't notice Herschel coming to me. It wasn't until he tapped me on my shoulder that I came to.

I said, shocked. "Herschel!"

"Hannah", he whispered.

"Sorry, I was in thought."

"Do you have something?"

"No, Herschel."

"Mrs. Krähling is looking for you."

"Oh, I forgot."

I got up and went to look for her. She was in the small drawing room, putting wood in the fireplace.

"Mrs Krähling! I forgot about you, but we can start right away."

"I have my list with me, Ms. Mangold."

"Good! When will the Rabbi come?"

"He's coming at six o'clock!"

I asked. "The guests?"

"Come at half past six!"

"The large drawing room will be ready by then?"

"Yes, and the chefs too!"

"Very good! Then I can change, but first, I check on Samuel."

I looked after Samu and then put on a nice but simple dress. It was greyish and had a white collar and long sleeves. I heard Georg when I was halfway up the stairs. Hans was already back and already finished. I went to Hans and greeted him.

It was so far! The Rabbi rang, and George went to open to him. Hans and I was nervous but also happy.

"Shalom, Rabbi!"

"Shalom, everyone, no one there yet?"

"They are still coming. We wanted to greet you first."

"Good! Where can I prepare?"

I said, pointing in that direction. "In the little drawing room."

Hans went to show him the way, and I became even more nervous. The doorbell rang again! Was that Martin and Ursula? Yes, it was them!

"Shalom, everyone! Nice that you are here."

"Shalom, Hannah! Where are the others?"

"In the big drawing room!"

Just as I said this, the bell rang. Everyone was there! Who else was it?

"Georg, please take the gentlemen into the large salon."

"With pleasure, Madam!"

I went and opened the door.

"Father!" I shouted with joy when I saw him.

Father said happily, "Hannah!"

"What are you doing here?"

"I can't let you do the Brit Mila alone."

"I am so happy that you're here!"

"Me too! Unfortunately, the others couldn't come with us. Mother is very sorry."

"You are Samuels Zeyde and an important part of our family. Come on, the guests are probably already waiting."

('Zeyde' is the Yiddish word for 'grandfather'.)

We went into the large salon. Everyone was already sitting there waiting for the mohel, the circumciser. Our mohel was Rabbi Silberstein. He was also a doctor and could perform the Milah. The guests were happy that father had come. Hans offered father a seat next to him - it was the place where the Mila took place. He handed Samuel to his Zeyde, and both smiled.

Rabbi Silberstein entered the salon and said a blessing. He only stopped in front of Samuel and my father. Next to him was a table on which lay the ritual knife and a goblet of wine. A few towels were also on the table to treat the wound.

Hans stood up and handed over his seat to Martin. He stood behind him and placed his hands-on Martin's shoulders. Martin was Samuel's Sandak (godfather). Father got up, kissed Samuel on the forehead, and handed him to Martin. The empty chair was for the prophet Elijah.

Rabbi Silberstein took the ritual knife. After saying blessings and invoking Elijah, Rabbi Silberstein severed the foreskin from Samuel with a sharp knife. He then recited more blessings over a cup of wine and announced the child's first name. "Samuel Yaron!" A drop of wine moistened Samuel's lips. The godfather and I also received the cup.

He ended Samuel's Brit with the saying. "Let him grow up to the Torah, the Chuppah, and good works." Meanwhile, Samuel was screaming like crazy, but it did not last long before his pain subsided.

Samuel was given plenty of presents at the banquet that followed. There were some very precious gifts. He received two kilos of gold from Martin as a symbol of wealth. He received the gold watch and some valuable things from his 'Zeyde'. Everyone gave him money or gold. Was that perhaps the incentive for Samuel's later career as a banker? (He founded the Mangold bank.)

We celebrated until late into the night. Eventually, it was almost morning, and the guests went home happy. The children were already in bed - except for Herschel. He took the opportunity to talk to the guests about possible research into his family. Two lawyers promised to help him, but this came to nothing. (If I remember correctly, Herschel never got an answer. Nevertheless, he went his own way - and successfully.)

Father spent the night with us. I had a room prepared for him.

The new morning was quiet and started with breakfast. Samuel was asleep, and I wanted to have a coffee first. My head still hurt, but the coffee worked wonders. Ah, the children were already sitting at the table enjoying their breakfast.

"Good morning everyone!"

"Good morning, Hannah!"

"Herschel is probably still asleep?"

"No! He has already gone into town and is meeting Mr. Hornmann."

"Good! Thank you, Olga, he is old enough."

Father joined us, and I was happy he was there. The children immediately made friends with my father, and father promised to take them to the park. Father just wanted to have breakfast first. I smiled and asked him if he wanted to stay with us for a few days. Father gratefully accepted and smiled.

"Ma'am, Miss Klein is on the phone."

"Good, George! I will come right away."

I went to the phone and talked to Sarah Klein. She wanted to tell me that Adam's mother had a permit and would come to us at lunchtime. How excited I was, and Adam would be happy! I wanted to make sure he was dressed properly and talk to him. The cook was supposed to bake a cake.

I went into the little salon and let Adam come.

"Adam, sit down. We need to talk."

"Has something happened, Hannah? I did not do anything."

"No, do not be afraid! Everything is fine. Your mother will arrive here this afternoon."

At first, he couldn't say anything, but then he burst into tears. But in the end, he smiled.

"You must make a good impression! Clean clothes and well-maintained hands are important, my son."

"Hannah, I have got everything clean. You don't have to be nervous."

"I know it will be exciting for both of you."

He said quietly. "Surely!"

"Then go, I'll call you when your mom is there."

"Thank you, Hannah. Can we go play football?"

That was a good idea from him. Then he'd come to other thoughts.

"Yes, but be careful."

With a "Yes!" Adam ran out of the salon. Right into dad's arms. "Well, my boy, what made you so happy?"

"My mom is coming! Hurra, hurra!", he shouted and continued to run.

I smiled and talked to Georg. "Georg, would you tell the cook to bake a cake? There will be visitors at noon!"

"Of course, Mrs. Mangold!"

I was sitting in the garden with father. Samuel was standing next to me in his stroller. The children played football, and two maids were employed as goalkeepers. I had to laugh as they acted and barely held a ball. A taxi arrived, and Adam's mother. A man came out and stopped the door. Then, a woman around thirty got out. She didn't recognize Adam, and Adam did not recognize his mother.

I called one of the maids to watch over Samuel. Father wanted to go to the lake with the maid and his grandson. Then I went to meet the lady. She smiled at me. The terrible atrocities she had witnessed were evident on her face. Nevertheless, I looked in a proud face.

"Good day! I'm Hannah Mangold. Are you Adam's mother?"

"Shalom! Yes, I am Anna Widawski."

"Please come! Do not be afraid. I am also a Jew." Anna breathed.

"Which of them is my Adam?"

"The one with the brown cap!"

Suddenly, she shouted loudly Adam's name, and Adam hardened. I begged him to come, and he came.

Anna cried when she saw Adam come in. He looked casual in knitted pants, shirt, sweatshirt, and brown slapped hat. She fell to the ground and remained on her knees. As Adam stood before his mother, he did not know what to do. He was too young and had no memories of his family and this terrible time that lay behind them.

"Mom?", he whispered.

"Yes! It is me. Please forgive me for not being able to protect you."

He didn't think long and jumped into his mother's arms. How good it was to see that! The two cried so much that I didn't want to disturb them. I asked the others to go into the house to cover the coffee table.

When I saw that the two got quieter, I went to them and helped Anna up.

"Is it okay again?"

"Yes, Mrs. Mangold. Thank you for helping Adam. May Hashem always protect you."

"I liked to do that, and it was a matter of course for me."

"Mom, did you come alone?"

"Yes, my son, the Nazis murdered them all. Whoever was still alive was thrown into one of the KZs and gasped. I was lucky: the Americans liberated our camp."

Anna cried again. Her nerves hurt too much, and then she continued, "Father, Lewek, and everyone else in our family is dead." Anna couldn't say anything else. It was a coincidence that Anna had survived. One of the camp supervisors liked her singing. So, it came that she had to give him daily. Anna was a trained singer and had given singing lessons before the war.

Adam also remained silent. He was overwhelmed by the whole situation.

"Let's go into the house! Coffee and cake will be good for you now."

In the salon, the children had already prepared everything. They were all sitting at the table waiting patiently.

"Children, you may begin."

One of the girls poured coffee and cocoa, and another cut cake and served it.

I asked Anna. "How did Adam survive all that?"

"My husband Jakob had hidden it under a hatch in the floor. He had enough food and water to survive. When the Nazis set fire to the houses, I thought he would die too."

Adam looked at his mom and took her hand. "Mummy! I'll never leave you alone again."

"You can't come with us at the moment. We need a passport first, then I'll get you."

"Promise, mom?"

"Promise, my son!"

Just as she said this, the door opened. Sarah Klein stormed into the room. She had an envelope in her hand and was very excited.

"Luckily, you're still here! I have something here for you, Ms. Widawski."

"For me?"

"Yes! Adam's exit permit and his new passport."

Anna didn't know what to say. She hugged Sarah.

"Thanks!"

"It's okay, that's thanks to Doctor Stöckli."

"Then can I come with you today?"

"Yes, my son!"

You could see how happy the two of them were. The other children were not enthusiastic. They had become a family over time, and now they were losing part of it. Of course, they were happy, too. But inside, they were crying for Adam.

"But you're staying here overnight! George can drive you tomorrow."

"Yes, gladly! Then Adam can say goodbye to his friends."

"Yes! An important one is still missing here. Herschel will surely come soon."

"I still have to tell the taxi that it can drive."

Sarah Klein interjected. "I could take both of them with me tomorrow, I have to go to Freiburg."

"Gladly! We also have to go to Freiburg. I'm living there temporarily in accommodation for Jews."

"Sarah, then you can stay with us too! There's enough space, and Hans will be delighted to see you."

"You're welcome, Hannah."

We adults were in the living room drinking tea when Hans returned home with Herschel.

"Good evening, everyone! Sarah, how nice that you are here! And you brought a guest, I see."

"Good evening, Hans! No, I came alone, but this is Mrs. Widawski, Adam's mother!"

"Good evening! Adam was happy about that."

"Shalom, Mr. Mangold. Yes, he was so happy, and so was I. I would also like to thank you." Then she turned to the younger man: "You must be Herschel."

"Yes! That's me. Shalom!"

"I have so much to thank you for, too! Without you, Adam certainly wouldn't be alive anymore."

"You don't have to thank me. We complemented each other very well. What I couldn't do, Adam could do and is still very good at it today."

Anna couldn't help herself. She hugged Herschel and kissed him on the cheek. (I still cry today when I think about this emotional moment.) We all had some fun, ate together, and drank. One might have been too much, but it was an evening to celebrate.

Another morning, another day. Was he even better? What would it bring? Anna didn't know! She stood facing me and was shaking. Was she ready yet? It was Adam. He stood at the bottom of the stairs with a packed suitcase and looked at us.

"Where are the others?", he wanted to know impatiently.

"They will arrive soon. Herschel has another surprise for you."

"There they are", he said, pointing toward the park.

Herschel shouted. "Luckily, you are still here!"

"Would I leave without saying goodbye? Brother, you must never forget me – and neither should you."

"I could never forget you, little brother." Herschel hugged Adam to him and couldn't hide his tears. The other children were crying, too. I cried, too. (G-d, that was a goodbye!)

"Stay strong, children!"

Herschel handed Adam a rolled-up piece of paper. Then he said quietly: "Open it!"

Adam pulled the ribbon. It was a photograph. When did they have these made? It must have happened overnight. Adam had to smile. Then he laughed, and everyone around him laughed, too.

"What you look like! Thank you, I can never forget you."

"You will never forget us like this!"

"Adam! It is about time we have a long way to go."

"Yes, Imma! I will say goodbye to everyone, and then we can go."

Adam shook hands with everyone, and in the end, it was my turn.

"Goodbye, Adam, and take care of your Imma."

"I will, Hannah! Shalom! I will miss you all."

Then they got into Sarah's car and drove off. I could see the boys and Olga having tears in their eyes.

"Come on, children, let's go into the house. Mrs. Krähling will make us tea. Of course, there will still be cake. By the way, the architect called and told me he would like to come by tomorrow."

"Hannah, can I be at the appointment?"

"Of course, Herschel!"

My father was coming down the stairs looking for me. "Dear, can George drive me to the synagogue?"

"Of course, father! I'll let him know."

"Thanks, Hannah, I'll wait outside the house."

"The younger ones can play football. It would be better if you and I walked around the house with him?"

"I think so, Hannah. Things are still going well."

It was midday, my father left us, and I waited for the architect. One of the maids came. "Ms. Mangold, a car is driving up."

"Thanks, Marie. I am going to the gentlemen. Go get Herschel, please."

"Yes, Ms. Mangold." I went to the front of the house and waited for the car. It was the architect Lehmann and his assistant. When they both got out, I greeted them.

"Good day, gentlemen!"

"Good day! You must be Ms. Mangold."

"Indeed, I am."

"My name is Bernhard Lehmann, and this is my assistant, Peter."

"Very pleased to meet you."

"The joy is entirely on my side, dear Ms. Mangold."

"We need a moment; my foster son is coming."

"We have time. Is that the object over there?"

"Yes! This gem there needs to be rebuilt. We want to build a children's and youth home there."

The two whispered among themselves. Then Mr. Lehmann said: "That sounds interesting!"

When Herschel joined us, we set off.

We stopped in front of the gardener's house. Mr. Lehmann examined the facade, and his assistant Peter took samples and examined the cracks.

"It all looks good! The facade needs to be renovated."

"Very nice, Mr. Lehmann, but now it depends on what it looks like inside." I unlocked the door, and I was surprised as I creaked it open: the inside was clean! Who had cleaned this place, and why hadn't I found out anything? Herschel grinned as I looked at him.

"We wanted to give you a surprise!"

"You succeeded, that is so nice of you!" I was visibly touched.

Mr. Lehmann and his assistant immediately got to work. They walked through each room, examining the plaster, beams, and floorboards. After 20 minutes, they came back to us.

"How does it look, Mr. Lehmann?"

"Not bad at all, Ms. Mangold. So, we do not have to carry out any major renovations."

"Good! Now, what does that mean?"

"I will draw up the plans and also make some sketches. This way, you can see what it should look like in the end."

"It's so kind of you. Get everything ready, and I will come to your office to approve the plans and sign the contracts."

"That means kindly, Ms. Mangold, but your husband has to sign the contracts."

I wanted to know. "Why?"

"Because in Switzerland, no woman is allowed to sign contracts. Otherwise, I would be committing a criminal offense."

A little annoyed, I said to him: "Okay, my husband will sign it."

"Gladly, and sorry about the signing thing. I am for reforms when it comes to women's rights."

"I understand already. Call us for an appointment. My husband will come then."

"With pleasure, thank you very much!" Mr. Lehmann shook my hand and said goodbye.

"These are Stone Age conditions here in Switzerland."

"Yes, Herschel, you are right."

"Still, you are in charge."

"That is probably true. I will talk to Hans later."

"I am going to have a juice. Do you like one too, Hannah?"

"No, just go. I will sit on the park bench and study the house."

"Is good! I will go into town later."

"Do that, but do not be back late."

"I will be back before dinner."

Herschel left, and I sat on the park bench. The weather was nice, and I sank into thought.

After a while, I came to again and felt a little shivering. I saw Hans standing at the top of the stairs. Had he called me? He waved to me, I waved back to him. Ah, well, he came to me.

"Shalom, dear, are you enjoying the sun?"

"Hans, my love! Yes, a little, but I'm thinking about what the house should look like."

"You'll do great, my love."

"I am a bit depressed. I am not allowed to sign any contracts."

"Yes, unfortunately! But I will do it for you, and you will take care of everything else."

"That's exactly how we do it, my love." I kissed him, and he took my hand. We went to the villa together. We went to the villa together. Dinner was served then as well.

Hans looked around and was surprised. "Dear, has your father left?"

"Yes! He took a flight to Berlin this morning. He must have already missed mother."

We went into the salon, where the young people and dinner were already waiting. Later we all went to the park and enjoyed the evening. Herschel and the others played catch, and Hans and I sat on the bench like an old married couple and watched them play.

After a while, I felt cold and wanted to go inside. The fireplace was already burning; I loved that kind of warmth. Little by little, Hans and then the boys came along. Olga had already said goodnight earlier. The boys had fun in the salon; Hans drank whiskey and smoked his cigar. I drank tea and was amused by the boys.

"All right, boys, time for bed. Sleep well!"

The boys went to bed. Hans and I finished our drinks and followed.

THE YOUTH CENTER AND THE YEARS AFTERWARDS

Three officials from the Department of Construction had announced themselves to inspect the construction site. Hans had the prospect of a financial subsidy. Did we need that? They should give us women more rights! (Fortunately, many things are better today than they were back then.)

Herschel swirled around the site. I had to go to him alone; Hans still had an appointment.

"Good morning, Herschel, you're already working."

"Morning, Hannah, I couldn't sleep."

"It all looks good!"

"Yes, but it could be better. I am not satisfied."

I asked him, surprised. "Why?"

"I would like the rooms upstairs already finished!"

"We have already made a lot of progress, so don't be so pessimistic!"

"I just want to finish. There's still a mountain of rubbish at the top that has to go."

"Good! Should I help you?"

"No! The boys are coming soon, and everything will be spotless by the time your gentlemen come. Olga still wants to clean."

"All right! Then I'll go to the park with Samuel."

I picked up Samuel and went to the little bench under the old oak tree. (What the old oak would have had to tell me if she could have spoken?)

I nodded off. One of the maids woke me up when the car with the gentlemen from the office building pulled up. Samuel slept peacefully in his stroller, and I slept on the bench. I quickly fixed my hair, adjusted my hat, and ran towards the house. From there, I waved friendly to the gentlemen.

I said to myself. "My g-d, they look grim!"

Herschel came to support me. "Everything will be okay, and you'll get your home."

"Of course, Hannah!"

When the gentlemen finally arrived at our house, one of three said: "Morning, are you Ms. Mangold?"

"Good morning, gentlemen, and yes, that's me."

"Is this about this little house?"

"Yes!"

"Good! My colleagues and first I will inspect it from the outside, then later the inside.

"With pleasure, gentlemen!"

It took almost an hour for the three to return to me. I sat down on the bench by the old oak tree with Herschel. Mrs. Krähling had picked up Samuel and wanted to go for a little walk with him.

"Well, Ms. Mangold, it looks good overall."

I was surprised and quickly said. "Do you think so?"

He answered me grimly: "Do you think I'm joking?"

"Of course not, but can I offer you coffee and pastries?"

"No! We don't have much time." One of the gentlemen looked at the other irritably, and then they shook my hand and left.

They hadn't even noticed Herschel at first.

"Funny officials!"

"Swiss!"

When Herschel said that, I laughed because I had thought the same thing. "Then we will receive the certification and a subsidy in the next few weeks?"

"That's what it looks like, Hannah!"

"Let's go inside, I need a coffee."

Hans came home later and was excited to see what the appointment had revealed. I sat in the drawing room with Herschel, and we talked.

"Good evening, everyone!"

"Good evening, my love!"

Herschel waved tiredly at him. He was tired and wanted to go to sleep. "Good night together."

"Night, Herschel!"

When Herschel left, Hans sat down next to me and kissed me. "How was the appointment today?"

"Terrible!"

"Why?"

"They were so rude!"

"They weren't rude, they were Swiss!"

"In Basel, the people weren't like that; they were cosmopolitan and nice."

"It doesn't matter, love; we get what we want."

"You're right, as always, my love."

"What is for dinner?"

"Lisa made a casserole. I'll tell her to heat a piece for you."

"Thanks! I'm going to take a quick shower. Are you coming with me?"

I replied with: "Little rascal!"

"I thought Samuel might need a brother."

"If there's a baby, then a little sister!" (We weren't granted that. Samuel didn't have any more siblings.) Hans went to take a shower; I went into the kitchen. Of course, I could have had one of the maids come. But I was never a real lady and did things by myself.

When Hans finished showering, he came to me in the salon. He ate, and I sat on the couch and watched him.

"You are not saying anything, love?"

"What would you like to hear?"

"We usually talk about the day."

"Haven't we already done that? Forgive! Do you think Herschel will get approval? He's already got high hopes."

"I guess so. Martin will take care of it; he wants to support Herschel."

"That's very kind of him."

"Yes, dear. Now it's time for bed. I have to get out early in the morning, and you have to do a lot too."

So, we went to bed and soon fell asleep. Slowly, the wild nights subsided.

After just one month, we were able to inaugurate the youth center. It turned out that the children loved it. A delegation from the city came, consisting of the representative of the city president and two of the gentlemen who had previously inspected our house. Two religious' representatives of the Jewish community and also many wealthy Jews attended. Of course, the entire board of trustees was present; even Mr. Rosenbaum came from Israel. Hans and Martin were happy with what I had created, and I was proud of what I could achieve as a simple Jew. The children moved into their rooms, and five more orphans joined them. Additional staff was still missing.

The festival lasted two days. I was exhausted by the end of the second day. I just wanted some peace. I quickly completed the interviews for additional staff. Then I went and lay exhausted on the sofa until Hans woke me up. He wanted to say goodbye; his trip to Geneva was coming up.

It was supposed to last five days, but I wasn't alone. Herschel was there, and the staff was. More and more often, Herschel stayed away; he remained with us. Herschel could finally begin his training. He received his residence permit and a foreigner's ID card. Herschel was one of the best in his teaching. That didn't surprise me; he also worked like a horse. Martin was proud of him because he was his mentor, and Herschel wanted to emulate him.

It hurt me a lot when he came to me a few months later to tell me he was leaving us. He had been offered a small apartment near his workplace. Of course, I couldn't be mad at him. He was 18 and ready for the big world. We saw each other regularly and went to synagogue together.

Martin made sure that he completed his training with top marks. At first, he worked as an assistant to Martin; He later qualified as a lawyer and became a partner in Martin's law firm.

One day, I got a call from Herschel. He wanted to tell me that he had met a young lady and wanted to introduce her to me. I was touched and agreed. When he came to me with her, I was amazed at what a beautiful girl he brought with him. She was Jewish, good-looking, and rich. They drank coffee with us, and we talked about their upcoming marriage. Her parents were lawyers in Tel Aviv. They had their law firm, and it seemed to be doing very well.

It was a wonderful afternoon that ended with a tremendous dinner. When Herschel and Tara left us that evening, everyone was happy. We gave them our blessing and planned the ceremony. (Herschel saw us as his parents; he had never learned anything about the whereabouts of his biological parents.)

A few months later, the two married in the Zurich synagogue. What a celebration it was, pompous and huge! Tara's parents paid for the whole party. After the festival, they honeymooned in Israel and stayed for a month. I would have loved to have gone with them both, but they no longer needed a watcher.

Life had to go on, and it did go on. New young people came from Germany. They had heard that our home was one of the best, and I was surprised at how quickly the word spread. I couldn't say 'no' to any soul who knocked on our door.

An idea developed in me. I wanted to build a network. Because if the houses communicated more with each other, more help would be possible. Since the technology back then wasn't as advanced as today, the whole thing went a little slower than I wanted. Instead of email, there were letter mail and phone calls. But little by little, we expanded the network. I went to our company less and devoted more time to our foundation. (Today, there is only one liberal Jewish children's home left in Switzerland. The Wartheim in Heiden is worth mentioning.)

Samuel became a wonderful boy. I enjoyed spending my time with him; he was clever and teachable. I can still remember when he started school. Hans and I were excited, but Samuel was calm. He wanted to learn, and he always did very well in school. Unfortunately, Samu couldn't stand the mixed school. He wanted to attend a purely Jewish school, which didn't exist in Zurich.

(Today, there are a few good Jewish schools in Switzerland. One of them is the NOAM in Zurich. If you have some time and inclination, visit the NOAM website. Like many Jewish institutions, this one only works through donations and sponsors. If you have some money left over and have nothing against us Jews, please donate something. Each of the children will thank you because your donation has gone well spent.)

Hans was worried; he suggested Samuel go to a Jewish boarding school. At first, I liked this idea, but when we heard that such a boarding school only existed near Tel Aviv. I was unsettled.

On the other hand, Samuel liked this idea so much that we agreed. He then went to the Mosenson boarding school in Tel Aviv from the summer onwards. School continued for more than ten years before Samu completed his university studies. In between, he often came home, and we enjoyed this time very much. We celebrated his birthdays and bar mitzvah. But we also had to live through the sad occasions together.

Father became ill and died a short time later; my world collapsed. Samuel came back to Switzerland without notice to support me. He already had all the qualifications in his pocket and wanted to do his banking apprenticeship in Switzerland.

We flew together to Berlin for the funeral. Father wanted to be buried in the Weissensee Jewish Cemetery. He had loved this place and had recently gone there often. He had suspected that he would die soon. Mother fell apart and died just a few months later. She loved him too much. It was a terrible time for everyone, and we went through an intense period of mourning. (I can understand it. I didn't feel any better when Hans died.)

Adam took over the apartment, but as xenophobia and anti-Semitism became worse, Adam and his family decided to leave Germany. They started a new life in Tel Aviv. He worked at a bank, Rosa worked part-time in a bakery, and at the same time, raised two other boys. Later, Rosa takes over the bakery and runs it together with Adam.

Ariel studied architecture and received tons of awards. He alternated between living in the countries where his building projects were. Ari (aka Ariel) didn't have a wife for a long time. At the time, I thought he was gay. Which isn't a bad thing; it even happens among us Jews, and that's a good thing. I have a suspicion about Aaron, my grandson, but I won't bring it up. He should reveal himself. I hope Samuel will still love him (mentioned in passing).

Ari then found a wonderful woman, a Christian, but Beate was never treated with hostility by us for it. They had two daughters (Olga and Samira) and later lived in Switzerland. Ariel had bought a villa on Lake Zug. We often and happily visited each other.

Samuel and Olga also liked each other. If Olga wasn't his cousin he would have chosen her and not Rachel. But I don't want to say anything against Rachel here. She is a wonderful mother and wife. Samuel never deserved her the way he treated her.

Hans noticed that I was feeling bad. To cheer me up, he decided to give me a surprise; our wedding day was approaching. I was surprised when he told me that we were flying to Berlin. I should pack quickly, and then we can get going. So, I packed, and Samuel was at work. I called him to tell him we were traveling.

When I had packed, Georg loaded all the suitcases into our car and drove us to the airport. We checked in and soon took off. On the flight, I wanted to know why we were going to Berlin. But Hans was good at keeping secrets to himself.

Our plane landed on schedule, deboarding was quickly completed, and our driver was waiting outside the airport. He drove us to our hotel. During the journey, I thought about my mother and father. How long had it been since I was here in Berlin? I had to go to their graves.

I didn't know whether it would be as easy as my parents' funeral. Because we had to cross the GDR border to get to the cemetery. Weissensee was in the GDR. But as a West German it wasn't that difficult, and you had reasons you could give.

Hans pulled me out of my thoughts. We arrived at the hotel at the zoo. How happy I was that we were staying at our engagement hotel! The car master helped us get out. One of the bell boys came and got our suitcases. We went in, and Hans went to the reception. We were always greeted very warmly here, and I always felt welcome.

We had the same room as before. Only the view had changed. The fallen war ruins had given way to an apartment block with a shopping arcade.

"Honey, we're going out to eat today. We're meeting a few people."

"Good! Can you tell me who with?" I was so curious.

"You'll see that!" That's all I got in response.

I didn't say much and went to unpack my bags. Hans was able to unpack his suitcases himself. I was always annoyed when it came to surprises. Hans didn't care. He then teased me some more.

In the evening the time finally came. Our driver picked us up; I was shaking with excitement.

The car stopped at the front entrance and the car master helped me get in.

As we sat, Hans asked me: "Darling, why are you shaking so much?"

"I am nervous! Leave me or tell me what you're doing!"

Hans smiled at me and kissed me. "Darling, it's a surprise and it's a nice one. So, calm down and be happy."

I nodded and bit my fingernails. We drove for 20 minutes until we finally arrived where the surprise was waiting. We had even crossed the GDR border. The border official had asked for the papers, but the driver had only handed him a document. The border guard read it, returned it, and let us go. That seemed strange to me.

I hated the GDR and was afraid. But I recognized the street and the houses. We were in our beloved Levetzowstrasse. There was our old house with a shop and workshop. My face started to smile. Sadness turned into joy. By Adonai, I was happy!

The driver stopped in front of the house. The shop was empty, and the wildest ideas began to develop in my head. We got out, Hans took my hand, said quietly: "Come on!" and smiled at me.

I wanted to know. "What's going on here?"

He pulled me towards the store. The light came on there. I was frightened and saw figures. Who was that? Hans took the door handle and pushed it down to open the door. We entered, and that's when I saw her. The vague figures became Eliam and Chajm. My heart was pounding. They had grown old!

Eliam smiled at me. I raised my hands and called out their names: Eliam! Chajm! What are you doing here?"

"Hannah! We wanted to surprise you. So: Surprise!"

Then Hans spoke, "Dear, today is our wedding anniversary, and I'm taking this day as an opportunity to give you this wonderful front building. Your family lived in this house and shop, so I thought you would like it."

I couldn't say anything. I always thought the house had been demolished. The GDR was never careful with such old buildings. Consider our beloved Levetzow Synagogue on the corner of Jagowstrasse. The GDR had it demolished in 1955, even though it could have been renovated without any problems. (This is one of the reasons why I never liked the GDR. Above all, the GDR regime did this with almost every Jewish building. It was not renovated. It was left to fall into disrepair or torn down.)

"How did you manage to buy the house? That's impossible in the GDR!"

"I know, but not entirely impossible, my dear. Relationships and lots of money!"

I kissed Hans and saw a car drive up out of the corner of my eye. Three men in leather coats got out.

"What do they want from us?"

"Don't worry, they're just the gentlemen from the State Security Service."

"Hans, I'm scared!"

Two of the gentlemen came into the shop and greeted Hans. "Dear, may I introduce you to Messrs. Marklein and Bauchitsch. It's thanks to them that we now own this building."

I smiled at the two gentlemen and thanked them politely. But I didn't want to have anything more to do with the Stasi. For me, the Stasi was almost like the SS in the Nazi regime. (Spy, torture, and murder!)

Later we went with Eliam and Chajm to a posh restaurant in West Berlin. I had to have a drink first; the whole thing had taken its toll on me. But it was still a nice evening with our dear friends. Only some years later, I found out Hans had paid two million francs for the front building. To make myself happy! If I had known this, I would never have agreed to purchase it. (Well, today the house brings a nice sum of return, and we can all live well on it.)

One of my first acts in the front office was to layoff notice to a family. She lived in our old apartment. Son Robert had smeared a swastika on the facade of the neighboring house. I mean the Nazi swastika, and not a swastika (a cross with four arms of equal length and angled at equal lengths), as his mother loudly claimed. I reported it to the Stasi, and the apartment was empty shortly afterward. I know I'm a bad girl. The apartment is still empty today, but not untenanted. The memories live on there.

(When I came to the empty apartment for the first time, I felt the past as if it were present. I saw everything in front of me as if it had just happened. I saw the family – my family! The Nazis took us away! This feeling burned like wildfire inside me! But I also saw happy things like my last birthday in peacetime.)

Before the fall of the Berlin Wall, the shop was also empty. I didn't want to rent it at any price, especially given its little secrets in the basement. After the fall of the Wall, I rented it to a lovely Vietnamese man. He ran a small grocery store and often sent me delicious things. When he gave up the shop, we rebuilt the shop again. Offices or practices could now move in. In recent years, a dentist has rented space, and it has been a pub around the corner.

Since Hans had such good relations with the Stasi, after such a long time, we had reached the place where our refuge once lay. You could still see remnants of the old tunnels. Eliam had done a great job back then. From then on, I had a bouquet placed there every month.

Of course, Hans and I also visited my parents at the cemetery in Weissensee. It was very emotional; I cried. Hans held my hand and remained silent. The gravesite was tidy, and the gardener did a good job. I put flowers on the grave, and when I couldn't take it anymore, we left.

We stayed in Berlin for a few days. But the day we returned to Zurich was a catastrophe for me. Samuel happily announced that he was emigrating to Freiburg. The community there was looking for a young assistant rabbi. Samuel fulfilled all the requirements - a university degree in Jewish studies/rabbinate, religious training at a rabbinical seminary, or studies at a Talmudic college (yeshiva).

I was overwhelmed, and my world collapsed. Hans noticed how much the matter bothered me. He suggested that we go to Freiburg with Samuel. I agreed, and Samuel didn't mind either. However, Hans wanted to live outside the community. For me, it wasn't a problem. I was also able to get involved in the community. I did it for years and always enjoyed that time.

Young community

(1976–2008)

[05 FREIBURG 1960]

VIEW OF FREIBURG AROUND 1960, SEEN FROM THE CITY GARDEN. (THE MANGOLDS MOVED TO FREIBURG IN 1976.)

MOVE TO FREIBURG

Of course, we couldn't emigrate overnight. It needed careful preparation. Hans first had to find a new home for us, which he did remarkably quickly - a wonderful villa in an older part of Freiburg, partly on a hill, the entrance secured with a wrought iron gate. A small avenue of old linden trees led up to the villa. When Hans showed me the photos, I immediately fell in love.

Samuel also had to have a say. He did this that evening at dinner. He liked the villa as much as us. Now, all we had to do was look at it on-site, and Hans had to sign the purchase contract. We planned the trip next week. I was happy; Freiburg had always been a beautiful city.

I still had to shop for clothes that fit. Ursula was the right person. But first, I had to win Hans over.

"Honey, I still have to go shopping. I don't have any suitable clothes for Freiburg."

He looked at me and said: "Women and their clothing problem!"

"I need to look neat and can't do that in old clothes."

"Go ahead, love, and take Ursula with you."

"I will, darling, I'll call her right away."

I arranged to meet her the other morning. There were currently a lot of new boutiques that wanted to be visited.

In the evening, Hans, Samuel, and I made our first plans for Freiburg in the small salon, and Samuel told us about Rachel for the first time. He had met her in Tel Aviv; like he, she was at this boarding school. As it later turned out, he immediately fell in love with the beautiful Rachel. We were so proud of our boy.

We talked for a long time, and eventually, we were so tired that we went to bed.

The other morning, I had breakfast early. I wanted to take Ursula into the city and explore all the new boutiques. Yesterday evening, Hans gave me enough money for some nice clothes.

I called Ursula and told her that I would pick her up. Said and done! Georg drove me to Ursula. Then we went straight to the city center. Georg let us get out and drove home. Finally, spend time with Ursula again!

After about five hours, we had everything together. We explored Bahnhofstrasse, Rennweg, and some boutiques on Paradeplatz. But before we went home, we had a coffee at Sprüngli's.

Then Ursula had her driver come. He took me back to our property. Hans was already at home and was waiting for me in the salon. Georg brought all the bags into the villa. I only carried one bag; it was a special gift for Hans.

"Dear, there you are. I was already worried!"

"Sorry, but you know what it's like when women shop."

"Exactly, that's why I'm not with you."

"I have a little present for you." I gave it to Hans; his eyes widened when he saw the contents.

"For me? How sweet of you!"

It was a tie clip with an engraving on the back, nothing special. But Hans loved things like that. What he liked was the engraving "Forever yours" in Hebrew: "שלך לתמיד." Hans kissed me and put the pin on his tie.

"Shall we have tea together?"

"Yes, with pleasure, love!"

"I'll go and tell Marie. Shall we go out on the terrace?"

"Gladly!"

I went ahead and set the table. Ms. Krähling joined me. She wanted to speak to me.

"Would you like to have tea with us? We could speak together then."

"With pleasure, but only if I don't disturb you."

"Not you!"

When Hans came with Marie and the tea, we sat down together.

"Okay, Ms. Krähling, what did you want to talk to me about?"

"I would like to end my employment here."

"Why?" I said in surprise. "Did we do something to upset you?"

"No! All three of you have grown on me. But I'm no longer the youngest, and my strength is dwindling."

"What are you planning to do?"

"I want to go to the place where I was once born. I love Beuren and I want to die there one day."

"Then it's certain. When do you want to leave here?"

"Next month, when it's convenient for you."

"Is it! My husband and I don't want to put any obstacles in your way. Even if we regret it very much."

"Thank you, and I'm very sorry."

"It's okay! You have to do what you have to do."

Hans said nothing. He was sad about Ms. Krähling's decision, but he accepted it. She had been very reliable over the years and had grown on us.

I took up the topic again later that evening. But Hans was so tired that he hardly answered. I soon fell asleep, too. In between, I woke up when Samuel came home.

The other morning, we were sitting at the table and having breakfast. Samuel joined us.

"You were late last night."

"Do you want to watch me now, mother?"

"No, of course not, but I heard you."

"I had a drink with some friends."

I noticed that Samuel was getting angry.

"Do we have everything together for the trip?" Of course, I only asked this to smooth things over.

"Yes, dear, I think we have it all together. The day after tomorrow we are going to Freiburg. Samu, do you have everything together, too?"

"Of course, father! I have to leave immediately. We're having a meeting at the bank."

"Go ahead, my son. Are you back for dinner?" Oh God! I monitor my son.

"Yes, mom, I'll be back by afternoon at the latest."

"Yes, me too. I have to go to the company too. Shall I take you with me, son?"

"With pleasure, father."

The men left, and I stayed behind. Now I had time to pack, and I also wanted to tidy up my office. A successor for Ms. Krähling also had to be found. She also had to take care of the youth center.

Isn't that too much for one person? We had to see, and perhaps the new maid would be of some help to her. I called the newspaper to place an ad. I'm curious if anyone will get in touch. Ms. Krähling was a stroke of luck.

There was a knock on the door. Georg wanted to speak to me. I hoped not for the same reason as Ms. Krähling.

"George, come in. What can I do for you?"

"Ma'am, I need to speak to you."

I looked at him questioningly: "Good!"

"As you know, I like Ms. Krähling very much. I would be sorry if she left."

He looks like he wants to leave, I thought, but I said to him. "I know you want to leave us too."

"Exactly, and I hope you and your family aren't mad at me."

"Of course not. We will miss you both terribly. All the best to you both."

"Thank you, madame, and I have a successor for me. He's very reliable and discreet, like me."

"Really? Make an appointment. I like to meet him."

"With pleasure, madame."

I was sad that they would both leave us. But I could understand it. Georg left, I did my mail, and soon Marie called for dinner.

Samuel came in the afternoon. Only briefly, as he quickly told me. He has to go to the synagogue; the rabbi still has a letter for him. He was supposed to give this to the Chief Rabbi in Freiburg. Samuel said goodbye until evening, and I relaxed in the drawing room.

The next morning, we had to pack. Just one day to pack all the things wasn't much. We wanted to stay in Freiburg for two whole weeks. During my first trip to Basel, I only had one suitcase. Today, everyone has a lot more suitcases with them.

While I was still dozing, Hans came back from his appointment.

"Dear, are you sick?"

"No. Can I not rest without looking weak?"

"You do, love. I'll have a drink."

"I have to talk to you."

"Do you have something on your mind?"

"No! Georg will leave us with Mrs. Krähling."

"There's only bad news today, and the day isn't over yet."

"Georg has a successor he would like to introduce to us."

"At least something good, dear. When is the good man coming?"

"Georg makes an appointment with him."

"Will Samu eat with us? I forgot that Martin and Ursula are coming to dinner."

"What?" I shouted in horror. "I'm sitting here doing nothing, and you forgot to tell me we're expecting visitors! I have to get ready!"

"I forgot. Where is my Hannah the way I met her?"

"It's still there, but understand: I want to shine by your side and not just sparkle."

Hans had to laugh when I said that. I went and kissed him, then got ready. Hans informed Mrs. Krähling that we were expecting guests for dinner.

After a while, I was ready. Hans came into our bedroom and marvelled at me.

"You are so beautiful, my dear Hannah."

"Thanks, my darling. Your compliments always sound like declarations of love."

"That's right, love. Are you ready? The guests will be coming soon."

"Go ahead, I'll follow right away."

Hans left, and I briefly fixed my hair. Ursula was always perfectly dressed, and I didn't want to look like a gray mouse next to her.

I finally was happy with how I looked and went downstairs. Just the doorbell rang. The Hornmanns were punctual, as always.

"Just leave it. I'll go open it."

"Good evening and welcome!"

"Hannah, my love, thank you for the invitation. It's nice to see each other again before your trip."

"Come in, it's already fresh."

Ursula and Martin came and took off their coats.

"We've got things ready in the drawing room, and the fireplace is already burning."

"What a weather today, quite cool."

"Yes, that's right, it's getting cooler earlier and earlier."

"Good evening, Hans. Thank you for the invitation."

"Good evening, Ursula, with pleasure."

"Sit down! Who likes a drink beforehand?"

"I would like to drink a whiskey. And you, love?"

"Nothing, there'll be wine soon."

"Okay, then a whiskey for Martin. And you, Hans?"

"I'm having a gin."

"Okay, come right away."

There was Zürcher Geschnetzeltes for dinner. (a briefly sautéed dish of veal in a cream sauce), Rösti, and salad. Everyone had dessert, and there was cheese and liqueur. Dinner with Ursula and Martin was lovely.

Afterward, we went into the small salon. The two men were smoking. We ladies drank espresso and spoke about the trip and Samuel. At around one o'clock, the two went home, and we went to bed.

Samuel didn't come home again until dawn. I had to accept it; he was old enough. He was already a young man and knew what he was doing. I should worry less about it.

In Switzerland, we faced almost no danger. In Germany, it would be different. Is it the right step? Didn't we leave Germany because of all the circumstances? But I would do anything to be close to Samuel.

"Good morning, Samuel; did you sleep well?"

"Yes! Mom, I don't want to talk right now. First, a coffee, and then you can beat me up."

Startled, I asked him, "Why?"

"Well, because I came home so late."

"Oh, Samu, you are old enough, and I had to learn this. At least you're coming home."

Samu said nothing. He just smiled at me and finished his coffee. "I still have to go into town. Do you need anything else for our trip?"

"No, I have everything."

"I'll be back in the afternoon. What's for dinner today?"

"There are still leftovers from yesterday."

"Okay, see you later, mom. Love you!"

"See you later, son."

Samu left, and I wanted to do a few things. Two of our suitcases smelled like a musty attic. I want to wash them out on the patio. It was harder than I expected. After my treatment, both suitcases smelled like roses.

I called Georg and asked him to bring the two giants into our bedroom. I could then grab them there. Hans only had two suitcases. He could easily take a few more things with him. That men always have to be so spartan!

I decided to add some underpants and undershirts. A few more socks couldn't hurt, either. Our suitcases were full to the brim, and I was tired. Hans had everything he needed, and it was the same for me. Samu packed his things himself. What would he say if I just packed his suitcases?

Just one more night, and then it starts!

Today would be leftovers from yesterday. Marie came and asked if we would all be there for dinner, to which I replied affirmatively. We wanted to leave early at five o'clock and sleep early.

In the afternoon, Samu came as promised and went packing. I went after him; maybe he needed my help.

"Samu, can I help you?"

"Mom, if you want to help me, you can fold my shirts."

"Gladly. You take three suitcases with you. More than your father, but you'll stay longer."

"Yes, mom, and I hope I'll enjoy the work there."

"You can do it, son."

After packing, we went to the terrace. Samu was thirsty. I could also use a lemonade. We could hear the young people in the park. They ran all over the park and played. More than 25 young people are currently staying in the youth center. I only occasionally helped in the youth center. We have found a replacement for me. Ella Stankowitz was a talented woman and could achieve anything with her strong will.

"Mom, do you hear that? The boys are calling for you. Do we want to go to them?"

"We can! Sure, they'll play hide-and-seek."

Samuel and I joined in the fun and joined the boys. They ran back and forth along the rose garden. Fast and almost too fast for me. I ran after Maurice; he was a gifted runner. He suddenly started limping as he realized he was running away from me.

"Maurice, that's unfair."

"Why? I have pain in my knee."

"Should I help you?"

"It's nothing! I don't want to be touched. Have you forgotten everything? Why are you leaving anyway, Hannah?" Maurice ran away limping; he was angry. I didn't understand why.

"Maurice, come back, talk to me."

Samuel noticed the situation. He waved to me and went after Maurice. He found him crying behind the small garden shed.

"Maurice, what's wrong with you?"

"Oh, Samu! I've had enough. I'll always be left, and now it's even worse. You go, and I stay behind."

"Hannah and Hans are only going for 1-2 weeks. Then they're back. That's short, and you're a man, not a little boy anymore."

"Don't tell Hannah I cried."

"No, I won't do that. Be strong and look forward to the future."

"I will, and thanks, Samu."

"Come on, let's go back to playing, and now you're running away from mom."

With a boxer to the side, Maurice ran past Samuel.

When they were both back with me, Maurice called out to me:

"Come on, Hannah, run with me."

I enjoyed his laugh. I hadn't forgotten why he had come to us. He was one of the boys who came to us from Bern. They had escaped from the Jewish boys' house in Bern. There, they had to follow the ultra-Orthodox faith.

I still condemn this way of teaching a religion today. I had raised Samu liberally. Hans and I had always advised Samu never to tolerate the strict way of life. One could and can also exist as a 'normal' Jew.

Maurice's call snapped me out of my thoughts again: "Hannah, what's wrong with you?"

"Come on!"

Just as I was enjoying the game, I heard Hans' car.

"Guys, I have to stop. Have fun."

I ran to Hans and was out of breath.

"Dear, you're panting like a steam locomotive."

"Hans, we played cops and robbers."

"Nice, what's for dinner?"

"Marie warmed up yesterday's leftovers."

"Good, come and kiss me, woman."

I loved the rough demeanor he had at times. I went to him and kissed him. You could hear the boys' whistles from behind. We waved to them and went into the house. Hans grabbed me there and kissed me again.

"That turned you on! Do we want to have another child?"

"I have nothing against it, but it always takes two to have children." (Unfortunately, we ran out of luck. Samuel remained our only child.)

Mrs. Krähling rang the bell for dinner. I was hungry, so I urged Hans and Samuel to hurry up. One of the girls served us food. I loved the wonderful smell of the delicious Zurich Geschnetzeltes.

Samu also sniffed the rising steam. "The Zürich Geschnetzeltes is so good. How I'll miss the chef's cooking skills."

"We can take her with us."

"Not that she has a George either."

"Oh, Hans, always you. Samu, will you join us in the salon for a while?"

"No, mom, I want to fix a few things and go to bed early."

"Then have a good night, my son."

"Night together, and I look forward to going to Freiburg with you."

"We, too. Night, Samuel!"

"Do you like a whiskey or brandy?"

"Whiskey with ice, love."

"Immediately! I drink tea. I'm somehow cold."

"Come to me, I'll warm you."

"Maybe later."

Hans laughed. (Why do men always have to think about it? Women don't think about sex as often as men, right?)

"I'm supposed to give you greetings from Herschel."

"Oh, how kind of him. He hasn't been here for a long time."

We had spoken about Herschel and Freiburg and how long it would take to get there. I began to yawn, and Hans asked me if we wanted to go to bed. I wanted to, and we still had fun together. I quickly felt warm again.

The other morning, I didn't want to get up, but it was the day of our departure. It was just five o'clock in the morning. Hans stood up as usual. We had abandoned our plan to leave at five o'clock because then we would have had to get up even earlier. When I also got up at the unusual hour, even Samuel was already up. He was still running around in his boxers.

"Samu put some clothes on! You will catch a cold!"

"Yeah, mom, I just had to pee." That wasn't exactly what I wanted to hear from my son.

Georg was already lugging his suitcases. "Good morning, Ms. Mangold. Did you sleep well?"

"Morning, George. Yes, that's fine, but I'm not a morning person, and especially not at this time." He just smiled gently and continued.

"Morning, dear! Would you like tea or coffee?"

"Tea. Good morning, my dear. I'm so tired but happy."

"Is it okay with you if we leave at six o'clock?"

"Yes, I'll be ready by then."

I took a roll and spread butter on both halves. Honey and jam were enough for me until there was more later. Add tea, and I was happy. Samuel also came and had breakfast with us.

At five to six, Hans asked impatiently: "Are you ready then?" For him, this was not an unusual time of day to leave the house.

"Yes, as far as I'm concerned, we can go. We still have to say goodbye to Mrs. Krähling and Georg."

"We'll do it, but they'll stay until we come back."

"Good, then we can go."

Georg had put all the suitcases in the trunk. And once we were seated, the journey to Freiburg could begin. Mrs. Krähling was still in bed, and Georg said goodbye to us.

We drove out of town, and Hans asked: "Do you want to take the highway or the country road?"

Samu said, "Country road!" You could almost think he was afraid of going to Freiburg.

"I do not care."

"Okay, then we'll go by land. It's much nicer, too."

It should be fine with me. There were at least a few Inns there. At lunchtime, we could safely stop somewhere and eat something delicious.

Two hours later, after a few traffic jams, we reached Basel. We had to cross the border in Riehen, but there was no time to visit Hans' father in Basel. It was still a long way to Freiburg, and we wanted to arrive during daylight.

We rented a suite in the castle hotel. Samu had raved about it. Although he had never been here himself, his girlfriend Rachel and her family always stayed there in Freiburg. And what good was for the Goldbergs was just good enough for us. (Wink in my eyes, my dears!)

I couldn't stand it any longer in a small town with the beautiful name of Auggen. I wanted to eat something.

"I'm hungry and have to go to the toilet too."

"Yes, darling, we'll stop at the next Inn. I'm hungry too, and I'm sure Samu is too."

When an Inn came, Hans stopped. We sat down in the gardening area. The innkeeper came immediately. He had seen our Swiss license plate and was accordingly eager. He kindly asked if we wanted to dine, too, and of course, we did. I was hungry; I could have eaten a side of beef. The innkeeper took our drink order and went to get the menus.

Promptly Hans said, "I eat roulades with potatoes and vegetables."

"No, I don't want that, but sauerbraten with dumplings and salad."

"So, my men have something, and I'm having chicken fillet with rice and salad."

When the innkeeper came, he took the order and served us the drinks.

"It's going fast."

"Sure, because we are Swiss."

"No, mom, because we're the only guests."

"You again, Samu! Psst, the innkeeper is coming."

"Why shush? Are you afraid he'll find out we're Jews?"

"No, but it's not appropriate to talk about others."

Samu looked at me but refrained from answering me.

"The Menus will come immediately. Can I bring you something else to drink?"

"Yes, a water and a Coke, please."

The innkeeper nodded and left. After ten minutes, he came back with the drinks, and a lady brought the Menus.

"Enjoy your meal!", said the waitress friendly.

We thanked and ate an excellent meal, and we spent an hour there. In the end, Hans paid the bill, and we set off again.

"Now, it's not far to Freiburg."

During the journey, we passed through many small villages, and in almost everyone there was wine. The area there was and is still known today for its excellent wines. "Spoiled by the sun!" A winemaker once said to me.

We finally got closer to Freiburg and saw the first parts of the 'suburb' as they called it - parts of the city that didn't yet belong to Freiburg. So, we came closer to our goal, meter by meter.

There it was, the beautiful castle hotel on Rotteckstrasse. It was not far from our future home.

"The viewing appointment will be tomorrow. This way, we can recover a bit."

"Yes, it's good, Hans."

"I still have appointments today. Please don't schedule me. The chief rabbi will certainly introduce me to his family."

"It's okay, son."

Hans stopped in front of the entrance with our car. A young man came and helped us. It was the wagon master. Once he had loaded the luggage onto one of the luggage carts, he sent for a bell boy to take it to the hotel. Then he took Hans' keys and drove away in our car. I didn't know about this service. The vehicle owner used to do this always himself. For a brief moment, even though the car master was trying to steal the car. He just took it to the hotel parking lot.

"Let's go in!"

In the entrance hall, I immediately noticed the wonderful fountain in the middle. I've never seen anything so beautiful before. I was all the way away.

With "Welcome to the Castle Hotel. What can I do for you?", we were welcomed.

Hans shrugged and said to the young woman. "Good morning, Mangold. We have booked."

"Come on, I'll see. Yes, there it is, a suite on the top floor."

"Exactly, where should I sign?"

"Your passports, please! I have to collect all the data."

Hans looked as frightened as I was. But it was a pure formality and had nothing to do with the persecution of Jews. Nevertheless, our reactions revealed that this trauma was still deeply embedded in us. Will this wound ever disappear, or will we always have to carry it around us?

We kindly handed over our passports, and the Lady kindly thanked us. After a few minutes, we received our passports back, and Hans signed the reservation paper. This Lady called a page who brought us into our suite. I was excited and amazed when the page opened the door. What a nice room, I thought.

But that was just the reception area. On the left and the right were the bedrooms and the bathrooms. All rooms were modernly furnished and had stucco work on the walls and ceiling. Now I knew why the Goldbergs loved the hotel.

The page took our luggage into the bedrooms, and Hans gave him a good tip.

"Puh, at last alone. What are we going to do now?"

"I'm going to our new congregation."

"Well, my son, we will make it a little cozy here. Will we have dinner together at night?"

"Yes, please, father. Except the rabbi planned something else."

"Just do it! You are already a grown-up, my boy. Have fun!"

"Thank you, mom."

"The boy has grown so fast! Yesterday a boy, and today a man."

"Yes, my love, but he will always be your boy. Come on, let's have a drink."

"Well, I want champagne."

"If you like. I'd rather drink whiskey with ice."

Hans ordered our drinks and fresh strawberries. They existed at this time of year. The man from the room service told us that they came from Israel. They immediately tasted much better.

"What time is the appointment tomorrow?"

"The broker said at eleven o'clock."

"So early! We have to get up early."

"Then we have more of the day, my love."

We spent some time together, and later, we wanted to have dinner together at the hotel. Of course, I wanted to be pretty first. Hans was in the bathroom taking a shower.

I haven't been a shy reef for a long time. I went to Hans and saw him as g-d created his Adonis. Oh, my g-d, he was still a handsome man!

"Dear, you don't look red anymore."

"Why should I?"

"Well, if you see such a magnificent boy, you will turn red."

"You get used to everything."

"Hey, you're ugly."

I had to laugh and kiss him before he had to cry.

Yes, we had it on, but only after an hour came out of the bathroom in a good mood.

"I love you, Hannah!" (I can still hear his words today. I miss him so much, my Hans.)

"I love you, too, Hans."

I could be grateful to this brown tyrant. Without him, I would never have met Hans. (Thank you, your brown bastard!)

"Dear, Samuel told me before. He will meet us at the bar."

"Well, I am very pleased."

"Will we?"

"Yes!"

We went downstairs and met Samuel at the bar.

"Would we have another drink or go eat?"

"I would be hungry, but if you want to drink."

"Next to the hotel is a nice little restaurant. Do we want to go there?"

"Yes!"

So, we went to the small restaurant that belonged to the hotel. A friendly waitress brought us to our table. The small restaurant was decorated in the style of the last era and therefore fitted in very well with the hotel. The waiter brought the card, took the drink order, and left.

"What are you eating?"

"There are so many delicious things."

"I eat ducks, red cabbage, and cloves."

"It sounds delicious, but I eat forel."

Hans thought, "And I will join Samuel."

We ordered the dishes and talked as the waitress brought us the drinks

"How did it happen to you with the rabbi?"

"Mom, the rabbi is very kind, and I also understand well with his auxiliary rabbi."

"I am very pleased, my son."

"Yes, I think I made a good decision."

"I think so. Don't you, Hans?"

"Yes, my dear. Of course, I am glad, Samuel, that you like it so well."

"Thank you, dad."

"Ah, the food is coming. Let you taste it."

"Samu, will you bless our meal?"

"Not here! People don't seem to tolerate such a thing."

"Well, then eat."

We sat together for a long time and talked about Freiburg. Samuel told us about the new congregation. This one was slightly ultra-orthodox, which did not fit me. But Samuel said at that time that there would be more Orthodoxy there. (This is a profound difference between Jewish schools of faith, even if it sounds like a gradual difference to outsiders.) Faithfulness was always good, although sometimes a bit too strict. The teachings of Scripture belong to every good Jew.

When we woke up, I looked forward to the appointment in Mozart Street, where our new house has waited. We had breakfast and got a few more things done. Then we went to the appointment. Samuel was still on his way; we wanted to meet there.

We were on time. At first, I thought we were wrong about the address. When I saw the villa, it was more beautiful than the photos. Already, that forged iron gate was impressive. Hans said nothing, but I could see that he liked the property. He had already seen it and knew the brokerage company.

We walked up the path to the villa, and we could see the agent waving at us. He must have been excited, too. It's not every day you sell a house like this. And thanks to the shade of the lime trees, the whole thing looked like something out of an old Hollywood classic!

A fountain was installed in the courtyard. The path led around the fountain.

The broker called to us: "The Mangolds, how beautiful!"

"Good morning, Mr. Lieberman! How are you?"

"Thank you, very good. What about you?"

"Also, good. All we have to do is wait for our son."

"No problem, we have time."

After ten minutes, Samuel came up the road and joined us.

"Well, then we can. We start inside, and then I'll show you the Outdoor area."

Mr. Liebermann opened the door, and my eyes almost fell out.

I said, surprised. "What a splendor!" (I never liked the entrance hall either. We later rebuilt it according to our ideas.)

We walked through the ground floor. There was a large lounge, a larger kitchen, an office, and a reception hall. On the first floor, there were several rooms and a very well-equipped library.

(Later, we discovered a small room – hidden behind a bookshelf – filled with once-forbidden writings. When we bought the villa, they were no longer banned.)

The staff's service rooms were on the ground floor. I liked the house more and more. I learned to love it later.

We walked through the little park. I noticed a small garden house. It was so lovely and even had its basement. The facility was old, but we had to exchange everything anyway. The ideal place for children to play in the sun.

A painted dragon was on a wall and reached almost to the ceiling in the interior. (Sometime later, I discovered the shallow depth of the dragon's head. I'm sure you could have hidden something there.)

"Well, that was it. Any questions?"

"Only one: when can we sign the purchase contract?"

"Tomorrow in my office."

"Well, we will meet with you tomorrow."

"Well, Mr. Mangold. Do you want to come at two in the afternoon?"

"Yes, that's right, I'll just pass by the bank and pay for the house."

"Very beautiful! I wish you a good day and till tomorrow!"

"Yes, until tomorrow, Mr. Lieberman."

When Mr. Lieberman had left, Hans asked me how I found the house. I told him I loved it. Samuel liked it, too.

As the weather was nice, I liked the environment. I wanted to walk to the hotel and look around the way. Hans wasn't right, but I was able to get through. It wasn't far, and who wanted to do anything to me?

Hans drove back to the hotel by car and slipped. Samuel still had appointments, and I got on my way. I walking the road alone. I met two women. They greeted me politely, and so did I.

Then I noticed the wonderful garden. It was huge; a lot of people crowded there. I wanted to take part in the rumble and run through the park. I saw many beautiful flower beds, a small lake, and – what I had never seen before – a cable car. She led from the park to the mountain.

There was a hotel over Freiburg. I planned to ride the cable car with Hans someday.

There was also a small pavilion where you could sit comfortably and drink coffee. I immediately closed the park into my heart. I learned later that it was the town garden.

I ran towards the city center and noticed our hotel was closer on this road than by car. I never liked driving. I loved public transport or taking a bicycle.

Hans was waiting for me. He had a little surprise for me. I was looking forward to it. I was still mad at him. At first, I acted uninterested, but when I saw the big straw rose. I couldn't help but hug him and kiss him. How quickly a thing becomes good again when you love each other!

In the afternoon we took a walk and went shopping. That evening, we met Samuel for dinner. He proudly told us that Rabbi Stein wanted him to be his assistant rabbi. He was allowed to continue his teaching as a bank merchant in Freiburg. It happened quickly, but if he was okay. I was it, too. (Today, he is a chief rabbi and resents this grinding position.) Around midnight, we went to our suite and ended the day with a drink.

The new day began gloomy; it was foggy. I was in a good mood anyway. In Freiburg, I slept better than in our house in Zurich.

Today, we had our big day. We signed the purchase contract for the new house, and Hans wanted to go with me to the synagogue. I was glad. I had not dared to ask him to do so. But Samuel was greeted in the synagogue today.

Since Hans was still in the bathroom, I took the opportunity and ordered our breakfast in the room. Just as he came out of the bathroom, breakfast came too – to the point.

"Good morning, my love. Have you slept well?"

"Good morning, my beloved, yes, and you?"

"Well, I was often awake. It must be because we are going to the synagogue today."

"So bad?"

"That's fine, but I'll endure it for you."

"Nice of you."

After breakfast, we finished and went to our appointment with Mr. Lieberman. Hans wanted to pay for the house today. The bank house Mayer had given us an appointment, although we had not been in the Jewish community until then. But they knew that Samuel was our son.

I asked as we stood in front of the brokerage office. "Do you think we're right here?"

But Hans replied briefly: "His name is on the wall." So, we went into the house. A whole house for a company, you've had to sell many properties already!

The Young lady at the reception asked us who we wanted to go to. Hans said that we had an appointment with Mr. Lieberman. Then, the lady became friendlier and more asked us to sit down. He'll come right away.

Lieberman said happily, "Ah, the Mangolds! I'm glad you are here!"

"Good morning, Mr. Lieberman. We are, of course, delighted."

"Please come with me! We have to go all the way upstairs."

"Ah, the boss has the best office!"

"Yes, but my son is here, the boss."

"What a wonderful view!" I said as I looked out. You could see the minster.

"Please sit down! Do you want coffee or something?"

"No, nothing, we just want to sign the contract. When can we come into our house?"

"Already today; The old owner has already moved out. You can take the keys with you right away."

"I will pay the house in full today."

"Well, I'm glad. The notary will come soon."

I sat in the background and listened to the gentlemen. After a while, the contract was signed and signed. In conclusion, there was a sparkling wine, not a very good one, but I didn't let myself notice it.

"Okay, then I'll go to the bank and have the money transferred."

"Do that, and here are the keys. Good luck in your new home."

"Thank you and goodbye."

When we were outside again, I noticed. "How long it had taken to get everything finished!"

"Yes, dear, but now we have everything, and in the afternoon, we can go into our house and look around."

"Well, but now to the bank!" I said, and took Hans with me.

"Dear, you don't even know where the bank is."

I pointed my finger north. "But there. You showed it to me before."

"Well, then let's go. The banker will wait."

We stood there and admired the sandstone figures on the old facade of the bank. Then we went in and were welcomed by our new banker, Mr. Grafeneck.

"Shalom, Mr. Mangold, and the wife are with you!" He whirled with his fingers in his beard and straightened his chin. I found it disgusting, so I had to take his hand to greet him. - He already gave me a hand.

"Greetings, Ms. Mangold. How are you, do you like Freiburg?" He looked at me questioningly, and I thought about the correct answer.

"Thank you, Mr. Grafeneck. I'm doing very well, and I also really like Freiburg. Isn't Grafeneck a noble name?"

He looked at me in shock and said something embarrassed. "No, no, Ms. Mangold. It just sounds like that. My family came from the Sudetenland, and we were driven out of there too.

I said casually. "That's interesting!"

"Then come with me to my office. Do you want coffee or tea?"

Hans replied, "I'd like some tea."

I sat on one of the two chairs. Mr. Grafeneck had pulled them to his desk, especially for us. Hans sat next and took the transfer form out of his folder.

"Ah, you have already prepared everything. That's how I love it, dear Mr. Mangold."

"Yes, such deals have to be completed quickly. We want to go into our new house today to see what we want to change."

We didn't want to do that until the next day, but Hans would have his reasons for pushing the pace like that.

"Do you already have an interior designer?"

"No, we don't need that. My wife does an excellent job."

"If you ever need someone, let me know. I know enough good artists."

When we finished, we said goodbye to Mr. Grafeneck.

"Goodbye, everyone."

"Goodbye, Mr. Grafeneck, we were pleased."

"Totally mine! I'll take you to the exit."

Finally, we stood in front of the bank. I could finally breathe in fresh air again.

"Shall we go to the hotel? It's time for lunch."

"Yes, with pleasure, dear."

We walked back to the hotel hand in hand. We freshened up there and then went to the little restaurant that was part of the hotel. Samuel joined us later. We ordered our food and chatted for a bit until the food came.

He had spoken to the rabbi for a long time. The official welcome in the synagogue was already in two hours. Hans didn't feel like it. But he would do anything for his son. I was looking forward to the synagogue. Finally, pray and sing again! (I've always loved singing, but now, at my age, I don't have to do that to anyone anymore.) Two hours later, we were standing in front of the New Synagogue with Samuel and were about to go in when we received a call from behind. It was Mr. Lieberman with his wife, Henriette. A kind lady, she was! The Liebermans were always very friendly. We met with them often. Sometimes they came to us, sometimes we went to them. With them, it was never tedious.

Samuel led the way. He had to sit in the front. We sat with the Liebermans in the middle of the room. The organ began to play, and the choir sang along. (I was in tears at the time. I was so emotional.)

The chief rabbi entered the bimah - the pulpit - and started to say a holy prayer. Then the choir sang again. Finally, another rabbi read from the Torah and welcomed our son to the community in Freiburg.

Hans was happy when we left the synagogue after more than two hours. Samuel had to stay; he had a few more conversations. Hans and I went out to dinner with the Liebermans. It was a beautiful evening that ended late.

The new morning has started very nicely. The sun was shining, and despite the cold, I could finally have breakfast outside. Hans didn't like this at all. He always thought that I might get sick. (A cold has never bothered me. It cleanses from the inside.)

At least after receiving a piece of fur as a pillow and a blanket to put over my knees, he was happy and even kept me company. Samuel had already left the hotel and wouldn't be back until the afternoon.

Hans looked at me for a while, then asked me. "Dear, should we go straight to the house?"

"Yes, I would like to see the kitchen. Maybe you don't have to change much there."

"Right, I thought so too. It looked pretty modern and tidy."

We finished breakfast and got ready. Hans was still on the phone; he spoke to Martin, who was preparing something in Zurich.

I whispered to him. "Say hi, dear." Hans nodded and adjusted them. When the conversation went too long for me, I kissed Hans on the neck, and he ended the "important" conversation. He looked at me and pulled me to him.

"I love you, my darling!" Then he kissed me.

After that long kiss, I had to take a breath. "I love you too, and if we live here, we will finally arrive."

"Weren't you happy in Zurich?"

"Yes, darling, but when I first entered this house. I felt a strange feeling of happiness."

He took my hand and said quietly: "I can understand you. I felt the same way when I arrived at the refuge." Hans' eyes became very wet, but he couldn't cry. (He didn't even cry when his father died.)

"Come on, let's walk to the house. You can show me this park."

"Gladly!" I shouted and went to get my hat. "Ready, can we?"

"Yes, dear." Hans took me by the hand, and together, we went into the reception hall to hand in our key.

Before the entrance, Hans wanted to know where we had to go. I pointed to the right and pulled him with me. It didn't take long until we got to the city park. Hans looked at everything carefully. He loved plants as much as I did. We stood at the cable car until he finally asked if we wanted to ride together.

I said, "not no!" We had more planned. But I promised that we would go together once we lived here. He accepted this, and we moved on.

We stopped again at the pigeon tower. Hans looked up and said. "I like pigeons, but they make a lot of mess."

"Yes, that's right, I just like to look at them from a distance."

A few meters further were the small lake and the orchestra pavilion. We stopped here, too, and Hans looked around again. "You can sit comfortably here on Sundays and listen to the orchestra."

"Yeah, that's nice, or you can have a little picnic."

Hans smiled, and then we continued walking. The exit from Mozartstrasse was in front of us. Just a few more meters, and we were standing in front of the heavy iron gate to our property. We walked down the narrow avenue. I admired the old Linden trees.

"The fountain would also have to be renovated. The previous owner had no interest in such things." (I later learned that the previous owner - the Weil family - was well-known in the art industry.)

"Yes, darling, I'll put it on the list."

"Do that, come on, let's go in."

The kitchen looked even nicer than I remembered. I went and looked in the cupboards; luckily, they were all empty. Just clean it up and re-arrange it, nothing more. However, the other rooms all needed modernization. The cellar was in bad condition; the old coal hatch was open. It had to be closed properly. After all, you were no longer in the safety of Switzerland.

"Darling, I'll make an appointment with a construction company. Maybe they'll have time tomorrow! They know best what to do."

"Gladly, but I want to be there. You know we women have a special knack for a cozy home." But I didn't hear anything more than a laugh.

"Dear, do we want to look around the garden?"

"Yes, I'd love to. Maybe we can take a look at the garden house. We didn't have that much time for that yesterday."

Hans took my hand, and we went into the garden. I always liked him. We redesigned the small garden house twice, the first time as we moved there and the last time as our grandchildren played there. Was the tree on which the swing hung older than the house?

I designed everything in the little garden house myself, and when Aaron was born, I decorated the dragon. At some point, I will hide a key for him in the hollow on his head. This key leads him to a chest containing items of personal value to me.

"Hans, let's leave this part of the garden a little mysterious. Samuel's children will play in the little house later."

Hans didn't think twice, nodded to me, and we kissed. "We could plant a few more fast-growing bushes. And when Samuel has children, things will be mysterious here."

I agreed with Hans, admiring the beautiful sculptures that decorated the back of our garden. (When I found out that these sculptures were by Hitler's favorite sculptor, I smashed them with my own hands and had them taken away. Nazi filth had no place and will never have a place in our lives. Hans was against it, but I didn't care. Even Samuel celebrated me back when I hit with a hammer in my hand.)

Hans and I had everything done. We had written everything down on a list and had an appointment with a construction company the next day. We didn't have much time because we were going back to Zurich on Sunday.

Samuel would stay and oversee everything. He could use our car there. We would take the train. The connections were now faster. When our villa is ready, we will move with all our luggage. However, we would not sell our villa in Zurich because we had the youth center there and wanted to expand it after we moved out.

We decided to walk back to the hotel. This time, via Mozartstrasse and a detour into the old town.

"These are nice houses on this street. Look, our neighbors." I looked at the nameplate. "Glauenstein, strange name. Well, Mangold isn't ordinary either."

Hans had to laugh. "Honey, whatever you have. When we move in, we throw a party and invite all our neighbors."

"Yes, I'm looking forward to that. What do we want here in the old town?"

"I just wanted to look at something. There's a new building where you can rent offices."

"Just rent and not buy?"

"No, we bought a villa and offices we do rent."

We walked along a picturesque canal. It almost looked like the Landwehr Canal in Berlin.

I saw a sign and read aloud: "It's called Gerberau, it's nice here."

Hans leaned on the canal railing and looked into the shimmering blue water. "Yes, I agree. Sometimes, I think you should leave everything behind and start over somewhere new."

"Honey, let's do that, and you'll see, it'll be wonderful."

Hans kissed me and took my hand. We continued walking together and enjoyed the sunshine.

"Are you looking forward to Zurich?" I wanted to know. I want to cheer Hans up a bit. He's been a little quiet since his remark about starting over.

"That's fine. I'd rather stay here and renovate the villa with you. Look, this is the new building. I like to rent the upper floor here with Martin."

"Nice, but it looks expensive."

I found the prices very high for the standards of the time, but Hans considered her normal. The property was on Augustinerplatz, an old and later expensive place. He wrote down the data, and we continued walking. Hans wanted to make an appointment for the next day. There were no cell phones back then. You had to go to a phone booth or call later from the hotel. (Hans wanted to call from the hotel. There was no rush.)

If you walked through the small streets of the old town, you could get to know new things. There were smaller shops and also the well-known Bächle. (I often stretched my feet into such streams in the summer. Some people from Freiburg found it strange, but I didn't care.)

When we arrived at the hotel, Hans made his phone call. I had a good time at the bar. I drank iced tea, freshly brewed, and cooled with ice cubes. The bartender had to make tea every time because of me. I was the only one drinking iced tea this time of year.

After the phone call, Hans came and had a drink with me.

I asked him. "Did it work?" He seemed a bit distracted.

"Yes, dear, but they don't want to rent to us. Martin will now look for another property."

"Is that because we are Jews?"

"No, they are afraid that we have too much public traffic. They are a peace-loving house where people don't want crowds."

"Well, it's their fault, and we'll get something better. Call Mr. Lieberman, I'm sure he can help you."

Hans looked up and blinked at me. "I already thought of that too. He is on a trip and will not return until Sunday evening."

"Yes, we are already on the way home."

"Samuel left a message at reception. We're invited to dinner with the Chief Rabbi this evening."

"Oh, did he do you a favor with that?"

"I'm sick. You can go alone."

"This is unacceptable. It's our boy, and we're doing it for him."

"But if the rabbi starts blessing everything, I'll get up and leave."

"Darling, father didn't do it any other way."

"I wanted to marry you too!" Hans looked ahead like a petulant child.

I tried to calm him down: "Let's go to our suite and get our clothes ready for the evening."

"I just need pajamas."

"That's enough, Hans!" I said in a firm voice, and Hans noticed this. He knew I would be angry if I said "Hans."

"Good, darling, you win. But only two hours."

"Go ahead, love!"

"Peter put the drinks on our bill."

"Of course, Mr. Mangold."

We went to our suite and checked our wardrobe.

"I'm putting on my black suit."

"Yes, that's good, and I'll wear the black dress with the long sleeves."

"I'm going to lie down for a bit. Today was a busy day."

"Go ahead! I'll go to the roof terrace and look at the area."

As I stood on the terrace and thought about that evening, I worried about Hans. Hans was so negative about our religion. What if the Rabbi wants to bless us? What if he wants to bless our new house? Let's let it happen to us! I have to make sure Hans doesn't start a fight.

"Honey, we have to get ready. Samu is coming soon."

"Yes, go to the bathroom. I'll come after you."

I went ahead, took a quick shower, and dried myself. Just Hans came and looked at me: "You are so beautiful. I love you very much."

"Thank you, darling, I love you too. You can take a shower. I'm ready."

While Hans undressed, I put on my bathrobe. My dress was on the bed in the bedroom.

"Honey, would you give me another pair of underwear?"

"Wait a minute, I'll go get them."

So, I went to get Hans a fresh pair of underwear. You couldn't say slip. He always wore the half-leg ones. Today it's boxer shorts.

He called from the shower. "Thanks, darling!" You could hardly see him because of all the steam.

I went to get dressed modestly, just as the Chief Rabbi liked. I put on subtle make-up. In this case, I didn't care whether he liked it. I very rarely go out without a well-groomed appearance.

Hans was ready, too. He smiled and even whistled to himself and put on his suit. He had already worn it at our wedding and his mother and father's funerals. But it still looked like new. Hans always wore his clothes for a very long time.

"But you're in a good mood."

"Why?"

"Well, you've been whistling the whole time."

"I'm just making the best of this situation, my darling."

"Aha, it won't be a funeral."

"No, and I'll survive for two hours."

Luckily! I thought, and the doorbell rang. Samu came to pick us up.

"Shalom, mom, dad. You look good—and so appropriate."

"Samu, we want to leave a good impression on your rabbi."

"You will. He already likes you. So, he doesn't know you, mom, dad, that well yet."

"Yes, and it could stay that way."

"Hans, please!"

"Rabbi Stein's driver is waiting for us."

"What, he has his driver?"

"Yes, why not?"

"Surely the parishioners have to pay for it."

"Father, first look at his household management, then you can criticize or praise."

"Samuel, you sound like one of them."

"Come one, father!"

We went to Rabbi Stein's car. The driver opened the doors for us, and we sat down in this magnificent car. It was a new model from Mercedes.

"So, you're Rabbi Stein's driver."

"Yes, that's me, Mr. Mangold."

"Well, I hope you get paid enough. Or do you have to give everything to the Rabbi?"

"No, Mr. Mangold, it's a normal job."

Samuel leaned over to Hans and said quietly: "Father, can you please behave, or do you want them to throw me out again?"

"No, please forgive me. Sorry, Mr. Driver."

"My name is Ben, and there is nothing to forgive."

Ben could handle Hans. Samuel was happy. His father had submitted and was quiet. Less than ten minutes before we arrived at the Steins' house.

"Nice shed!" Hans started, but Samuel stopped him immediately.

"Stop complaining, father!"

I stayed calm. The house was a bit pompous. But wasn't ours more pompous? Those who live in glass houses shouldn't throw stones. Hans looked at me irritably. I took his hand, and we walked to the entrance. A gentleman was already waiting for us there. Oh, they have a butler, too, I thought.

"Mr and Mrs Mangold, I greet you. Shalom and welcome to our home."

"Father, mother, may I introduce you to Rabbi Stein."

I was overwhelmed by him. A short man around 60 with a black yarmulke. He smiled at us: "Come in, blessings be upon you, my dear guests."

Oh, he's doing it, I thought. He blessed us, and Hans' expression became even fiercer than it already was. The rabbi took us to an anteroom where we could take off our coats. We heard a woman - Certainly, it was his wife.

"Dear, the Mangolds are already here. Come and say hello!" A pretty girl came and greeted us.

She politely shook our hands and said sweetly: "Good evening. I'm very pleased that you came."

"Dear, is everything prepared?"

"Yes, father, we can go to the drawing room."

When Hans stood next to me, he took my hand and squeezed it.

He whispered in my ear: "This is his daughter. Doesn't he have a wife?"

We went into the drawing-room, and I looked around. No servants, no wife, nothing. What was happening?

"Sit down, the food will be ready and served soon." We sat opposite each other, Samu opposite the young woman, and Rabbi Stein sat at the end of the table.

Aha, servants, after all, I thought, and then the door opened, and three gentlemen came in carrying something that looked delicious.

When the food was on the table in front of us, Hans wanted to start, but the rabbi had other plans. Full of joy, he asked Hans to bless the food.

Hans jumped up and was about to scream, but Samu had his father under control. "Rabbi, shouldn't I bless the meal?"

"Isn't it rude to your father if you deny him the opportunity?"

"No, no, dear Rabbi. Let him say the blessing, I'd rather listen to my son."

Phew, I thought. The turn was very sharp and narrowly avoided disaster. Samu stood up and took a piece of bread in his hand. Then he began the kiddush: "Blessed are You, G-d, our G-d, King of the universe, who brings forth bread from the earth."

Then he sat down again. It was a brief blessing; it wasn't a holiday. The meal was good. There was duck breast, and we also were served potatoes and carrots. I do love these veggies.

After we finished, we went with Rabbi Stein to his salon for a drink. There were also cigars, and of course, Hans took one.

"Rabbi, may I ask you if your wife is indisposed?"

"Dear child, my wife suddenly left us six months ago. Now, all I have is our daughter Liesel."

"That's terrible, please forgive my curiosity."

"There's nothing to forgive, Ms. Mangold. Adonai just had better plans for her." But in reality, he looked sad as he said these words.

Even Hans felt sorry for him and tried to cheer him up: "Rabbi, let's smoke a cigar together and maybe drink some whiskey. It eases the nerves."

"Yes, with pleasure, Mr. Mangold."

Liesel served the two of them the drinks. She made me iced tea, and Samu had table water. Later, she sat down with him and spoke with him about the training.

Hans and Rabbi Stein got along surprisingly well; they often laughed and occasionally slapped each other's thighs. I didn't listen but dreamed about our villa. When I got bored, I asked Hans if he wanted to go.

Only he didn't want to! We were with the Steins for more than five hours, and those who did not want to come stayed the longest. It wasn't until after midnight that Rabbi Stein's driver drove us back to the hotel.

When we were already in bed, Hans suddenly asked me: "Dear, are you angry?"

"No! Why?"

"Well, because we just left now."

"It was nice, and considering we only wanted to stay for two hours, it was fine."

"I love you." Hans kissed me and turned around.

"I love you too, darling." I snuggled up to him and quickly fell asleep.

The next day was Sunday, our departure day. Hans still had an appointment with the construction company. He was glad he found time on Sunday. We had breakfast and got ready. Then we took our coats and left. I accompanied him because I also had a say. We were already standing at the main entrance to the villa when the car with the two men from the construction company drove up. They got out and greeted us.

"Hello, everyone. May I introduce you to my son Fritz? He'll be taking over the company soon."

"Good day, everybody. You have a nice house," Fritz politely seconded.

He was right, so I happily confirmed: "Thank you, yes, it will be wonderful."

"Come on, let's discuss the points in the house."

There, Hans showed the gentlemen what we wanted changed. It took more than two hours. Only then did we put everything behind us and were back in front of the front door.

"I'll get everything ready and send it to you. Your son can sign the contracts, Mr. Mangold."

"Yes, I would say that too, I'm happy that everything worked out so well."

I said politely. "Goodbye, gentlemen."

"Goodbye, Ms. Mangold, Mr. Mangold."

When they left, I said to Hans: "Nice people! They'll do a great job."

"Yes, I agree. Let's go back to the hotel. We still have to pack."

I linked arms with Hans, and we walked to the hotel together. Hans went to the reception; I went upstairs.

When he entered, I was already packing! "Have you started yet?", he asked me.

"Yes, I'm almost finished. Did you get the information?"

"Yes, darling, everything is booked. Samuel will take us to the train station."

"Fine, I thought he didn't have time."

"Rabbi Stein wanted it that way. He thinks very highly of our son."

"I'm glad it happened this way. It's unimaginable if he were unhappy here."

The doorbell rang. "Can you open the door? That should be Samuel! I still have to get my things from the bathroom."

Hans opened the door, and I disappeared into the bathroom. When I returned, a bellman and Samu took the suitcases out of the suite. I put the things from the bathroom in one of the bags and took one. Hans carried the rest into the lobby. He settled the bill; I went to the car.

"Ben, what are you doing here, and where is our car?"

"Rabbi Stein wanted me to drive you."

"Mother, you're already here. I've been looking for you. I wanted to tell you, and dad didn't mind."

"Me neither, but it's a nice car too."

I quickly got in. Hans came and got in, too.

"Shall we go?"

"Yes, dear!"

Hans joked with Ben, and I was lucky he did it! "Ben, step on the gas!"

The train station was only a ten-minute walk away. It was quick by car. As soon as we enjoyed the luxury, it was already over.

"You go ahead, Ben, and I will take the suitcases to the platform."

"Where do we have to go?" I asked, a little confused.

"Platform 3, that's where the express train arrives. We can then drive directly to Zurich."

"Alright, darling, let's get going. The two of them are already doing it."

The express train was already on platform 3. I thought the train would drive away without us. No matter what, to be worried, the train had these waiting times.

"Ah, the train is here. We have to go to wagon 2. We have reserved a compartment there."

Ben and Samu drove these modern luggage carts to the second wagon and lifted our luggage in. Hans and I had nothing to do - he went and looked for the compartment. I stayed with our luggage. Samu then helped us bring everything to the compartment. Hans gave Ben a tip, who declined but then accepted it. Finally, they shook hands, and Hans got in.

"Son, please take care of yourself. I'm not used to being without you."

"It's okay, mom. I have people here to look after me. Please don't worry and we can talk on the phone too."

Samu wiped away my tears. Like all mothers, I found it difficult to let go.

"Dad, take care, and thanks for behaving. It means a lot to me."

"It's okay, Samuel, I was wrong about the rabbi."

"I'll be in touch about the renovation work."

"Yes, do that. We are reachable. Love you, my son."

"I love you too, dad. And of course, you too, mom."

Finally, he hugged us and then left. I immediately ran into our compartment and opened the window. Ben shook my hand, and Samu gave us one last wave. The conductor whistled, and our train started. I only closed the window when only small dots were visible on the horizon. I sat down and picked up the book I was reading.

Hans was reading the newspaper and asked: "What are you reading, darling?"

"A book by Thomas Mann."

"Aha, should I read it to you?"

"No, I'd rather read myself. You read your newspaper."

Hans' head disappeared behind his newspaper again. The train was passing a small town. It was a stunning technological achievement, such as an express train. He only stopped in the bigger cities, and we would soon arrive in Basel.

I opened the window and looked out. People were milling back and forth on the platform. A couple of baggage handlers ran from our train to the one on the other side. A little girl smiled at me, and I waved to her. A whistle sounded at the front of the locomotive, and a conductor raised his trowel and whistled twice in succession. Then the train started moving with a jerk.

"Honey, we're going again."

"Yes, I noticed it. We'll be home soon."

Hans scratched the back of his head. "I hope Georg will pick us up at the train station."

"Did you tell him?"

"Yes, dear, of course."

I just nodded at him and continued reading my book. It was good what this man wrote in his novels. Hans was bored.

"Do you have to go to the bathroom?"

"No, dear, why?"

"Well, you shift around in your seat. You might think you need to go to the toilet."

"No, my rump hurts, and I'll be happy when we can finally get out."

"Yes, me too. There is still a lot that needs to be done."

Hans took his briefcase and placed it on his knees. Then, he picked up a white sheet of paper and a pen.

"Do you want to write me a love letter?"

"I could, but I'm sorry to disappoint you, love. I'm just writing down everything I need to do in the coming week."

"It's a shame, but that's also important."

Hans was writing his list, and I looked out the window. Finally, we drove past Altstetten. We would arrive soon. I enjoyed the sight of the simple houses. They were in the suburbs, all had a small garden next to them, and children often played in the garden or on the street. Ah, the announcement from the train conductor that we are about to arrive at Zurich Central Station!

"Honey, the suitcases! We're almost there!"

"Yes, love, I'll take care of it."

I put my book in my bag, and Hans prepared the suitcases. Things had to happen quickly because the train continued directly to Interlaken.

The commotion on the train made it clear that the train station was not far away. Hans was already there and ready to lug his suitcase. As always, I only carried the bags.

The train pulled into the station, and Hans brought the suitcases to the exit. I went behind and helped him. Luckily, Georg was on the platform and saw us.

Georg said, "Hello, everyone," almost out of breath. "I was almost late!"

"Hello, George, but you did it."

"Come on, darling, give me the bags."

I gave Hans my bags, and he helped me get out. I sighed and was happy to have finally arrived.

"The car is at the side entrance. I wasn't allowed to park in the front."

"Renovation work?" asked Hans calmly.

"Yes, Mr. Mangold."

At the car, Georg packed all the suitcases into the trunk, and we sat in them.

"Can we?"

"Yes, George!"

Georg drove off to our property. I was looking forward to the young people and Ms. Krähling.

It was already late afternoon when we arrived home. I was hungry, and I'm sure Hans was too.

"Honey, I'm hungry, are you?"

"Yes, my dear, ask Ms. Krähling what's available."

I went and asked her. It was nothing special planned. That's why I wanted Shakshuka. It was more of a breakfast, but I also eat it when I'm not hungry. Soon, we were sitting in the salon eating our delicious shakshuka.

(Shakshuka is a specialty of Arabic and Israeli cuisine; translated from Arabic, it means something like 'mixture'. The dish consists of poached eggs in a sauce of tomatoes, chili peppers, and onions.)

"Darling, I'm going to sleep early this morning. Let's have another drink and then go to bed."

"Yes, dear, you are right. I am tired, too."

We enjoyed our drinks, Hans smoked another cigarette, and then we went to sleep.

I slept late and didn't get up until around ten o'clock. My back hurt; I wasn't 20 anymore. Hans was already in the office and had a lot of things to do. He also wanted to meet Martin; he had to rent the offices.

I enjoyed the beautiful morning. It was a sunny and pleasantly warm day for this time of year. Mrs. Krähling came and gave me some company. I asked her to have tea with me. We talked about her imminent departure. I still couldn't get used to the fact that she and Georg would soon be gone.

In the next few days, a new butler wanted to introduce himself. Can he replace Georg? I do not think so. He also has to go with us to Freiburg. Everyone else would stay and work for the youth center.

"Ma'am, a truck pulled up."

"It's good, Marie. These are the moving boxes."

"Should I go?"

"No, just leave it, I'll go. Please ask Georg to come to me."

"I will, ma'am." Marie left, and I looked at the boxes the truck was bringing.

The driver stopped and got out. "Hello, am I in the right place with the Mangolds?" he wanted to know.

"Yes, if you bring the boxes."

"Yes, I do, and they're big and heavy."

"Our butler will help you. He'll come right away."

"Yes, don't rush, I have time."

The driver went into his truck bed and unloaded the boxes. When Georg came, we could get started. The two unloaded all the boxes. Later, the driver got a coffee and a good tip.

"Well, that's a lot of boxes! Thank you, George."

"You're welcome, but now my back hurts."

"Take some time off and treat yourself to a hot bath."

"I do."

Georg limped away, and I looked to see which box I could take first. When Maurice and Tom came around the corner, I had them carry boxes. Tom was annoyed, and Maurice enjoyed the boss role and chased Tom around. After five boxes, Tom didn't want to and couldn't do it anymore. Maurice raised his arms in triumph. Then they both went to lunch, and I looked to see where we could take the boxes.

Towards the evening, Hans came home and was amazed when he saw how far we had already come. Maurice wanted to help me, but I told him he could go. He was just a boy and should have some fun, too, and he had that with Tom. They often and happily fought with each other. Then, they ran through the park and ended up completely exhausted.

"Honey, let's bring the rest of the boxes into the rooms tomorrow. Today we don't do anything and enjoy the evening. Shall we go over to the teenagers?"

"If you like! They play together a bit."

So, we went to the youth center together and enjoyed the time with the boys and girls. We played Catch the Hat! Black Peter and Memory. I was happy and forgot about longing for Samuel. Hans kept losing and was annoyed. I made fun of it and teased him.

When we had finished playing, the children went to bed. We headed home. Hans wanted something to drink and smoke; I drank some tea. We were tired and went to sleep together, but not without chatting. I liked talking with Hans in bed. He usually dozed and usually just said 'yes'. When he dozed off, I pushed him.

The other morning, it was raining, foggy, and cold. I had to sneeze. Oh, G-d, was I about to get the flu? Just not now! I thought as I blew my nose. I went into the kitchen and asked for some tea. That would be good for me now.

I took it and went into my study. I wanted to spend half the day there and pack a few boxes. Samuel had called the evening before and told Hans that the construction company had already started the renovation. I was happy. We will be moving soon.

Hans carried boxes with Maurice and Georg. Now, there was a large box in almost every room, and countless boxes were throughout the house scattered. I went to check on the noise the men were making. Hans and Maurice carried a box up, and Georg, still damaged, carried a box. I didn't even want to think about how to get the boxes down again, but the moving company was responsible for that.

"Darling, don't you want to take a break? Look at George. He can barely walk upright anymore."

"Yes, dear, we wanted to bring this box into Samus' room. Now everything is done, and we can slowly start packing."

"Just to think that we'll be moving in three months. I'm so happy!"

Hans just looked at me. Then he went for a drink with Maurice and Georg. I went to my study and continued.

The telephone rang. It was Ursula. "Ursula, what joy! … Yes, I'm home, yes, we can do it. … Then I'll wait for you here. …Is Martin coming too? … Ah well, then just us. … See you soon, Ursula." She wanted to come over and bring something with her. Well, who knows what she'll have again.

When Ursula came, I was curious to see what she had with her. Her driver brought her. The gift, she said, was in the trunk.

"Let's go inside. Do you like coffee or tea?"

"Tea, please, and Julius, please bring the present to the drawing room."

Julius, their driver nodded, and Georg came to help him. We already went in and enjoyed the warm tea.

"So, I think your present is already in the drawing room. Come on, let me show you."

Before I could say anything, Ursula pulled me along. Only in the drawing room did she stop. I saw it; it looked like a bronze figure. I felt my eyes sparkle.

I asked her in surprise. "Oh, Ursula, what is that?"

"Take the cloth away and look at her."

I pulled out the silk cloth and saw this beautiful bronze sculpture. So uniquely beautiful and elegant! It was a good 70 cm high and heavy; I tried to pick her up, but she was unusually heavy.

I asked Ursula. "Who is that?"

"Well, don't you recognize her?"

"No!"

"This is me, a design for the large marble statue in our garden."

"Yes, I remember them well. Why are you giving us this precious bronze?"

"Well, I don't want you to forget me in Freiburg!"

Her gesture touched me so much that I had to hug and hug Ursula.

"I will never forget you, and we have a telephone."

With tears in her eyes, she said. "I will miss you very much."

"I am very sorry about that. I don't have such a beautiful sculpture to give you as a gift."

"It doesn't matter, my love."

We went to have our tea. When Hans came with Maurice and Georg, Ursula left. Hans thought the little bronze figure was beautiful.

Did I have to be jealous? Hans just laughed and kissed me. Maurice's eyes widened; after all, the sculpture was half naked.

"Let's go do some packing."

"But only for an hour; we want to talk to Samuel on the phone."

"It's okay, dear."

Three months later, it happened. Mrs. Krähling and Georg left us, and we were about to move. The farewell between the two was heartbreaking, and everyone cried. Although, the two men were the tough ones and tried not to let it show.

"Should I drive you to the train station?" Hans asked Ms. Krähling and Georg.

But the two preferred to take a taxi. Didn't want a big goodbye? Ms. Krähling promised to write to us. We would stay in touch that way. (We wrote for a while, but at some point, there was no reply from Beuren. Maybe we should have checked, but we often do things differently.)

The butler that Georg recommended to us was not for us. He was a complete disaster and wouldn't take any instructions from me. Nevertheless, I gave him a chance, and he was allowed to go to Freiburg.

We had loaded three vans and had now arrived in Freiburg. They stood at the gate and waited until Hans let them in.

"I hope the trucks can fit through the gate."

The driver just nodded. He was used to narrow spaces and skillfully drove his van through the gate. Neither driver caused a scratch. (When I had gotten my license, I crashed Hans' new Mercedes. I thought it was funny; Hans was upset. Men and their toys!)

It got pretty tight in front of our house. Hans parked his Mercedes on Mozartstrasse. When he returned, we were already unloading our furniture! I stood in the entrance hall and directed the movers. Luckily, we finished everything after about five hours.

Not all the furniture was in place yet, but that didn't bother me. We had enough time.

It was more important to hire new staff. The replacement for Georg didn't do well in Freiburg either. We decided to fire him and look for a new butler. Something was missing from him. Was Georg even replaceable? Difficult! It had to be love at first sight if it could even succeed.

At that time, there were still agencies through which you could hire domestic staff. I applied there and got some housemaids. We couldn't find another George. (It wasn't until a year later that we ran into François. It was practically love at first sight. Whatever he could do, Georg's skills surpassed him. We didn't need a new Mrs. Krähling; François also fulfilled these tasks.)

So, in the end, we managed to get our house the way we wanted it. Soon, we had a housewarming party, had our home dedicated, and would hopefully be very happy here for many years.

I had invitations designed. They showed off our new home along with the date and time of the party. When the time came, and almost everyone came, I was excited. It was almost like my first day of school in Berlin.

Many people from our new community came, including almost all our new neighbours, except the family from the adjacent property. They were committed to the Third Reich. They greeted but kept to themselves.

Rabbi Stein blessed our house; we ate and were all happy. The party continued late into the night, and we had made new friends by the time our guests left.

Hans was also still able to rent the offices he wanted. However, they were too small, and we bought a building on Bertholdstrasse. There were little commercial units on the ground floor (a health food store and a pharmacy), and the offices were above. We had the attic converted into a penthouse - as a retreat when we handed the villa to Samuel.

But it wasn't that far yet. There were other challenges. One of them was almost too much for Hans. Samuel wanted our household to run according to Kashrut rules, and Jewish dietary rules. That determines what one can and cannot eat - no pig, separate milk and meat, and use separate cutlery, dishes, and pots for them. He even wanted to hire a new chef specifically for this purpose.

There was a lot of trouble. Hans said: "If you don't stop, we'll move to Bertholdstrasse. Then you can live here like an ultra-Orthodox Jew." (I can still hear his words clearly.)

Samuel didn't speak to Hans for several days. At some point, Samu found it too ridiculous and asked his Father for forgiveness.

He went into his study, where he sat as he often did, over books and papers.

Samu asked cautiously. "Father, may I speak to you?"

As he often did, Hans said understandingly: "Of course, my son. What do you want?"

"Father, the way we are behaving is ridiculous. I did things without thinking about what I was doing with them. I am a guest in your house, living with Rachel under your roof. I've now spoken to her, and we are looking for our own house here in Freiburg."

But that was out of the question for Hans. "You are meschugge, my son", he replied. "We also bought this villa for you and planned the garden for your children. You and Rachel are family. If so, we'll leave the villa to you and move into our penthouse."

"No, father! Can't we compromise?"

"Good! Speak, my son."

"I still have a lot to do and want to take over this community at some point. So, I follow all the rules and be a role model. What if I send for the kosher food and eat it separately from you in the little parlor?"

"That could work. Let us try it! You know I have always been proud of you and continue to be so."

"Of course, father! Come and let me hug you. I love you, Tate!"

Hans stood up and took his son in his arms. He said quietly: "I love you too, my son."

So, Hans accepted the compromise proposal. Samu adhered to the kashrut rule and ate separately from us: we were in the large salon, and Samu was in the small salon. We couldn't think of a better solution.

But things didn't go well for long. Hans became angry. He missed having his family at the table. However, Samu did not want to return to the table and demanded his rights, as they had both agreed. He even became hot-tempered and wanted to move out. Rachel said nothing. She always did what Samu wanted.

At that time, Samu said that worried me: "The women in our community are only there to have children and raise them. They must serve their husbands, just as Adonai did."

Was Samu still my son? I had to ask myself. I didn't raise him that way, always admonishing him to be kind and respect people. I soon realized that moving to Freiburg had been our biggest mistake. Our family disintegrated.

Samu now often stayed late in the office and avoided his father. Sometime later, he offered to move into the penthouse apartment with his wife and leave the villa to us. After all, he and Rachel wanted to get married soon.

We felt insulted. Samu wanted to get married, and we didn't know about it! Our son later apologized, but this wound didn't heal for us - never again. Hans got very involved, became ill, and suffered a mild heart attack.

Completely distraught, I called our doctor. Doctor Schmitt immediately rushed over and examined Hans. Luckily, he didn't find anything more serious. However, Doctor Schmitt didn't want to take risks and forbade Hans to fly. But our son wanted to get married to Rachel in Tel Aviv. He soon did because he still had respect for Rachel's parents.

Unfortunately, that soon changed, and he only spoke of Rachel's father with hatred.

So, our parents stayed at home. After all, Ari and Adam attended the ceremony with their families and took videos and photos. (What a beautiful couple Rachel and Samu were!)

Samuel and Rachel stayed there for 14 days and traveled through Israel on their honeymoon. Hans didn't speak very much. It was not possible to find out whether he was angry or whether his health was unwell. I offered him to move to Bertholdstrasse and leave the villa to Samuel and Rachel. For the sake of peace, Hans agreed.

We didn't have to take much with us. The personal belongings, clothes, and a maid. However, if I had known that this was the beginning of Hans' death, I would have spent every second with him from then on.

When Samuel and Rachel returned, we asked to speak to them. We didn't want to explain the injuries. It was too late for that. We had to draw a line under this period of life. Hans could no longer take part in an active life.

We invited Samu and Rachel to dinner. I had reserved four seats in the restaurant at the hotel. Samu and Rachel agreed. Only after his prayer, because he couldn't pray there. No problem! We just ate after 7:00 p.m. Hans was already walking with a cane, and it was getting worse every day.

We took a taxi to the restaurant. I didn't dare drive, and Hans couldn't do it anymore. Samu and Rachel were already there.

I said happily. "Hello, children, it's nice that you came." I was happy that we could finally talk together again. Hans didn't say much. He didn't speak much after his heart attack.

Samu stood up and took his hand. "Father, I'm glad that we can finally talk about everything. Mother, thank you for arranging everything."

When Samu said this, Hans looked at me sharply. I had been using a little white lie, but now it had been discovered. Nevertheless, I remained calm and smiled at him, undeterred.

Samu was curious and asked his father. "So, father. Do you want to talk to me?"

Hans cleared his throat. "We will move out. I will arrange to renovate the penthouse apartment tomorrow. You get the villa, and we retire."

Samu reacted irritably. He had thought everything was fine. But now this!

Samu was already bubbling over. "What have I done now?"

"Nothing!", replied Hans weakly. "But think about it: you have your own life now, and we have no room in it anymore."

Contrary to her custom, Rachel also speaks out. "You can't go! I can't run a household on my own yet. Please!"

But Hans had made up his mind and didn't want to change his mind. He explained brusquely: "Then hire staff, or we'll leave ours there. All we need is a maid."

Now Samu also became stubborn. He replied: "Then everything has been said. You can still stay here, we go. Mom, I'll call you!"

I cried, and Samu saw it. I was worried. Rachel was magical. She wanted us to stay in the villa if only to support her. But Hans refused. He wanted to be left alone, and I wasn't, asked.

Samu and Rachel left the restaurant. We stayed seated. Hans wanted to finish eating. So, it was decided we would move again.

Was it worth the effort to start over in Freiburg? If we ended up staying alone, we could have stayed in Zurich. (For a moment, I thought about moving back to Zurich because we were happy there.) But Hans didn't want to go back. He called the construction expert we trust and had some renovation work done on the penthouse apartment. Luckily, it took a while.

I became friends with Rachel. She was always a nice person, and I liked her a lot. I often went for coffee with her. There was a small café on the site of the place of Old Synagogue where we met secretly – yes, secretly.

I never figured out why Samu started to change so much. He was now often irritable, even quick-tempered, and also had problems in the community, not just with us. And the higher he rose in office, the more he was no longer himself.

He often traveled to Israel and met significant people there. Days later, he came back with a lot of money. Was this the reason for his change? He told me they were former boarding school friends who now wanted to invest in Germany. The chief rabbi at the time was happy about such contacts, as he was able to build the new synagogue. This project - and its sponsors - was well received by the Rabbinical Council. So Samu steadily rose in office.

He had long since left his own family behind. When Rachel's parents announced a visit, he got angry. Rachel explained quite harmlessly: "Samu, Mame, and Tate are coming to visit us. Tate is not feeling well and wants to see a doctor here."

I know because I was there. But Samu immediately became indignant: And he shouted at Rachel. "Now! I don't have time for your parents. They should stay in the hotel! Our house was never good enough for them anyway!"

She said quietly and was already starting to tremble. "But!"

"But what? I want to be left alone. Go and do your work!"

Samu stood across from her and raised his hand. I was just able to prevent it and warned: "Samu! Not! If you do that, you'll lose my respect."

I didn't know why he suddenly reacted like that. When Rachel's parents arrived, he was traveling and supposedly had to pick up something in Goslar for the Chief Rabbi - Was it something that couldn't be postponed? Did he feel guilty - Or was he hiding something from Lior, Rachel's father?

The Goldbergs didn't care. Lior could never tolerate Samu. Esther told me when we were traveling together in Munich at some point. Lior wanted a lawyer as a son-in-law and not a banker - especially not a candidate rabbi. He had no interest in religion and often covered his ears when Samu began to preach. I thought that was funny because it made Samu extremely angry.

Little by little, Esther Goldberg became a good friend who supported me during this transition period. Lior, her husband, on the other hand, was more buttoned up, but he wasn't in Germany often anyway. The Goldbergs had an apartment in Munich but lived in Israel and were rich and powerful there.

But Lior died soon – two years before Hans. He suffered a stroke and died on the way to the hospital. Since then, Esther lived in Munich and often visited Rachel and Samuel. Funny: Samuel liked Esther. He even wanted her to move in with them. But Esther politely declined. She preferred to come to visit, and when she was there, we met for dinner and often drank coffee together.

Meanwhile, Hans left the house less and less. I was worried about that. I called our doctor and asked him to speak to Hans. After all, Hans wasn't doomed to die; he was old but not dead nor terminally ill.

The doctor initially prescribed him a course of treatment so that he could learn to think again. But instead of going to the spa, Hans wanted to go to Ascona and experience Lake Maggiore again. He blossomed again, walked without a cane, and wanted to get back into life. We stayed in Ticino for three weeks and enjoyed the Mediterranean life. We talked a lot about Freiburg, and Hans mentioned for the first time that he would give up our company. I was kind of happy about it and thought of Herschel.

When we got back, Hans asked me and Samu to talk. I was surprised: he was so formal, almost distant. I worried again. I called Samu and asked him to come to me and Hans. Hans wanted to have a conversation with him. Samu came, and we sat down with Hans. Finally, everything was clarified, and everyone was happy about this solution. Samuel offered to help his father. Samuel offered to help his father. All business was currently at a standstill due to Hans' illness. Hans has accepted it.

Samuel was good at business. He founded a Jewish private bank and took over our company. Martin organized the takeover of the company. He also was supposed to support him legally and help Samu with everything else. He drew up the contracts, and these also regulated our retirement. We kept the penthouse apartment and received a fixed monthly payment from Samu.

Martin and Herschel brought us the contracts personally. What a joy! Even Hans woke up from his torpor; he was so happy that Herschel was there. He asked Herschel for a personal interview. He gave him a letter. He was only supposed to open it after his death. Herschel swore and stuck to it. That was the last time they saw each other. (Oh, I'm in tears right now.)

All takeover contracts have been signed and certified by a notary. Samuel was now the legal owner of our company and bank director. I was so proud of him and what he had achieved. A few days later, he was elected chief rabbi of the community, and from now he regulated the community's banking transactions through his bank.

Of course, this was a reason to celebrate. Samuel invited everyone and wanted every one of rank and name to be at the celebration. Even Hans wanted to come, but he was now in a wheelchair. He was already weak, and he was relieved that Samuel was taking over the business and he could retire.

Again, the alleged investors came from Israel. Samu always tried to please them. They behaved like they were kings. Samu sweated in her presence. I never found out what they had on him. It was unimaginable to me what could be behind it. It was none of my business.

I had a few more delightful years with Hans. Our first grandson, Elias, was born in 1995. But then he suffered another heart attack. I prepared for his death, but he didn't want to die yet. The doctor who had been advising Hans for years suggested that he live in a nursing home from then on. I was against it and had our apartment remodeled again so that he could continue to live there. He had two carers who were there for him around the clock. I moved in with Samuel. I was there every day with Hans and rarely left his side.

Finally, Hans asked me to let Samuel come. I called Samu in his office. When he came, Hans was already weak. But he wanted one last conversation with his son. I walked out of the room and left Hans to Samu. When Samu came out of the room where Hans was lying after half an hour, he was distraught. He had tears in his eyes and an envelope in his hand. I wanted to talk to him, but he just shook his head and left our apartment.

I went to Hans. He looked at the ceiling.

"Honey, is everything okay?"

He looked at me and said quietly: "Now, yes! I clarified what needed to be clarified. Now I can go."

Hans died of a pulmonary embolism five long and agonizing years later. A blood clot in the pelvic vein had broken loose and washed into the lungs. His organs were now simply too weak and no longer wanted to work. I held his hand until he closed his eyes forever. I can still remember the time exactly. It was 4:37 a.m. (I wanted to die that day!) When I was practically crying dry, I covered every mirror in the house with a black cloth. For us Jews, this is a sign of mourning.

(It is an old custom of the Jews that the mirrors went covered in the mourning house. Mourners do not leave the house until the funeral. Afterward, they sit at home on low chairs for a week, they do not shave or cut their hair for a month, and don't change their clothes. They don't have to cook for the first week either. Other relatives or close friends take care of that. At least that's how it's taught.)

The funeral was simple, as Hans had wished. Hans stipulated in his will that he must cremated. Samuel said - I remember clearly - that it was against the Jewish faith - due to the biblically based idea that on the Day of Judgment, all the dead will be resurrected. Therefore, the body must be buried intact. But since Hans was never really a believer, he wanted to annoy Adonai again during his last walk.

Samuel still gave the eulogy for a very long time. We then met at the Jewish center right next to the cemetery. There was a funeral feast there. Samuel wanted this because it would once again show how generous he was. But he hasn't been that way for a long time. It was just a display for the public.

At least I met friends again that I hadn't seen for a long time. Among them were Herschel, his wife, and one of his sons, Ruben.

I went through three of Hans' four stages of grief with great care.

Phase 1 Aninut: Between death and burial. This first period of grief is the most intense. During this time, the family is released from religious duties.

Phase 2 Shiva: In the first week after the funeral. The mourners do not leave the house, do not go to work, and avoid joys of all kinds. Neighbors and acquaintances provide meals and services held in the mourning house. It is traditional to cover the mirrors in the house. Not buying or wearing new clothes, skipping haircuts, and shaving are among the traditional duties during the mourning period.

Phase 3 Shloshim: 30 days after the funeral: The mourner returns to everyday life, but some restrictions (ban on music, joyful celebrations such as weddings, hair cutting, buying and wearing new clothes) continue.

Phase 4: The year of mourning did not apply to me because Hans was my husband. If a parent dies, the practices of shloshim continue for a year. However, after thirty days haircutting is permitted again if criticism comes from an outsider. There is a very extensive procedure depending on the faith. I chose the above. (Samuel had to go through the complete repertoire since he lost his father.)

Many friends supported me during this time. They provided me with all sorts of delicious food, and the children often came to me and comforted me. Esther came especially from Munich to support me. On the seventh day, she went and took all the clothes from the mirrors and dragged me out into the fresh air. We went to the synagogue together and prayed Kaddish. (**"Exalted above all praise and song and praise and consolation that is, carried out in the world, and say: Amen."**)

It took me a long time to get used to the time without Hans. We had such a good time and kept going through bad times. But the good times exceeded the bad times. I still remember talking to him in the first few weeks after Hans died. I enjoyed talking to him at the Jewish cemetery almost every day. As a sign of peace, I placed a white rose on his grave.

Hans and I had bought the grave a few years earlier; I will also lie there one day. It's nice to know where you can find peace at some point. (I hope that Samuel carries out what my will states.)

The day of the execution of the last will came. It wasn't anything wild; I was the sole heir. Samuel and Herschel also inherited a part - in return for which they had received the letters from Hans - including the youth center and vineyards on the Golan Heights. There was nothing more, which certainly annoyed Samuel. What did he want with vineyards and then in the Golan Heights, where it was always cold?

Herschel was doing better with the youth center. However, he was never allowed to sell the property. With Herschel, I was sure that he would always take good care of this legacy. He then expanded the system and improved the organization by adding youth centers similar to ours but with slightly different training.

(Hans some years before his death)

[07 VILLA MANGOLD]

(VILLA MANGOLD IN ZURICH AROUND 1950)

FAMILY, GRANDCHILDREN: ELIAS, AARON AND LEAH

After the grief, I decided to travel. I loved traveling, went to Africa, and got to know many people there, their customs and traditions. I was thirsty for everything new, trying to forget, to find myself. I found myself in an empty room, surrounded by high walls, hearing my screams, almost drowning in my sea of tears.

I spent a year in Israel and enjoyed it, met my relatives, made new friends, and got to know Esther's past better. She also had a different life there. A villa with vineyards, dates, and olive groves, worked by many employees. Back then, I didn't want to leave this little paradise. Just imagine: a lawyer's wife lived in the countryside surrounded by vineyards and olive groves!

We two widows decided to do something together. She wanted to open a gallery in Munich and wanted me to help her with it. I was happy to do so and made many high-profile contacts for her. At least I knew some wealthy people through Hans and Martin. In other words, she made the big money, and I did the work.

I don't want to complain, but that's how Esther Goldberg was always. I didn't care, but eventually, I had enough and returned to Samuel and his family. Samuel and Rachel with their sons Elias and Aaron, both beautiful. Real Mangolds or sometimes Epstein.

I often played babysitter for them both. They were sweet; Samuel wasn't as calm as the two at that age. They often played at the little garden house. A swing was hanging on our old oak tree, and a sandbox was next to it. They sat there, baking sand cakes or throwing the wet sand at each other.

I remember Elias throwing sand at me, and he claimed it was Aaron. But Aaron cried, and Elias took the blame. I told them we were playing. Something could go wrong. Soon after, Elias went to the Jewish kindergarten and was gone almost all day. I then played with Aaron and often went with him to the ice cream parlor in the old town.

That's when I started writing down my experiences. There was a lot to say about our refuge. However, I didn't publish the book after all. I wrote it down and put it away. I placed my hope in Aaron. I was hoping he would bring it out. I still hope so because it's in the box where I collect jewels and valuables to give to him.

When Aaron also started kindergarten, I no longer had anything to do. I started a new hobby, but painting wasn't for me. Ursula had once advised me to find a young man and run away with him. But of course, I didn't because I never wanted any other man except my only man.

One day, I accidentally barged into a seemingly secret meeting with Samuel. He was sitting in the drawing room with three men. They looked so ultra-Orthodox that just looking at them disgusted me. They sat there with their dark faces and looked at me - as if I had caught them.

Samuel yelled at me to get out. The last word was far from spoken. I withdrew for this moment. The men from Israel started laughing, and I didn't feel like confronting them.

But after this appointment, Samuel mutated more and more into a tyrant. I often thought now that every time he became more powerful, he also became fiercer. So, what's the point of money and power? Nothing! Health and a happy family, on the other hand, are priceless.

I carried this thing around with me for over a week. When I met Samu in his study, I dared to speak to him. "Samu, I have to talk to you."

"Mother, if you want to apologize to me about the other day, everything is fine."

"No! I don't want to apologize. I want you to apologize! It's not acceptable for you to treat me so rudely. I never raised you like that. What's wrong with you?"

"I don't know what you want, mother. I was having a meeting with representatives from another community, and you barged in. You're the one who should be apologizing."

I understood. In order not to escalate the matter unnecessarily, I gave in.

"It's fine, sorry!"

I went and left him sitting. He made no move to ask me to stay. I was sad. What happened to my dear Samuel?

I pulled back and kept my distance for a while. Rachel didn't like it. I told her the reason. Rachel was sad and afraid for the children and herself. However, I believed that Samuel could never harm his family.

At some point, Samuel came to me and asked for my forgiveness. I wasn't sure if I could believe him. He was acting strange like he wanted to get rid of me. He even asked me if I wanted to Tel Aviv go for a while. I politely declined. Samuel left.

Later, I found out the reason. Once again, a strange delegation came from Israel, and Samuel sold himself again. He took a lot of money from them to build the New Synagogue without loans. Once again, I had to stay in the background. The rabbis didn't like me, Samuel told me.

So, I retreated into private life. Esther occasionally came to Freiburg and took the little boys on vacation. They liked it, and I liked it now and then, too. Either I went along alone. Or I enjoyed my free time without my grandchildren.

Sometimes, I also met with Ursula in Zurich. I visited the youth center and lived with Ursula. Martin died a few years after Hans. Herschel and Viktor Hornmann – the second son, next to Ruben Hornmann – took over the law firm.

Rachel told me that she was expecting another child. I initially thought that everything would get better. Samuel traveled a lot; his anger was not on the house. The older children went to cheder, a kind of primary school, from the age of three. Rachel finally had some peace and quiet.

Since I had nothing to do, for the time being, I turned back to Israel. Tel Aviv was and is one of the most beautiful places in the world. I enjoyed being there often. Adam, my brother, invited me. The bakery that Rosa had once taken over was doing well; his children had just taken over. They also had grandchildren, all boys. They spent a lot of time with me, and I loved spending time with them.

Adam asked me then if I wanted to stay. There was enough space in his house, and you could enjoy the sea view. I declined his friendly invitation. Hans wouldn't have wanted it if he had still been by my side. But I enjoyed the weeks there, went for walks at the harbor in Jaffa, and went to the synagogue to pray.

There, I met a young rabbi. He looked familiar, and he recognized me too.

"Shalom, Ms. Mangold."

"Shalom, Rabbi? I'm sorry, but I don't know your name."

"Weinstein, Rabbi Weinstein. Yes, we will see each other more often soon. Your son ordered me to Freiburg."

"Well, how nice! I have to move on, Rabbi."

The rabbi nodded politely, and I left. I wondered what he was up to. I couldn't get his cocky grin out of my head. I decided to return to Freiburg, I wanted to talk to Samuel. Adam had told me nothing good about Rabbi Weinstein. And I can do Samuel's circles well enough myself.

I came back when Leah, his youngest, was born. Finally, a girl and beautiful! What joy that was, and she screamed more than the two boys in front of her! Finally, I had a job again. I was happy to take it on. When you are needed, you stay young.

In light of Leah's birth, I also abandoned my plan to talk to Samuel. Only later did I remember why I had returned to Germany and decided to ask Samuel about Rabbi Weinstein.

I made my way to Samuel. He was in the synagogue, studying his books. I knocked softly on the door; Samu invited me in.

"Samu, can I speak to you?" I asked him gently. Not that he immediately flared up again.

But this time, he was calm. "Of course, mother, you always do! What's on your mind?"

"It's about Rabbi Weinstein. Do you know him from Israel?"

"Yes, he was a fellow student and became an assistant rabbi at the Great Synagogue in Tel Aviv. Did he do something?"

"No. I met Rabbi Weinstein and was surprised that he knew me. Then he told me that he would be coming to Freiburg soon."

"Yes, that's right. He was visiting us at the time and saw you when you came into the salon. I asked him that evening if he would like to join our church. He accepted my offer and has been in Freiburg since yesterday. He will particularly promote youth work. The last rabbi let them go."

"Then it's all right, my son. I have to get going again because Rachel wants to go to the city park with Leah and me."

"Have fun!"

I said nothing more, left the room, and closed the door behind me. I hadn't remembered that unfortunate evening for a long time didn't want to remember it now. I then headed off to meet Rachel. So, I had other thoughts.

Leah developed very well, and I contributed my part. Rachel was happy about that. She could have done it on her own. After all, Elias and Aaron became wonderful boys, even without my support. But she gladly accepted my help.

Now Elias was approaching the age of his bar mitzvah. He attended religious classes almost every day and was diligent and inquisitive. On the day of his bar mitzvah, he was so excited! He couldn't sleep the night before, he was so happy. On Shabbat, we all sat in the synagogue and celebrated the service for the young people who had their bar mitzvah.

Rabbi Weinstein called out four names, and four boys came onto the bimah. Each of the four went wrapped in his tallit, the prayer shawl.

The rabbi alternately pointed to a section of the Torah with his silver Torah finger. Then the child touched these places with the fringes of his prayer shawl, kissed it, and began to read to everyone in a clear voice. Two even sang. Elias left it at reciting. The rabbi then gave a speech with the blessings for the four boys.

Samuel threw a party for all four boys. Many guests came, and Elias also had an appointment with Rabbi Weinstein that day. He wanted to talk to Elias about a place at the yeshiva, a Jewish college where mostly male students devote themselves to the study of Torah, particularly the Talmud. That had always been Elias' goal; He also wanted to study. (He is now studying art.)

A high-ranking rabbi from Israel came, particularly Rabbi Weizmann. Esther reported that he was a strange fellow. She knew him from her husband.

Elias was so happy when he told me he got a place at the yeshiva! He often and happily went to see Rabbi Weinstein. But when he came home at some point, I noticed that he had teary eyes. I asked him what was wrong. He just said he had problems with his girlfriend.

He didn't want to see Rabbi Weinstein the next day and refused to leave the house. I was worried whether he wasn't hiding something from me. But a few days later, he went back to him. He said at the time that he was overwhelmed.

Aaron had his bar mitzvah a year later and was just as excited as Elias was at the time. Again, we were sitting in the synagogue on Shabbat, and Rabbi Weinstein called out his name. Aaron was the only one who had his bar mitzvah that day. He went to the bimah, covered himself with his tallit, and Rabbi Weinstein pointed to a passage in the Torah with his silver Torah finger.

Aaron touched the fringes of his prayer shawl, kissed it, and began to read in a clear voice to everyone: "Blessed are You, G-d, our G-d, King of the world, / who has given us the doctrine of truth / and eternal life planted in our midst, / blessed are you, G-d, giver of teaching."

Rachel and I were so emotional! I was crying. Samuel sat as always apart from the family next to the bimah and stared straight ahead as if petrified. What world did he live in? What had happened to him and when?

When Aaron finished, Rabbi Weinstein gave Aaron the final blessing and left him in the care of the family. Samuel and Rachel donated a snack. This was handed out after the ceremony.

The next day, Samuel gave a large banquet in Aaron's honor with hundreds of guests. There was celebration, eating, and prayer. Samuel celebrated from the Torah and was blessed non-stop. It was a lovely celebration, and I thought that maybe Samuel had changed after all. **(He didn't!)**

His father promised Aaron that he would get a bank account with money that would later finance his studies. Aaron wanted to study architecture after graduating from high school, but at the same time, he helped his father in the synagogue. Aaron wanted to learn everything about the Torah and the Talmud. But he was not disappointed when Rabbi Weinstein told him he would not admit to the yeshiva. He was never as religious as Elias or Samuel.

Leah was now at an age where she had to go to cheder. At first, it was difficult for her. She was sensitive and timid, but over time, things got better, and she was happy to go. I usually dropped them off and picked them up, even though the cheder had its transport service. She had fun, and so did I. Because we often made trips to our favorite ice cream parlor downtown.

Of course, there were bad days too. One day, Aaron came to me. He pushed around, and I asked him what was wrong. He asked me back then whether Jews would go to hell if they coveted their gender. I asked him why he wanted to know such a thing. He just said he just had this at school.

It never occurred to me that my little Aaron preferred his gender to the female. Only after two years did I find out he loved a boy and didn't know what to do. Because I am liberal, I told him to carefully consider who he reveals himself to and who he doesn't. I suggested he talk to Rabbi Weinstein. He had always been well-disposed towards Aaron, and Aaron liked him too.

But Aaron became more and more quiet and thoughtful. I saw him cry and saw the bruises. When I asked him about it, he replied that he had fallen and couldn't tell anyone about it. Rabbi Weinstein forbade him to talk about being gay. I suggested that he live his life on his terms and not listen to a rabbi. I thought he would be happy with that. (But ...)

I've long been on the sidelines of the events and no longer the center of attention. At the beginning of 2009, I had my first heart attack. I took medication and had to slow down. (I had always been healthy until then.) In the hospital, I thought a lot: would I see Hans again dying in pain? Would we wake up in another world or on another level? I also read a lot about these topics, but I didn't come to any conclusions and had to continue living in uncertainty.

After being discharged from the hospital, I turned my life around. I ate healthily, stopped drinking alcohol, and only thought kosher. I sorted out my life and the things that were still open. I had made my last will and signed over my front building on Levetzowstrasse and my assets to Aaron. He's supposed to get it on his 21st birthday. Half of the shares and shares went to Elias and Leah. Samuel and Rachel were only supposed to get the penthouse apartment because they had enough.

A good friend suggested that since I had experienced so much. I could write a book. (I did. You are reading it right now, my dear readers.) But the story is not over. It always starts again.

Aaron has disappeared! Nobody knows where he is. His father doesn't seem to care, and my daughter-in-law must also care. Otherwise, her husband would be angry with her. I'm the only one worried about the boy.

Of course, I asked Rabbi Weinstein if he knew anything. He replied, "To hell with that gay bastard! He only disgraces our community and on you Mangolds."

I was beside myself with rage and called him a long-haired slob and told the golem to take him. (My blood boils just thinking about it.)

Where was Aaron? Was something done to him? I had to ask Esther. Only she was well disposed towards him.

But slowly my will to live dwindled. I was in my late seventies and deserved to die. (What does a person do when she's ready to die but can't because her brain says 'no'? Think about it! When you have an answer, write it down and burn the piece of paper. I will read it in heaven. Just don't expect an answer from me.)

Then Esther called me to tell me that Aaron was with her; he was fine. He will not return to Freiburg. Things had happened that meant he couldn't come back. I had to promise not to say anything about his whereabouts and I stuck to it. I also didn't tell anyone that Aaron was closer to the male gender than the female gender.

Until Samuel told me that Aaron was going to study in Berlin. He would join the liberal community there; Samuel would provide him with monthly support. The family owns an apartment in Berlin that he can use.

I was relieved. I knew Aaron would have a much easier time there than in Freiburg. He never liked Freiburg. Munich or Berlin were the cities of his dreams. I had always loved Aaron. I signed over a bank account to him. I gave him access, and he had more freedom. So, this story has a happy ending, and I can die in peace.

It is now 2017. Everything is going well in the family. Samuel often has business appointments in Berlin. Sometimes I think he's just faking it. In reality, he wants to be close to his son. He meets him for coffee, or they go to dinner together in Feinsberg. What a nice restaurant, delicious food, and great wine! I was there once with Esther and Aaron for his 19th birthday.

One of my last big wishes was for Samu and Aaron to get closer again. I tried to mediate always and everywhere, no matter the situation or the time. I was always there for everyone and ready to help.

My inner values dictated this to me. Kindness and my humanity made me strong - alongside my pride. I was given this in my cradle by my lovely mother. My father gave me the will to survive, and he was the one who said: "Every tunnel has a light at the end that shines for you so that you can find your way."

Today I was at Hans's grave; Elias took me there. For me, at 85 years old, things aren't moving so quickly anymore. Elias is patient and never talks much. We understand each other even without many words. He lives in seclusion, perhaps because of his studies. He studies modern art at the university here in Freiburg. He has a great girlfriend, Katja. I like her and hope he and she will go together their way.

I hired a gardener to look after our two graves starting next month. Rachel said she would take care of it, but she has so much to do she shouldn't be tied up with such things. I also prepared my funeral and arranged it in my will.

I feel weak and ready for my final journey. I hope Hans is still standing at this bridge and is waiting for me.

I would give you one little thing along the way: **"Never swim with the flow; swim against it. Don't let your dreams get in the way! Only those who dream can achieve great things. Every great deed began with a small dream."**

(08 Our beloved Hannah)

With love, your Hannah Adriana Mangold (née Epstein), born on April 27th, 1932, in Berlin - died on October 19th, 2017, in Freiburg.

"Some of the names and characters are fictitious. As are some of the scenes. But there is always a large amount of truth in such a story. The changes are for the safety of real people."

(THE SYNAGOGUE TODAY)

Epstein   Mangold